KILL THE MAN

Kevin Reilly had never shot a man before. He kept repeating this fact to himself as he sat before a half-open window of a rented room in Quebec City, an AR-15 Armalite rifle cradled between his knees like a cello. He had to steel himself to commit murder—no, it wasn't murder; it was an act of courage for the welfare of his people. That was the phrase.

A raw November wind drew the dampness of the streets into the darkening room. Reilly shivered, although his skin felt hot, and his knees began to shake uncontrollably . . .

CHAIN REACTION

A thriller by GORDON PAPE and TONY ASPLER

Chain Reaction

A novel by Gordon Pape and Tony Aspler

BANTAM BOOKS

TORONTO · NEW YORK · LONDON

CHAIN REACTION

*A Bantam Book / published by arrangement with
The Viking Press*

PRINTING HISTORY
Viking edition published April 1978
Book-of-the-Month Club edition published October 1978
Bantam edition / June 1979

*We acknowledge with thanks Intermède Musique
for permission to use a line from "Mon Pays"
by Gilles Vigneault. We also thank Carnaval
de Québec Inc. for permission to use two lines
from the official song of the Québec Winter
Carnival.*

Chain Reaction

Kevin Reilly had never shot a man before. He kept repeating this fact to himself as he sat before a half-open window of a rented room in Quebec City, an AR-15 Armalite rifle cradled between his knees like a cello. He had to steel himself to commit murder—no, it wasn't murder; it was an act of courage for the welfare of his people. That was the phrase.

A raw November wind drew the dampness of the streets into the darkening room. Reilly shivered, although his skin felt hot, and his knees began to shake uncontrollably. He leaned forward, placing his elbows on the ancient radiator, careful not to let the rifle barrel come in contact with the hot metal.

The draft from the window made his eyes water. With great deliberation he wiped a tear from each with the base of his thumb, one at a time so that he could keep a continual watch on the street below. His hooded eyes followed the line of traffic which was starting to thin out now as the lemming-like exodus of civil servants for their comfortable homes in Ste. Foy and Sillery began to ease. He stole a glance at his watch—5:34 P.M. Can't be much longer now, he told himself. A mixture of fear and exhilaration seemed to inflate like a balloon inside him. He tried to stop his knees from shaking by picturing himself walking in the street below. He could do it blindfolded: he had memorized every detail of Grande Allée for the better part of a week. To his far right, an expanse of lawn rising to the Quebec National Assembly building, a luxuriant green in summer, now brown and mottled awaiting the first winter snow. Next, a small driveway out of which the car would come if The Target was driving. (In his mind the victim was no longer a man, but a target.) In the middle of the view from his window vantage point was a vast block of government offices built of Quebec limestone, newly sandblasted, a perfect backdrop to set off The Target if he was walking (as was his habit). The building occupied an entire city block. Next, an intersection. To the far left were a drugstore and a newsstand where The Target often stopped to buy an evening paper. If he had no time to get off a shot before, he could always shift his aim to the well-lit doorway there. Once again, he checked the Armalite's magazine and safety catch, then wiped his damp hands on the lapels of his jacket. He pressed the rifle's front sight into the hollow of his cheek, willing The Target to appear.

He had chosen the ideal time of year, he noted with grim satisfaction. More by luck than judgment. In the summer the trees along Grande Allée would have been thick with foliage. Now their leaves clogged the gutters, mixed with the droppings of the horses that pulled the *calèches,* candidates for the glue factory, all of them. The trees, black and skeletal in the autumnal gloom, did not hinder his vision, but they would obscure him if anyone were to look up from the street. He had an unobstructed view of the sidewalk right up to the National Assembly building.

The chair he sat on creaked as he shifted his position. He had been sitting, watching, for over four hours, and his muscles began to protest. He wanted to stand up and stretch, to have a good crap, but he did not care to break his vigil: The Target might appear at any moment and his opportunity would be lost.

He rubbed the back of his neck and flexed his toes to relax himself. He watched the cars below as they began to turn on their headlights. Some of them had their windshield wipers going against a light rain. A soft night, his father would have called it. That meant The Target might use his car instead of walking, and Reilly cursed the rain and the forecasters on the radio who had made no mention of it. The Target on foot would make for a simple shot; in a car the odds would lengthen. He looked at his watch again: 5:41 P.M.

The Cabinet Room was full of smoke and acrimony. At the head of the highly polished conference table the

Premier sat tapping a pencil against his teeth as he listened to his Minister of Social Affairs, Guy Lacroix. He's the only one of my ministers who stands up when he speaks in cabinet, the Premier said to himself; I might have mistaken it for good manners if it weren't for the demagogue in him. He watched Lacroix clench his fist and bring it down on the silky tabletop, causing pencils and note pads to bounce.

"You tell us to wait, to be patient. We've been waiting the best part of two years!" The young minister's voice cannon-balled off wood-paneled walls and echoed around the vaulted room. Poor Jean-Claude, thought the Premier. Still, he has been shouted at before. The object of Guy Lacroix's anger, Jean-Claude Belmont, the Minister of Education, sucked on a dry pipe and doodled on the paper in front of him.

"We won the referendum. We have a mandate for independence. What the hell else do we need?" thundered Lacroix. "Do you think the feds are going to hand it to us on a plate? We're in the driver's seat now. I would like to remind my honorable friend, if you've got them by the balls, their hearts and minds will follow."

There was laughter around the table and even the Premier smiled. Jean-Claude Belmont knocked his empty pipe out into the ash tray to give himself a few seconds before speaking. The cabinet was quiet, as it always was when the Minister of Education was about to address it. Belmont had been a highly respected figure in the party for many years; along with the Premier and the former leader, René Lévesque, he had been the architect of the policies which had finally given the Parti Québécois political credibility in the eyes of the electorate.

Belmont let his eyes travel down the table before replying. Many of his colleagues, perhaps a majority of them, were becoming increasingly impatient with Ottawa's prevarications. Lacroix's extreme position was gaining support both within the cabinet and among the grass roots of the party. But Lacroix was wrong, and the action he counseled could only be fatal to the party and to Quebec. A former law professor from the University of Montreal, Jean-Claude Belmont had an advocate's approach to political realities. Both sides lose in a stand-up fight; there was always a compromise for sensible men.

"What my honorable colleague states so colorfully is, in essence, correct, except for one not inconsequential detail. Yes, we won a referendum which gave us a mandate for independence. But, my friends, there was a rider attached to that which too many of us choose to ignore these days. Our mandate is valid only in the context of economic association with the rest of Canada. That was the commitment we gave to our people at the time of the referendum. That is the only reason, and let us be honest, gentlemen, that the referendum went in our favor. . . . "

Lacroix was on his feet stabbing his finger at Belmont, but the Premier motioned him to silence.

"So we are committed to that position, both morally and by law. Now, if we wish to change the rules, we have no option but to consult the people of Quebec." There were murmurings from some of the ministers. Guy Lacroix passed a note across the table.

"You have heard the Minister of Social Affairs. He would have us emulate that pariah among nations, Rhodesia, and proclaim a unilateral declaration of independence next week. You know where that would lead us. To economic ruin and most probably military reprisals."

"Who from, the Eskimo?" interjected Lacroix. The Premier noted that several cabinet members were grinning. "The symbol of our new freedom," continued Belmont undeterred, "would be the bread line, like thirty-one. We owe our people more than that. It is our duty, our sacred trust, that we work to ensure a secure future for them and their children, a future in which they can enjoy both prosperity and freedom."

Belmont relaxed against his high-backed chair. The Premier watched him and saw how his friend had aged during these last five years. At fifty-seven his energies were soon dissipated, but he was still a voice of reason in troubled times. Predictably, the room exploded in a babel of voices the moment Belmont had finished speaking. Lacroix was on his feet again, eyes wide with Messianic fervor. The Premier had to rap his gavel for order. "Gentlemen, gentlemen. A little decorum." Belmont frowned. He knew the cabinet was deeply divided over the issue. And for the first time since he had helped to found the Parti Québécois, he could not predict which way events would move.

The anniversary celebrations were less than a week away, and it had become traditional for the party to mark the date of its accession to power with a major policy statement—a tactic designed to show its followers and the world at large that the dynamic new government had lost none of its momentum or its reforming zeal. Only this year there was nothing to announce. Negotiations with Ottawa and the other nine provinces were not going well; not even Belmont could pretend they were. The Canadian Prime Minister had from the outset adopted a hard line with Quebec. He had not refused to negotiate—he was too astute for that. Federal obduracy would hand the Parti Québécois the pretext it needed to jettison the "economic union" clause of the referendum. Instead, the Prime Minister was acting with punctilious correctness in public while making impossible demands at the bargaining table. He had asked for the return of the mineral-rich Ungava territory of northern Quebec, ceded to the province in two stages in 1898 and 1912. As well, he wanted neutralization of the St. Lawrence Seaway under an international authority. Was the Prime Minister really so naïve as to think the Québécois would accept such a proposition? And that four-hundred-mile-plus land corridor to the Maritimes cutting through the heart of Quebec's Eastern Townships. Ottawa must be dreaming! What else would they want? Self-determination for the English in Quebec? Westmount, the new Berlin? It was absurd, of course. Lacroix did have a point, and Belmont could understand the man's frustration. Were he a generation younger he might be pounding the table too. But UDI was not the answer. He became aware that the room was quiet again and the Premier was speaking.

" . . . so I understand very well what our Minister of Social Affairs is saying." The Premier had to pull the two factions of his cabinet together. "I share his unhappiness. . . . "

Belmont observed his leader closely. The tall frame supported a small emaciated head on drooping shoulders suggesting the skull beneath. He looked like a spent force. His fingers, twisted with encroaching arthritis—as much a part of his appearance as his slight limp, a legacy from a childhood bout with polio—traced appeasing arabesques above the table in an effort to unite all views behind him.

The turned-down mouth seemed to pull his whole face into an expression of total exhaustion, accentuated by the graying mustache and the shaggy eyebrows. He should have stepped down years ago, but without him the party would fly apart into those clever and energetic elements which the force of his personality had welded together to realize the dream of Quebec's independence.

" . . . yet I cannot endorse Monsieur Lacroix's recommendations. There are other options to be exercised before we play that final card." The Premier raised his voice to be heard over the low rumblings around the table. "Furthermore, we have made a fundamental commitment to our people. As leader of this party, I am pledged to that. If you want to change it by short-circuiting the democratic institutions by which we gained power, then it will be done without me. If you wish, gentlemen, I shall put the matter to a vote. But I can tell you now that if you vote in favor of UDI, you will be voting for my resignation as Premier and leader of the Parti Québécois."

"Traitor! Judas!" Lacroix was on his feet, the veins in his neck standing out like ropes. Belmont had never seen him lose control of himself like this.

"What the hell's the use in voting! You've blackmailed the majority of your party into silence. Where's your democracy now? You're a spineless old man who's turned his back on his people. And now you bend over for Ottawa. You'll regret this moment, I promise you!"

Lacroix swept his papers off the table and stuffed them into his briefcase. He stamped out of the Cabinet Room, slamming the door behind him.

The Premier reached for a cigarette to mask his anger. "Monsieur Lacroix has spared me the necessity of calling for a closing motion." Turning to his secretary he added, "I would like the minister's remarks not to appear in the minutes—for his own protection."

Belmont watched the Premier rise wearily to his feet. He felt no satisfaction in the victory he had won. The lingering question was, at what price?

The glare from car headlights sent shadows dancing across the ceiling above Reilly's head. He rocked slowly back and forth on his chair, a motion which drew his cheek up and down the barrel of the Armalite. The clicking sound of a woman hurrying in high heels drifted up to him from the street below, and he craned forward to catch a glimpse of her. All he could see was the floral circle of her umbrella. The sound of high heels had always excited him; she always wore them around the apartment for him even when she was naked. On the pretext of making coffee in the kitchen, she had left the table for a few minutes and then returned behind him, her hands over his eyes. Don't peek, she had said, I have nothing on. She took the candles from the dinner table into the bedroom. Only the lower classes make love in the dark, she had said. The flames seemed to leap up to her as if to wash her body in fire. The clack of her heels on the hardwood floor made her buttocks bounce as she led the way into the bedroom without even looking back to see if he were following. . . .

Reilly felt a sharp pain in his cheek. He had scratched himself on the rifle sight. He shook his head. He had been daydreaming; he was angry with himself for drifting off. He checked his watch—5:52 P.M. He raised the rifle to his shoulder and peered through the night-sight. Objects he could hardly see in the gloom suddenly became visible, darkly defined against a blood-red glow. Night turned to a strange red twilight that seemed to wrap itself around bodies like a curtain of blood.

Just holding the rifle in preparation for firing eased the tension in his stomach. He had eaten nothing for two days; he had been unable to keep the blandest food down, as if his very insides rebelled against his plans. But he knew he was right; in his twenty-two years he had never been more certain of what he had to do.

She had first opened his eyes to it. They had lain awake in bed talking late into the night. They had sat cross-legged on the floor listening to music, discussing it. They had talked about it in bars, she nursing a single Kir all evening, he downing bottles of Export Ale as he became angrier. She had helped him to see his own life as it really was. He understood now how his people were being victimized, driven from their homes, their land by a racist government. She had triggered in him the revelation that here in his own country, his own province, his own city an entire way of life was being systematically eliminated. There was none of the overt brutality that charac-

terized the Nazi persecution of the Jews, but instead a
slow bleeding, a more subtle form of genocide.

The anger she had awakened in him aggravated a
deeper, long-dormant pain inherited from his father. Cathal
Reilly was a Catholic born in Belfast. In 1952 he and his
wife, Maura, sold their house at a loss to escape the blind
prejudice and open hatreds of Ulster. They emigrated to
Canada with their meager savings to start a new life in a
country full of promise and the opportunity of fulfillment
—according to the immigration posters. They had settled
in the Point St. Charles district of Montreal among other
first-generation Irish immigrants. Life had been hard for
them, especially when Maura gave birth to their son,
Kevin; but however impoverished they might be in their
newly adopted country, they could lead a life of dignity
without having constantly to be looking over their
shoulders.

Kevin Reilly had never been one for politics. Things
happened for better or for worse; he cared little for those
faces in the newspapers that made them happen. But the
endless stories his father told him on the way to Mass
every Sunday of the Catholic's lot in Ulster had etched
themselves deep into his subconscious like a Jesuit sermon.
"Never forget," his father had told him, "and never forgive."

She had drawn these memories from him as surely as
she had drawn him into her body. By persistent analysis
of the situation in the province, she had suggested to him
the link between the Belfast his father had turned his back
on and the political realities of Quebec. She brought newspaper clippings to show him workers being forced from
their jobs because they could not speak French, the
language of the newly powerful majority. She drove him
around Montreal and pointed out the number of houses
for sale at give-away prices because their English-speaking
owners could no longer find work. She showed him reports on the English school system which coldly predicted
that bureaucratic attrition would in the end force it to
close down. And he told her how his father had been subjected to abuse from French-speaking officials at the unem-
ployment-insurance office because he could not speak their
language—his own co-religionists! And how his mother
had been refused service by salesgirls and waitresses for

the same reason. Shades of Ulster, and only the beginning; but here he could do something about it, she had said. Yes, he could do something about it, but what? As they made love, she had suggested that one bullet could wash away the stench of oppression that hung about his father and himself. . . .

He checked his watch again—6:04 P.M. The balance would soon be corrected for all time.

In the hallway of the National Assembly building Jean-Claude Belmont slowed his pace so that the Premier could catch up to him. He wanted to thank his leader for backing him, but he knew that in doing so the Premier had played the most powerful card in his hand—the threat of resignation. Was he bluffing or would he really step down? Belmont had to find out.

The Premier approached him and linked arms, an ambiguous gesture of friendship or political solidarity not wasted on the Minister of Education.

"Ah, Jean-Claude, the Chinese have an ancient curse which says 'May you live through interesting times.' I think we are all cursed."

Belmont sighed. "I want to thank you for what you said in there. At least sanity prevailed."

"Yes, but for how long?" replied the Premier. "I feel rather like that missionary in the cooking pot, *mon ami*. That fox in Ottawa has the torch in hand, and my own party is just waiting for the water to boil."

"Why don't we slip out and have a Pernod? You remember that bar we used to haunt when we first dreamed up the Parti Québécois with Lévesque?"

The Premier shook his head. "I would love to. I would also love to play golf, fish for trout, and see more of the woman I love. But we are so close now I cannot relax for a second. But I'll walk with you a short way to clear my head. Wait for me, I'll just tell Touraine."

While the Premier informed his bodyguard of his movements, Belmont left a message with the doorman that he would not be needing the car, in spite of the rain.

The two old friends paused on the steps of the Assembly building and buttoned their raincoats. Sergeant Touraine of the Quebec Provincial Police stood with both hands in his pockets three paces behind the Premier and scanned Grande Allée.

"I suppose I shall have to reprimand Lacroix," said the Premier wearily as they moved down the steps. "I could move him from Social Affairs to Sport, but he would only become a rallying point for the St. Jean Baptiste mafia."

"He's young and impetuous," said Belmont, not wishing to appear to influence the Premier's thinking.

"Always the lawyer, eh, Jean-Claude?"

The rain, driven on the wind, slanted into their faces as they turned right up Grande Allée. They leaned into it, chins pressed against their chests. Sergeant Touraine strained to hear their conversation, but it was lost in the wind.

Kevin Reilly watched the three black shapes move toward him in a strange blood-red circle—two in front, one tall, one short, and a large man behind. He waited for them to approach, counting to himself to steady his nerves. When they were two hundred yards away he centered the cross-hairs on The Target's chest, held his breath, and gently squeezed the trigger, once, twice. Through the night-sight's crimson globe he saw the body turn, then jump up and arch over backward into the street. The first bullet had hit the left shoulder; the second had struck the right cheek, tearing the flesh away and rendering unrecognizable the face of the Premier of Quebec.

Reilly stood up at the window, the rifle still in his hands, looking down on the two men who knelt over the fallen leader. He could hear the blood pounding in his ears. A wild surge of triumph passed through him momentarily. The anger flowed out of him and in its place a sense of amnesic numbness began to take hold. The sight of his victim lying in the road, his blood diluted by the rain, seemed to erase all details of his escape plan. But he must act. He wished she were there with him to tell him what to do now.

The third man, who had walked behind, was beginning to rise now; he had pulled out a gun and was running up the street in the direction of the shots. Reilly pressed himself back into the shadows, although the man could not have seen him at the darkened window. Suddenly there was an aggressive knocking at the door. Reilly threw the Armalite onto the bed in panic. He rushed at the door, his only means of escape, and clawed at the chain. He flung it open, and there in the hallway stood the landlady, her knuckles raised. The panic in her face mirrored his own. She began to scream at him, her wizened old hands pulling at his jacket. He pushed her backward and she caught hold of the banister, gasping for breath as he dashed down the stairs. He could hear her screeches echoing down the stairwell after him as he raced into the street.

Jean-Claude Belmont wept as he took off his raincoat to cover the Premier's face. "Oh my God," he kept repeating to himself. Suddenly he became aware of Sergeant Touraine running, gun in hand, up the street, and his thoughts turned to the assassin. He was still out there somewhere—perhaps drawing a bead on him. Involuntarily, he crouched down beside the body of his friend. He saw a man run from a building ahead. Touraine dropped to one knee and leveled his Smith & Wesson .38 in both hands, arms extended. The man stopped and turned, hesitated for a second, and then raced off up Grande Allée.

"Don't kill him!" yelled Belmont. "We want him alive!" But before he could complete the sentence, Sergeant Touraine had fired. The bullet hit Reilly square in the back, and as he fell on the greasy sidewalk two more shots found their mark in his kidney and right shoulder. Reilly rolled over in the gutter, the blood running black down his neck.

At 7:26 P.M. the Canadian Broadcasting Corporation interrupted its local programs across the country with a flash announcement:

"We have just learned that the Premier of Quebec has been shot down in the street outside the National Assembly building. He was pronounced dead on arrival at Quebec City's Hôtel-Dieu Hospital. A man believed to have been involved in the assassination was shot by the Premier's bodyguard while trying to escape. He too was dead on arrival at hospital. The man has not yet been identified. We will bring you further details as soon as they are available...."

In Quebec, viewers were stunned and bewildered. In homes throughout the province families left food untouched on the tables and went out into the streets. Men and women cried unrestrainedly. The switchboard at Radio-Canada, the CBC's French network, was jammed with calls seeking confirmation of the story. Local radio stations and newspaper offices were also deluged with pleas for information. A howl of grief arose in the province. Almost without exception, blame for the murder was pinned on *"les maudits Anglais"*—the goddamned English.

In the other nine provinces the news was greeted by a mixture of outrage, satisfaction, and concern for the repercussions. "He had it coming to him," one Ontario tavernowner remarked. In Calgary, a schoolteacher turned off her radio and said to her husband, "Perhaps the frogs will come to their senses now." But most Canadians were shocked by the violence; no political figure had been assassinated in Canada since the murder of Pierre Laporte by FLQ terrorists in 1970. The fact that that had also happened in Quebec was not lost on the English community.

The Prime Minister of Canada sat at his desk with a chicken sandwich and a glass of milk, holding down the corners of a map of the Yukon and Northwest Territories. Standing beside him was his youthful Minister of Northern Development, Avery Walton. Great stretches of the map had been shaded orange, red, and blue—land claimed by the native groups, the Dene, Inuit, and Metis. There was a crisis in the North, and it had to be settled quickly before the joint American-Canadian pipeline project could start. The native peoples had refused to allow a gas pipeline to be constructed across land they claimed as theirs. Negotiations with the three groups were to resume the next day, and Ottawa still did not have a firm counteroffer to the vast compensation claimed by the native communities. Work on the twice-delayed gas line was scheduled to start in the coming summer and work on an oil pipeline would begin two years later. That did not allow the government much time to settle grievances generations old; grievances which five years of hard bargaining had failed to resolve. And without a satisfactory settlement the prospect of sabotage and even attacks on construction crews was very real. Avery Walton had reviewed the native people's claims and was about to outline his proposed counteroffer for the P.M.'s approval.

"The key to the question, sir, is not so much cash as federal investment in local industry, to keep the young people from drifting south. . . . "

The buzzer on the Prime Minister's desk interrupted him.

"A moment, Avery." The Prime Minister picked up the receiver. "What is it, Miss Marston? I asked not to be disturbed."

Walton could hear the secretary's agitated voice on the line.

"All right. Send her in." The P.M. hung up. "Doris Faber. Something urgent. No, don't go. We have to finish this tonight."

Walton was annoyed. At any other time he would have been delighted to see the Prime Minister's attractive executive secretary, but a successful outcome of these negotiations would ensure his swift advancement in the cabinet. His proposal was extremely complicated, and he needed the P.M.'s full attention. The old boy was an arch-politician, but he tended to be rather slow on the uptake when discussions got technical.

The door opened and Doris Faber came in; she tried to affect her customary cool demeanor, but she was betrayed by the high color in her cheeks.

"There's something—" She broke off when she saw Walton, but an impatient wave from the Prime Minister told her to continue. She found difficulty speaking.

"The Premier of Quebec, sir. He's been shot."

The Prime Minister's groan was barely audible. "Is he dead?"

"Yes, sir. Outside the legislature. They killed a man running from the scene."

"Have the police made a positive identification?"

"He appears to be an English-speaking Montrealer." She looked at her notes. "Kevin Reilly. Lives in Point St. Charles."

"The stupid son of a bitch," roared the P.M. He brought his fist down on the desk with such force that the glass of milk toppled and spilled over the carpet. Walton jumped around the desk, ready with the handkerchief from his breast pocket.

"Leave the goddamned stuff. And get this map out of here."

"But the native claims, sir," protested Walton.

"We have a potential civil war on our hands, and you talk about native claims!" The P.M. sank back in his leather armchair and covered his face with his hands.

Secretary of State Lawrence Wilde's Washington office was lined with maps. He could have had paintings on loan from the Library of Congress, he told visitors, but he preferred maps. He was fond of indicating positions of strategic importance with a billiard cue merely by swiveling his chair. While other members of the President's circle had photos of wives and children on their desks, Wilde had an etching of Disraeli, a statesman whose diplomatic skills he dreamed of emulating. The doings of the former political-history professor from Columbia were as well documented by the foreign-affairs journals as they were in the tabloid gossip columns. And the fact that the Secretary of State was still at his desk at 7:35 P.M. was itself worthy of mention in both.

The problem of Britain kept him at his desk that night. The national coalition government had proved as ineffectual as its predecessors at reversing the economic decline. Last month's balance-of-payment figures, about to be released, were the worst in British history. The pound had sunk to $1.09 and threatened to drop below the dollar mark once the new figures were released. Unemployment would reach the two-million mark by Christmas, and inflation had spiraled back to twenty per cent, despite huge loans from the International Monetary Fund and drastic price controls. British industry was ravaged by communist-inspired strikes, some of which had led to violence at the docks and the mines. Both the dockworkers and the miners had returned communist slates at recent elections for union officials; and the indications were that the railroad and transport workers would do likewise. Without massive American intervention immediately, the British labor movement could be within the communist orbit inside six months.

The President had requested a comprehensive program which he could bring before a joint session of Congress by the end of the week. And this time massive American or German-Japanese loans would no longer do the trick; "No more goddamned Band-Aids," was the President's phrase. "I want another Marshall Plan." So Lawrence Wilde had to forego the cocktail party for a visiting Argentinian soprano to work on a political and economic package that would ensure that communist influence in the trade-unions movement would be neutralized without opening the United States to the charge of direct interference in the domestic affairs of another nation.

As he studied the ballot system of the Transport and General Workers Union, the teletype machine in the corner began to clatter. A small bell rang to signal the urgency of the message. Like Pavlov's dog he responded to the machine only if the bell rang. He read the message and immediately raised his night secretary on the intercom.

"Get me the President right away. Find him wherever he is. Tell him the Quebec situation has gone critical."

Holbrook Meadows, C.B.E., chairman of International Consolidated Enterprises Incorporated, known on the Stock Exchange as IntCon, had two tables reserved every night at the Unicorn Club in Mayfair's Curzon Street. One table was situated on the raised aisle of the brocaded room, where he could see everyone who came and went; the other was tucked away in an alcove where he could discuss his business affairs in private or dine his "lady friends" with discretion. He had had especially large chairs placed at both tables for himself to ensure that his ample frame would not be constricted and his weight would be supported. His personal assistant called the club after lunch each day to tell the maître d' which table Mr. Meadows would occupy that night.

Since Jan Maadan, executive vice president of South African Gold Limited, a wholly owned subsidiary of IntCon, had flown to London that day in order to meet privately with Meadows, the table chosen was in the alcove. He had asked Maadan to fly to London, but he didn't particularly want to publicize his presence by having him visit the office. The South African principal normally came to England once a year to present the report of his company's activities at IntCon's annual meeting. Maadan's presence in London four months before the AGM might give rise to gossip that could reflect in adverse share-price movement.

In the alcove Maadan spread his reports and geological surveys on the table, safe in the knowledge that no club member would invade their privacy. Between the *pâté de fois*, roast duck in black-cherry sauce, and *crème brûlée*, Maadan briefed Holbrook Meadows more fully on the confidential report he had forwarded to the IntCon chairman a few weeks earlier.

"There's no doubt about it, Mr. Meadows. I've had my men in the field check and recheck. It's just as I said. The Red Veldt is worked out. There's no more than three months' gold there at full capacity." The younger man was apologetic but adamant in his evaluation.

"The Red Veldt is the company's most important mine," murmured his host, staring into the ruby eye of his Château Margaux '61. "What if you went on fifty per cent capacity?"

"Within two years it would become unprofitable to mine it, however much we slowed production."

Meadows had known before the meeting that the news would be bad. Maadan was a cautious man; he would never have submitted such a potentially damaging report if he had any doubts. But Meadows had to be sure and had insisted on new samplings being taken. Now there was no question.

If news of the Red Veldt field leaked out it could do irreparable damage to IntCon, all the more so since most of the company's other international holdings were not performing profitably. Copper production in Chile had yet to stabilize after almost two decades of political turbulence and labor unrest in that country. As far as IntCon's tanker fleet was concerned, the Law of the Sea Conference had passed such Draconian legislation limiting passage and docking facilities to supertankers that IntCon's smaller ships hardly paid for their upkeep. The company's Canadian mineral holdings were assets in the ground, largely unexploited because of bureaucratic red tape and hostile geography. Only the munitions plants made money; they always did. But South African gold had been IntCon's lifeblood for the past twenty years. Now it was running out.

"I need hardly remind you, my good chap, that the slightest whisper of this would—shall we say—be indiscreet." Meadows looked quizzically at the tanned face of the Afrikaaner.

"Yes, I understand. A stock-market plunge. Liquidity problems within the parent company. Mass layoffs. Perhaps an enforced sale of major assets."

"Succinct and to the point," murmured the Englishman. But Maadan was a company man. Meadows had hand-picked him, promoting him out of the laboratory and into the board room at the age of thirty-seven. Maadan was his man, completely loyal and dependable. A waiter approached and Meadows motioned Maadan to silence.

"Excuse me, sir. There's an urgent call for you. Long distance, from Canada. Would you like to take it here?" The waiter produced a phone and plugged it into a socket in the wall.

"Thank you, Jefferson," said Meadows, and he allowed the waiter to retire out of earshot before he picked up the receiver.

"Excuse me, Jan. Hello, Meadows here. . . . " Maadan watched the corpulent features of his chairman metamorphose into a cunning grin. "Thank you for calling, good night." Holbrook Meadows replaced the receiver in its cradle as if it were made of glass.

"That was Ross Anson of the Montreal office. I think our problems may have been solved. Some obliging nutcase has just assassinated the Premier of Quebec."

The clash of sabers echoed through the *salle d'armes* at the exclusive Club des Sports on Rue St. Honoré in Paris. The opponents moved crablike along the mat, parrying attacks to the head and torso. The taller of the two held his free hand imperiously at his waist, while his opponent favored the traditional stance of the forearm in the small of the back, to reduce the target area.

There was something of the strident bully in the style of the aggressor. He shouted through his mask as he pressed his challenge and stamped his leading foot with each lunge to further intimidate his opponent. The speed of response kept the opponent safe from the vicious cut and thrust of the attack, but clearly the forceful nature of the aggressor would triumph in the end.

As if to forestall that victory, the loudspeaker above their heads broke through the sharp rhythm of steel on steel.

"Monsieur de Luzt, telephone, Montreal calling," said the disembodied voice. "Urgent, Monsieur de Luzt."

As his opponent stepped back, dropped guard, and made a move to remove the mask in deference to the loudspeaker, de Luzt pressed his attack, lunging forward to strike the vulnerable wrist.

The opponent tore the mask off in a fury, revealing the angry features of a beautiful black woman. "That was hardly sporting, monsieur," she snapped.

De Luzt stepped back, handed his saber to a second, and smiled at her.

"One wins as one can. A lesson in survival, my dear."

He drew a Hermès silk handkerchief from his neck and ran it across his forehead. "You handle a saber well, mademoiselle."

"I was a member of the French Olympic team at Montreal," she replied, unbuttoning her tunic. "But quite frankly, monsieur, I have never faced an opponent who had such contempt for etiquette. It is, after all, only a sport."

De Luzt studied the jet-black hair, shiny with sweat, the full lips, the velvet-brown eyes, the glistening skin, a deep coffee color. Probably the French West Indies, he thought, or Mauritius, perhaps. Her family must be wealthy for her to have taken up fencing, or maybe she had a rich patron. She was not a woman to be dismissed lightly. It wasn't easy to find such agreeable opponents at midnight in Paris.

"They are waiting for you on the phone. Why don't you answer it?"

"Your skill with the saber and your beauty made me quite forget. Excuse me. In the meantime, I hope you will allow me to offer you a glass of champagne. Steward, a bottle of the Dom Pérignon. I know we have not been formally introduced. My name is Antoine de Luzt, soldier of fortune and your servant." He affected an ironic bow.

The woman's annoyance gave way to curiosity. She was intrigued by this tall, aristocratic man with his close-cropped white hair, the iron gray eyes, and the thin, angular nose. Taken together, the features resembled an eagle searching for prey. There was a line of cruelty about the mouth and the corners of the eyes, accentuated by the pockmarked cheeks, which repelled her yet excited her.

"Thérèse St. Rémy," she replied, shaking her hair free, "and all I will tell you about myself is that I am thirsty enough to accept your champagne."

"Splendid. You will forgive me if I take the call." He backed away with mock courtliness and disappeared into the dressing room. A steward appeared with the champagne and two flute glasses. Carefully, he poured the wine into the glasses and handed one to the woman. Almost immediately de Luzt appeared back in the room. He slapped his thigh and whistled like a young boy who has an agreeable secret he cannot share. He raised his glass. "A toast, my dear, to the victor."

The Prime Minister of Canada had called an emergency session of his inner cabinet, requesting members to be in his office by 8:30 P.M. sharp. It was almost nine o'clock, and André Lafontaine, the P.M.'s Quebec lieutenant, had yet to arrive. Lafontaine was congenitally late. Usually his leader was prepared to overlook the fact because of Lafontaine's unique grasp of the political realities in the province. But tonight the P.M. drummed his fingers impatiently on the desk, awaiting Lafontaine's arrival. There was no point in starting without him. Around the Prime Minister were the members of a small group of advisers hand-picked by him to reflect the major sectional interests across Canada and to provide an inner council representing key factions within the party.

Avery Walton spoke for Ontario and the young professionals of the party, John Penny, the Minister of Agriculture, was the voice of the West, a veteran politician, pragmatic and calculating, the perfect counterbalance to Bill McVee, a former fisherman from the Maritimes who had a sailor's way of expressing himself. And then there was the ever tardy André Lafontaine, who could take the pulse of *la belle province* better than any politician of whatever persuasion. He had managed to retain the common touch which so many Quebec ministers seemed to lose after a short time in office.

"Finally," said the Prime Minister, as Lafontaine hurried into the office and sat down, breathing heavily. He mumbled his apologies.

"Gentlemen, the unfortunate death of the Premier of Quebec has created a situation the seriousness of which I don't have to impress upon you. Before I ask for your thinking, I would like to tell you one or two things which may not be common knowledge to you all. There are good reasons for not having kept you informed. However . . . The Premier of Quebec and I held four secret meetings at Harrington Lake over the past eight weeks in an effort to clear the log jam of the formal negotiations. I believe we were close to an accommodation which would have ensured the future of Confederation. At the same time it would have allowed the Parti Québécois a formula which would give Quebec sovereignty of a kind within the Canadian constitution. Unfortunately, we had not finalized the deal to the point where we could present it to our respective cabinets. And now some idiot with a rifle has destroyed all the progress we made by a single stupid act. What we now have is a flashpoint crisis in Quebec. The question is, gentlemen, what are we to do? First of all, André, how do you read it?"

"Well, sir, the PQ will want to elect a leader as quickly as possible. There's a provincial election due within eighteen months, and they cannot afford to wait. There are only two likely contenders for the leadership—Belmont and Lacroix. Of the two, only Belmont would be acceptable to us. In the light of your Harrington Lake talks, sir, Belmont might be able to finish the business with you. Lacroix, never. The man is very dangerous—more so because he is popular with the people, especially the trade unions. He speaks their language. They respond to his bogus Marxism; worker councils, profit-sharing, price codes, worker-directors. They eat up that jargon. The man is not a card-carrying communist but the next best thing. And we all know where he stands on the constitutional issue—complete and total independence for Quebec. No economic ties, no deals. Trade links with the Francophone countries and probably guns along the St. Lawrence Seaway as well.

"His supporters within the party are the radicals—the people the Premier had managed to keep on the fringes and away from influential portfolios. If Lacroix becomes leader, they will dominate the cabinet and the civil service as well. He must be stopped."

The Prime Minister listened to the gloomy prognosis, making the odd note on the pad in front of him. "Other comments, gentlemen?"

Predictably, Avery Walton was the first to reply.

"Seems to me that a political vacuum has been created in Quebec. We could take advantage of it and exploit it for our benefit. After all, we have a decided asset: a Prime Minister who is fluent in French, who is well respected and popular in Quebec. I think you should become actively involved in the Quebec situation, sir. A major policy statement on national television."

"The buggers are out there already," interjected

McVee, pointing to the door. "Beats me how they can hump those cameras around so fast."

"I think you should use your prestige and political leverage to ensure Belmont's election," Walton continued. "You might even let it slip that you and the Premier were an ace away from sewing the whole thing up, and Belmont is the only man to see it through. I'm sorry if I sound callous, but that gunman may have played the Péquistes into our pockets."

Bill McVee concurred with a roar of approval.

"Damn right. Them bloody Quebeckers have been asking for it. Now we've got them by the gills, we should stick the gaff in. You kin talk to 'em, sir. Use your power. We might never get another chance if that son of a bitch Lacroix takes over."

John Penny poured himself a third cup of coffee from the urn and waited for the Prime Minister to turn to him now that everyone else had had his say. He brought the coffee back to his chair, took a sip, and set it carefully on the floor beside him before speaking.

"I'm afraid you can't do it." The statement was final and brooked no opposition. "André would tell you the same thing if he weren't so scared of the bogeyman Lacroix. Sure you speak French, Prime Minister, sure they like you in Quebec. Sure they voted for your candidates. But you're not one of them, sir. You're an outsider. A foreigner. You're English."

The Prime Minister sighed. Penny was right. Quebeckers could accept an English-Canadian leader in Ottawa if he showed himself sympathetic to their province. Hadn't they once given John Diefenbaker fifty seats in spite of his atrocious French accent? But the provincial government in Quebec City was off limits. Let a federal Prime Minister try to interfere there and he would find out very quickly where the real interests of Quebeckers lay.

"Walton and McVee counsel disaster," Penny continued, staring into his coffee cup. "Show your face in the province and you'd drive the voters into Lacroix's arms just to demonstrate their independence from Ottawa. And where would we be? An enemy of Confederation at the helm in Quebec and a damaging blow to your prestige in the rest of the country, sir."

An atmosphere of gloom hung over the meeting; they knew Penny was right.

"What do you suggest, John—that we do nothing?" The Prime Minister began to play with the ring on his little finger, a nervous habit which those close to him could interpret as the anxiety that springs from tiredness.

"Well, we could play double bluff and come out strongly for Lacroix," Walton interjected. "The Quebeckers might back off then. They're a perverse bunch."

"Too risky," Lafontaine said. "The press would see through it."

"But we've got to fight, goddammit," roared McVee, who was ready to storm the Plains of Abraham all over again.

"The trouble is that whatever we do, it's going to be wrong," the Prime Minister said dejectedly. "There is another matter we have to take into account. The United States is extremely nervous about the Quebec situation. The President speaks at great length on the subject every time we meet. He's almost paranoid about it. The prospect of an unfriendly regime taking over the province scares the hell out of Washington. And when they get scared they're likely to go off in all directions. I guess you're the only one who was around during the Bay of Pigs, eh, John?" Penny nodded.

"I agree that in domestic terms, our best course of action is no action," the P.M. continued. "At least nothing overt. There may be other ways to ensure Belmont's election. But bear in mind there's always the danger that if we fail to show initiative, Washington will interpret it as weakness, an inability to control events, and that could be serious. The President has a tendency to shoot from the hip, remember. With that thought, gentlemen, good night."

The sealed file landed with a thump on the President's desk. *"DEPARTMENT OF STATE—TOP SECRET."* A weary Lawrence Wilde lit a cigarette as the President broke the seal and riffled through the daunting pile of paper.

"We've been watching the Quebec situation since nineteen sixty-three," Wilde said and, seeing the frown on the President's face, added quickly, "I asked them to include only the most recent and relevant material. The briefing paper on the top is an abstract of the rest. You'll notice it contains reports from the European Desk on the probable impact Quebec independence would have there, as well as an assessment from the Canada Desk. Just how quickly this assassination will accelerate matters is something we have to determine. I'll get the department at work on an update first thing in the morning."

"That's all I need, Larry. We're just a year away from an election and what's happening? There's Britain reduced to a banana republic, Spain about to blow up again, the Warsaw Pact doing their dervish dance along the Yugoslav border, the Russians swarming over Africa, OPEC about to turn off their taps again, and the Khmer Rouge ready to descend like locusts on Thailand. Now these bunglers in Canada have created a crisis right on our doorstep, for God's sake. And my wife wonders why I forgot our anniversary."

"Congratulations, sir."

"What? Oh, thank you. . . . But this Quebec business, this is bad news. We've got another Cuba on our doorstep, only worse. The Canadian government hasn't got the steel in their bellies to . . . " He left the statement unfinished as he began to read:

> *Department of State*
> *Document: ACD-18174-326H*
> *Classification: Top Secret*
> *To: Secretary of State Lawrence Wilde*
> *From: L. Munroe Fawcett, Assistant Secretary of State for European Affairs*
> *Report to the Secretary of State on the implications of an idependence declaration by the Province of Quebec, Canada*
> *This document updates and enlarges upon document ACD-14523-255A. Compiled by the North American Desk of the Department of State, in collaboration with senior officers of the European Desk.*

The first pages of the report were background, chronicling the rise of the independence movement in Quebec, the 1976 electoral victory of the Parti Québécois, and the

1978 referendum in which sixty-three per cent of Quebeckers approved independence within a framework of economic association with the rest of Canada.

"I don't think you'll find much there you don't already know, sir. The real guts is from page thirty-eight on," advised Wilde.

The President flipped through the report. There, neatly summarized, was what he wanted to know.

IMPLICATIONS

The consequences of Quebec breaking away from Canadian Confederation to establish a separate and independent state would be as follows:

1. POLITICAL:

Instability along our 3000-mile border with Canada. There is no certainty that the Canadian Confederation could survive a rupture of this magnitude. The splintering off of Quebec could encourage other provinces (ie., British Columbia, the Maritimes) to do likewise. In some cases, provinces or groups of provinces might invite annexation by the United States. In the case of British Columbia this could work to our advantage, enabling us to establish a land link with Alaska. But should the provinces attempt to go it alone we would be faced with the danger of economically weak and fragmented states along our northern border. In this event, our strategy should be to make client states of these new countries before a major power unfriendly to our national interests does so before us.

This risk is especially grave in the case of Quebec. The province has become highly radicalized in the last two decades, especially in the trade-union movement, the universities (faculty and students), and the working press (print and electronic media—see attached report on separatist bias within the Canadian Broadcasting Corporation). The present Quebec leadership has succeeded in holding the radicals in check. But it is our estimation from intelligence reports that they remain potentially strong and could gain control if Ottawa refuses to compromise.

2. RESOURCES:
Threat to our energy supplies. Canada and the U.S. reached agreement in 1977 and 1979 on the construction of gas and oil pipelines across the Yukon and the provinces of Alberta and Saskatchewan. These pipelines will feed the lower 48 states with the energy resources of the Prudhoe Bay area (see map). Construction has been delayed, but once these pipelines are fully on stream we estimate our dependence on imported energy supplies will be cut by 78% (accounting for estimates of alternative energy sources).

The fragmentation of Canada could seriously threaten the construction of these pipelines. Unless we are able to annex corridors along the routes, we run the danger of being forced to renegotiate pipeline treaties with new states of unknown political persuasions. Such a development could set back the completion of the pipelines by several years, throwing us back on the mercy of the OPEC countries.

3. ECONOMY:
Almost as serious from the economic standpoint is the danger of an unfriendly Quebec gaining control of the St. Lawrence Seaway. Several of our midwestern cities depend in large measure on the waterway for their economic vitality (e.g., Buffalo, Cleveland, Detroit, Milwaukee, Chicago, and Minneapolis-St. Paul). The threat of excessive tolls, or Seaway closure, could cause acute economic disruption. An unscrupulous government in Quebec could hold us to ransom in any negotiations over the right of passage. At this point in time, the Seaway is more critical to our economic well-being than the Panama Canal.

4. INTERNATIONAL REPERCUSSIONS:
History has shown that successful independence movements encourage similar attempts elsewhere. At the time of writing there are several move-

ments seeking autonomy in Europe alone: in the United Kingdom (Scotland and Wales; to a lesser extent, Cornwall), in Spain (Basques and Catalans), Italy (Tyrol), Yugoslavia (Croatians), and Belgium (Flemish). Each of these countries is of strategic importance within our European defense perimeter. Each is suffering domestic problems which would be further exacerbated by a sudden upsurge of independence movement activity spurred on by the example of Quebec. Intelligence sources indicate Soviet influence and support in a number of the above-mentioned nationalist groups. It is our assessment that Soviet agitators will seek to exploit the situation in these countries in the event of Quebec independence. We regard the situations in Yugoslavia, Spain, and Italy as hypercritical. With the expansion of the Soviet fleet in the Mediterranean, any political disruption in this area could bring us into direct conflict.

5. STRATEGIC IMPLICATIONS:
Quebec occupies a critical position within the North American Air Defense Command (NORAD). If an independent Quebec were to adopt a neutralist posture, the result would be to compromise severely the effectiveness of our early warning system centered on the Pine Tree Line in the northern part of the province. Loss of that segment of our aircraft- and missile-detection system would leave the American Eastern Seaboard vulnerable to surprise attack from across the North Pole. A neutralist Quebec could also impede the monitoring of foreign shipping in the Gulf of St. Lawrence, exposing the American Northeast to the possibility of nuclear submarine buildup in coastal waters.

An independent Quebec would also compromise Canada's effectiveness as a NATO partner. Major defense-production facilities would be lost: munitions plants in the Montreal area; aircraft factories in Montreal; shipyards in Sorel and the Quebec City area. It would take several

*years for new manufacturing facilities to be
developed in other parts of Canada.*

SUMMATION

*It is our opinion that the potential advantages
of Quebec independence (the possible annexation of territory from a fragmented Canada)
are far outweighed by the disadvantages. We
recommend that, in the American national interest and the interests of our NATO allies, our
government give the strongest possible support to
the government of Canada in any measures it
deems necessary to prevent separation by the
province of Quebec, up to and including direct
military intervention. We further recommend that
the Quebec government be made aware of the
U.S. government position in this matter in an
appropriate way as soon as possible.*

The President set the paper down on his desk and
ran his finger over the bald highway of his head. "Well,
that's unequivocal enough. I'll read the rest later, Larry,
but how do you think we should approach Quebec—
through Ottawa, or do we deal direct with the bastards?"

Wilde outlined for the President the PQ leadership
battle that was shaping up.

"I think we ought to let Ottawa know our position
and offer every assistance possible to them. Between us
we might be able to devise policies that will keep the
radical left out of the Quebec government. In the longer
term we should be working toward squeezing the PQ
out of office entirely to make room for a regime committed to Confederation."

"Very diplomatic, as always, Larry. But, dammit,
I've had it up to here with diplomacy. Everyone seems
to think they can push the U.S. around and we'll just
observe the diplomatic niceties and turn the other cheek.
We've been afraid to stand up for ourselves since Vietnam—but no more, if I've got anything to say about it.
Go ahead, draw up the statement. But while you're doing
that, I'm going to get the CIA in there and ask the Secretary of Defense to place the entire Northeast sector on

Yellow Alert. This mess is going to get solved, and it's going to be done our way for a change. Clear?"

"Clear."

"Good. Get to it."

The *Montreal Chronicle* building squatted soberly over an entire city block, a testament in more optimistic times to the power of the press. From his scruffy office on the eighth floor, Taylor Redfern, senior reporter and columnist, could see the St. Lawrence and the island ruins of Expo '67. As those pavilions had slowly fallen into decay so too had the fortunes of his newspaper. Fifteen years ago the *Chronicle* had enjoyed the reputation of being Canada's finest, but circulation had fallen off drastically, beginning with the exodus of English-speaking people after the Parti Québécois victory in 1976 and accelerated by the referendum results. As more English businesses relocated their head offices in Toronto and Ottawa, the paper's advertising revenue diminished. And so the noon edition that Redfern flipped through, to see what butchery the proofreaders had wrought on his copy, was flimsier than he would have wished.

At thirty-eight, Taylor Redfern was the last of a nucleus of award-winning journalists whose style and energy had made the *Chronicle* the envy of editors across the country in an era known ironically at the newsdesk as "B.F.P." Before French Power. While his colleagues had forsaken the province, lured by the security of flourishing newspapers and magazines elsewhere, Redfern had stayed. If his friends asked him why, he would say that he had too many books to pack. Not that he had any burning loyalty to the *Chronicle,* but he felt at home there and he enjoyed the distinction of being its best journalist—even if there was little competition now. An essentially tenacious person, he told himself that if he moved, he would have to learn all over again; his vast knowledge of Quebec and the network of contacts built up over the years would be almost useless elsewhere, as would the French he had absorbed in the streets.

And then there was the inducement of a fat bonus from his editor, Cameron Craig, as well as the freedom to pick his own assignments. Redfern took home more money than the *Chronicle*'s publisher, but the investment was considered worth while by the board of directors. Without his popular column and investigative stories the *Chronicle*'s circulation would have plummeted even further.

Redfern scanned his copy, looking for typesetting errors. He had been up all night, along with the rest of the *Chronicle*'s staff, preparing a special section on the assassination. He had written a personalized obituary of the murdered Premier as well as his regular column, in which he speculated on the future course of the Parti Québécois.

Irritated at the composing-room errors, he was marking corrections for the second edition when Cameron Craig's voice summoned him on the intercom. He grabbed the marked copy and headed for the editor's office.

"How is it those typesetters down there never make a mistake when it comes to French names, but they can't even spell 'dialogue'?" he complained as he entered Craig's office. "It's the same damn word in French."

"Maybe if you'd learn to use the video display terminals you wouldn't have so many problems," the editor said, without taking his eyes from the portable television set on top of the hospitality cabinet.

Redfern shuddered. He was one of the last holdouts against typing stories directly into the computer.

"What're you watching?" he asked, changing the subject.

"News," mumbled Craig. "Just want to see if we missed anything."

The inscrutable face of the CBC announcer stared out a livid red.

"Why don't you tune that thing in? Jesus, I know that guy and he doesn't suffer from beriberi!"

"Shut up and listen."

". . . shot and killed by Sergeant Auguste Touraine of the Provincial Police has now been positively identified as Kevin Reilly of the Point St. Charles district in Montreal."

"Good, we got that," said Craig.

". . . Police believe that Reilly was acting alone; however, they are investigating a report that a second assassin may have been involved. One eyewitness testified that he saw what could have been a rifle flash from the roof of a nearby government building at the time of the killing."

"Yeah, I got that from one of my people in Quebec," said Redfern, rubbing his red-rimmed eyes. "Our bureau there's working on it."

"No motive for the killing has yet been established. Police are working on the theory that the assassin may have been part of a radical English-speaking terrorist cell committed to the elimination of the PQ leadership. Security for other leading members of the party has been strengthened. Rumors of the existence of an Anglophone terrorist group, reminiscent of the old FLQ, have been circulating throughout the province for the past year."

"That's weird, they can't find a motive," said Redfern. "From what I could dig up, Reilly had no political connections. And there's nothing to say he was a psychopath."

"What about a terrorist group?" Craig asked.

"Well, if there is one, they're keeping pretty quiet about it. No one's claimed responsibility. No calls to the radio stations. You'd think they'd want to crow. Still, anything's possible in this best of all possible worlds."

". . . So far CBC reporters' attempts to contact the late Premier's bodyguard, Sergeant Touraine, have been met with steady refusals by the man who has now become the central figure in the assassination. Sergeant Touraine is reported to be suffering from severe emotional strain."

"You know, I once played gin rummy with that guy," Redfern said. "Outside the Cabinet Room. He always carried a deck with him and played solitaire to pass the time. He wasn't the type to go to pieces because he shot a man." He took out his pad and scribbled a note with the stub of a pencil.

As the voice droned on, the camera cut away to a still photograph of a rifle.

"Police ballistics experts have identified the murder weapon as an AR-15 Armalite, a lightweight, highly versatile rifle which used to be standard issue to U.S. and British forces under its service designation as the M-16. The Armalite, which has an effective range of four hundred yards, can be purchased at gun shops and sporting goods stores."

"Why the hell didn't we get that photograph?" demanded the editor. "How come the CBC got it and we didn't?"

Taylor Redfern squinted at the screen. There was something about the rifle that seemed odd. But the picture was blurred, his new contact lenses were bothering his eyes, and he moved forward for a closer look. What was it? The sight? Just as he approached, the camera cut back to the announcer.

"Damn."

"We'll have further reports on our bulletin at six. In other news today, the Energy Minister . . ."

Cameron Craig levered himself from his leather chair and snapped the set off.

"They got us on the murder weapon. I'll kick that Morgan's ass. Damn kids I have to employ these days. All he had to do was sweeten the police photographer. Don't they learn anything at journalism school?"

"You know, Cameron, that's what keeps me here, your shining integrity."

"Yeah, meanwhile we get scooped by the CBC, marvelous. Anyway, what do you make of it?"

"You mean the conspiracy theory? I dunno, it sounds like Kennedy all over again. Someone fires off two shots on a dark wet night. Both find their mark. It's possible. They never found the second bullet. The one they did came from the Armalite. Could be another gun. A cross fire makes more sense."

He felt the two-day beard on his cheeks.

"But I tell you what bothers me. Touraine. Why did he shoot Reilly in the back when the guy was plainly unarmed and running away? Not once, mind you, just to wing him. But three times, Cam, three times!"

"Yeah, I thought of that too. No wonder he doesn't want to see anyone."

"And then there's Reilly himself. If he shot the Premier, what was the reason? Was he part of some terrorist group? Was he a nut? A hired gun? Was he part of a conspiracy? If we only knew that."

"How would you like . . . ?"

"I know what you're going to say, Cam. How would

I like to do an in-depth profile on Reilly? Talk to his parents, his friends. His employer. Read his high-school yearbook. Check out his hobbies, interests, right?"

"You took the words out of my mouth. You should be able to peddle it to the States. The *New York Times* syndication service has been clamoring for stuff."

"You just talked me into it. But right now I'm going home to sleep. I've been in these clothes for two days."

"Funny," replied Craig, "and I thought you were looking particularly elegant today."

"Thanks very much," said Redfern from the door. "Oh, and by the way, if I do find an English-speaking terrorist group, I'll make sure this place is on their list."

Jean-Claude Belmont had not slept either since the death of his leader. His doctor had advised him to rest, but even in the moment of his deepest grief he could not abandon the party and the province to the machinations of Guy Lacroix. Now, as the senior minister, he sat in the Premier's chair, presiding over a cabinet meeting to decide upon the funeral arrangements.

Strange, he thought, when *he* sat in this chair he held the party together like glue, and now less than twenty-four hours after his death, we're at each other's throats over a question as trivial as the date of his funeral.

The Premier's mistress, with whom he had lived for five years, had requested a private ceremony followed by cremation. But she had no legal standing. The dead leader's wife and children had been content to leave the decisions concerning burial arrangements to the cabinet.

Rejean Normand, the Minister of Tourism and a strong supporter of Lacroix, was arguing for the funeral to be held on November 15, the anniversary of the party's accession to power. The fallen Premier would be presented to the world as a martyr in the sacred cause of Quebec's freedom. The emotional response in Quebec would force Ottawa to back down and grant independence on the province's terms. The scenario was ideal for Lacroix, so much so that one could almost suspect *him* of having arranged for the assassination.

Belmont dismissed the thought. However much of a demagogue his cabinet colleague might be, Lacroix could never be party to such an act. Yet the doubt lingered. The

Premier, his friend, deserved a dignified burial befitting a statesman of his accomplishments, not a three-ring circus designed to generate mass hysteria and to further Lacroix's political ambitions. It would be Lacroix who would ride the flood tide of passion right to the leadership of the party; and with that momentum Lacroix would carry Quebec to immediate separation, and the hell with the consequences.

As Normand pressed the case for a November 15 funeral, Belmont's mind began to wander. He tried to analyze his own motives. He did want to be Premier; had he not earned the leadership through his years of service to the party? Was he not, with the Premier and Lévesque, the prime mover behind its foundation? The thought of the mantle passing to a man like Lacroix was anathema to him.

He rapped his pipe on the table to interrupt Normand.

"Gentlemen, it is clear that we are getting nowhere. We have been here for four hours. I suggest a ten-minute recess. Perhaps Monsieur Lacroix and I could meet during that time to see if there is a way around this impasse." From the corner of his eye he saw Lacroix give a deprecatory shrug.

The two candidates for the leadership faced each other alone in a small antechamber off the Cabinet Room.

"We don't seem to be getting anywhere, Guy," remarked Belmont wearily.

"I don't understand you. Have you no sense of public relations?" The younger man pushed the hair out of his eyes with an impatient gesture.

"He was my friend. I will not have his funeral cheapened."

"What good can your friendship do him now? We are this much away from what he wanted." Lacroix held up his thumb and forefinger, an inch apart, to Belmont's face.

"I have a proposition," began the older man. There was a businesslike tone in his voice. Lacroix knew he was going to compromise.

"We will hold the funeral on November fifteenth, as you wish. But on one condition. There will be no speeches. No mass demonstrations. No rallies, no politics. Do you understand? The service will be simple, as he would have wanted, with no histrionics. I will not agree to anything that smacks of show business."

Lacroix thought for a moment. He could see one hundred thousand French Canadians on the Plains of Abraham singing the Quebec anthem. Television cameras bringing the message to the world that Quebec would be free. If he agreed to Belmont's proposition there could be none of that. But to get the funeral held on November 15, that was the crucial victory. He could exploit the moment after the fact.

"Very well. I accept. Now let's get this damn meeting over with."

Belmont was somewhat taken aback by Lacroix's ready acceptance; he had thought he would have to do more arm-twisting. Had he overlooked something? He was tired and the cabinet meeting had gone on long enough. He would worry about it later.

"All right," said Belmont. "All that's left, then, is the question of the eulogy."

"Kevin Reilly? Yes, he work here before." The hulking French Canadian breathed a mixture of beer and garlic over Taylor Redfern as he pumped gas into a Japanese car.

"How long?"

"Eight month, maybe. He serve gas and do some repair. But I never knew him. *Tabernac.*" The burly man spat on the forecourt. "If I knew what he did, I would have broke his legs like dat." He snapped his fingers.

"Did he have any friends? Did he see anyone, a girl perhaps?"

"No, he come in and he go out, never talk much. I think he was a little . . ." He placed an oil-encrusted finger to his head and rotated it in a small circle. A woman driver tooted her horn for service.

"Dat's all I know. I'm busy."

"Okay." Redfern put away his notebook and began walking. He hunched his narrow shoulders against the north wind. The swollen gray skies and the biting wind promised snow. Finding out everything there was to know about Reilly was proving more difficult than he had thought. No one would admit to knowing the man. There was definitely a girl friend. Several of Reilly's acquaintances had testified to that. "A knockout" was one description. But no one knew her name.

From public records he learned that Kevin Reilly was born in Montreal on May 22, 1958.

The boy had received his elementary education at the Blessed Virgin Elementary School in Point St. Charles. School records showed an unexceptional child, cooperative but shy. No sign of rebelliousness. If anything, he seemed something of a follower: "lacks initiative," "should be encouraged to develop his own self-expression," and "easily led" were typical comments on his report cards. The picture Redfern drew was of an introspective, intelligent boy, lacking self-confidence and apparently devoid of any ambition or drive.

A visit to Reilly's old high school confirmed the portrait. An English teacher at St. Stephen's remembered him as a "gangly lad who used to pick his nose. I had to keep telling him to stop. No, I don't recall him being much interested in girls. Not like some of the others in his class. I think he was afraid of girls."

His graduation yearbook carried the photo of an eighteen-year-old with long hair and a sallow, acned complexion. The caption read: "Kevin Reilly. Interests: Hunting, thinking. Girl friend: None (although Joanne would like to be). Best subject: Shop. Ambition: To make some money. Probable destination: A philosophical big-game hunter."

Very little to go on. Joanne, he discovered after lengthy inquiries, was killed in a car crash in Vermont the summer after graduation.

The mention of hunting. Reilly was obviously fascinated by guns from an early age. A former classmate recalled that Reilly had an uncle or cousin who had a shack in the Laurentians where they would hunt in the fall.

After high school there was no information whatsoever. Redfern could find no one who could tell him what had happened until Reilly surfaced several years later at the gas station. Reilly's parents would be the only ones who could provide the answers, but they had refused to have anything to do with the press in spite of large financial offers from competing newspapers. Their telephone had been disconnected.

As matters stood, Taylor Redfern, the top investigative

reporter left in English Quebec, had very little to show for his researches. There was nothing to be lost by having a crack at Reilly's parents. He took a taxi to their Point St. Charles tenement. At his knock, he heard the chain slide across the door.

"Who is it?" The weary voice of a middle-aged woman with the unmistakable cadence of Ulster.

"My name is Taylor Redfern. I knew your son, Mrs. Reilly."

There was no sound from the other side of the door. He could smell stale frying fat emanating from the apartment.

"He often fixed my car. We used to joke because I had my St. Christopher stuck on back to front."

"What do you want?"

"I work for the *Chronicle* . . ."

"Go 'way. I'll have nothing to do with the papers."

"No listen, please. Kevin has been badly treated by the press. I'd like to tell his side of the story. I know he wasn't like that."

He could hear a stifled sob from the other side of the door.

"May I come in? I can help Kevin. Put things right in my paper."

He waited for the sound of the chain sliding out of the bolt. But there was none.

"You can trust me, Mrs. Reilly. I knew Kevin at the Blessed Virgin years ago. Then I ran into him at the garage just a few months ago. Please, I can help him."

The door opened slowly and Mrs. Reilly, her greasy hair piled up in a bun above a careworn face, stood aside to let him in. He entered the living room, taking in the heavy Victorian furniture, the coconut matting on the floor, and a menagerie of carved wooden animals on every available surface.

"My husband does them," said Mrs. Reilly, motioning him to sit. The moment she sat down she burst into tears.

"You knew my boy. You know he'd not do such a terrible thing. He was a good boy, a quiet boy. He went to Quebec to see a friend. They shot him because he was running. You knew him at school. He could never do a thing like that."

"Who is it, Maura?" a man's voice called from the bedroom.

"It's a friend of Kevin's. Come to see us." The man, in a dressing gown and carpet slippers, entered the room, leaning on the furniture as he went.

"Taylor Redfern, Mr. Reilly. Those carvings are very impressive." The man looked at the journalist with empty eyes and sank down on the overstuffed sofa next to his wife.

"He says he can help Kevin by writing in the newspaper—the truth."

"The truth," repeated the man, staring vacantly in front of him.

Redfern proceeded cautiously to interview them about their son's background, but their answers did little to fill in the gaps. Finally, he said, "May I see Kevin's room, please?"

"The police went through it and took everything away," said Mrs. Reilly softly. "There's nothing there."

The sentence ended in a wail. Her husband looked at her briefly and sighed.

"I'm sorry, I didn't want to upset you. If you'll just show me where it is."

The woman waved a hand toward the hall.

The room was small and dark, more like a cell than a bedroom. A single bed made up neatly, covered by a carefully mended bedspread. On the boxwood table, painted white, was a reading lamp made from a Chianti bottle. The floral wallpaper added the only touch of color, apart from a vividly painted crucifix over the bed. The few articles of clothing in the closet dangled from wire hangers, emphasizing the owner's absence. A turned-out pocket was the only indication that the police had touched them. On the bookcase were a few paperback novels, some old car-maintenance manuals, and a heavy, leather-bound family Bible. The inscription in the flyleaf revealed that it had been presented to Maura and Cathal Reilly on their wedding day by the bride's parents. Presumably they had passed it on to their son on his majority. Redfern thumbed idly through it. Kevin's birth was recorded, as was the birth of a daughter two years later. The deaths record showed the little girl had died at six months. The passing of Kevin's grandparents was recorded in the appropriate place; the life cycle of the family was all there. A faded blue ribbon marker divided the book of Judges, chapter 16. A passage had been underlined and then obviously rubbed out, as the trace of the pencil was still visible. The quotation read, "And the house fell upon the lords, and upon all the people that were therein." In the margin next to the lines Redfern could discern numbers which had also been rubbed out. He carried the book to the window. Very faintly he made out the seven digits of a phone number. He made a note of it and continued leafing through the Bible. There was nothing else of interest.

"Please, help my son," said Mrs. Reilly as she accompanied him to the door. "They said some terrible things about him, but he wasn't like that at all."

Redfern breathed more easily once he was in the street again. He was not proud of himself, intruding upon parental grief. At times like these, he hated his job.

"Ladies and gentlemen, we will be landing at London's Heathrow Airport in a few minutes. Kindly fasten your seat belts and place your seat backs in the upright position. . . ." Ross Anson opened his eyes. A British Airways stewardess stood over him with a trayful of steaming towels. With a fixed smile, she held one out with a pair of tongs. Dutifully he took it. It burned his fingers. He dropped it involuntarily on his papers and retrieved it too late to stop the ink from smudging over the IntCon letterhead.

The stewardess had disappeared by the time he looked up. He cursed the airline for not having a first-class seat available for him. As general manager of La Société Minière du Québec Ltée., known as SoMin, IntCon's Canadian mining subsidiary, he was used to traveling everywhere first class. But the imperious summons by Holbrook Meadows necessitated his catching the first available plane out of Montreal. He had been sitting over breakfast reading newspaper reports of the assassination when the phone call had come. Meadow's executive assistant would give no indication as to why a meeting was so urgent— just arrive in London on the next plane.

All the way across the Atlantic, Anson had been rereading the most recent correspondence he had received from Meadows. The old boy always handwrote his letters to senior management, an eccentric affectation, Anson had always thought. He tried to speculate on the nature of the emergency that called for his immediate presence in London. He was aware that SoMin's operations had not met profit projections, but that was beyond his control. The Quebec government had been slow in granting development rights for the iron and copper deposits held by his company. Quebec was insisting that IntCon build processing plants in Quebec before licenses would be issued to SoMin. London was understandably lukewarm about investing some forty million dollars through their New York bankers to develop secondary industry in an area of uncertain political climate. The result was a standoff.

No, it was more likely that Meadows wanted a complete briefing on the incredible uranium strike his geologists had recently confirmed on Concessions 41, 44, and 46—parcels of land along the eastern shore of Hudson's Bay where SoMin held exclusive exploration rights. According to the chief geologist, the find could conceivably be the largest bed of uranium ore ever discovered; if so, it would double the proven world reserves of the mineral, including those in the Soviet Union. Meadows had had a confidential report of the find at least a month ago. Why the sudden panic?

"Ladies and gentlemen, as we are making our final descent to Heathrow, would you kindly extinguish all cigarettes and refrain from smoking until you are in the terminal building. Thank you."

The 747 dipped into the cloud bank and splashes of rain cut across the windows. Ross Anson shuffled his papers together and tucked them into his briefcase. The plane broke through the overcast and Anson looked down on the muddy ribbon of the Thames and the drab suburbs of London. He wished he were back in Montreal.

Holbrook Meadows's chauffeur was there to meet him as he came through customs. He handed him his suitcase, and at first the man seemed reluctant to take it.

"Where am I booked into, George?"

"You mean the hotel, sir? I don't know that, sir. Mr. Meadows is here at the airport. He's waiting in the car outside."

Anson stopped in his tracks. Meadows was never even out of bed at this hour of the morning, let alone waiting for an underling at Heathrow Airport.

Holbrook Meadows was indeed at Heathrow, sitting impatiently in the back seat of the company Rolls-Royce Silver Cloud, slapping the palm of his hand with a rolled copy of the *Financial Times*. His greeting to Anson was perfunctory, and he wasted no time in getting to the point.

"Someone should have told you not to pack a suitcase. You won't need it, Anson. You're booked back to Montreal on the eleven-thirty flight."

Anson sank back into the luxurious comfort of the Rolls.

"Are you serious?"

"I didn't bring you all this way to joke with you. Now listen to me very carefully. Ever since your phone call two nights ago I've been thinking about the situation in Quebec as a result of the assassination. From our corporate point of view, events are exceedingly fortuitous. We must take advantage of them."

"I don't understand."

"Simply, my dear Anson, we must do everything in our power to ensure that Monsieur Lacroix becomes the next Premier of Quebec."

"But the Parti Québécois is antibusiness, and Lacroix's the worst of the bunch." Anson was tired and he couldn't follow his chairman's reasoning.

"I didn't fly you over here to argue politics with you, Anson. All I am prepared to tell you is that in the long-term interests of IntCon it is essential that Lacroix win the leadership." The voice trembled on the edge of anger. Ross Anson was about to express his indignation at the way he had been treated—flown over with no information, told he was returning two hours later, and the wiser only for some seemingly absurd diktat by his superior. Meadows patted him on the knee.

"I'm sorry, Ross. You must be tired. I'm afraid I cannot go into details. The fewer people who know, the better. Just trust me that what I have told you in the strictest confidence is for the good of the company and its future. I have a lot of faith in you. That's why you are here. I could have sent someone from headquarters to do what I am asking you to do."

Meadows's soothing words acted like a balm on Anson's frayed nerves.

"What do you want me to do?"

"Good man. I want SoMin behind Lacroix's campaign. You are to make available to the Lacroix campaign fund any money they may need."

"Up to what limit?"

"I said nothing about a limit. I repeat, any money they may need."

"But sir, there are laws in the province governing donations to political parties."

"For elections, yes. But this is not an election. It's a leadership contest, which does not come within the act. I have had our legal department check into it. The Parti Québécois has rules governing the amount of money a candidate for the leadership can spend. But these are party regulations, not laws."

"But what if it got out that SoMin or IntCon was throwing money at Lacroix?"

"It would be most embarrassing both for Monsieur Lacroix and for us. That is why the matter must be handled with the utmost discretion. Which is why you are here and why you will be bringing this back to Montreal with you."

Meadows leaned down and picked up a new leather briefcase from the floor of the car. He drew a key from his pocket and unlocked it. He lifted the lid and there, neatly stacked, were bundles of Canadian one-hundred-dollar bills.

"One million dollars, Anson. There will be more if it is needed." He locked the briefcase again and handed the key to the amazed Canadian.

"Sir, don't get me wrong, but why all this charade? Why couldn't I simply draw the money from the company account in Montreal instead of flying six thousand miles to bring it back? And God knows what I'm going to do at customs!"

"You must be more tired than I thought. In the first place, we want no record of this transaction, either through our banks or in our own books. This money comes from a special IntCon contingency fund which I alone control. The only way to get it to you without any bookkeeping entries was this way. Unorthodox, but essential."

"But what about customs?"

"As far as British customs is concerned, exchange-control regulations apply only to sterling leaving the country, not foreign currencies. In Canada, well, if you went through the green area and they asked you to open up you'd have some explaining to do. But I have saved you that trouble. When you pick up your baggage at Mirabel Airport you will go directly to the customs officer at position thirty-two. Hand him your passport before you display your luggage and you'll have no problem. Providing, of course, you are on the eleven-thirty plane."

"What about security?"

"There's no law about carrying a briefcase full of money onto an airplane, as long as there isn't a gun in it."

Anson lapsed into silence. Holbrook Meadows had thought of everything.

"Are you satisfied, my dear chap? Splendid. You have two hours and forty minutes until your departure." He handed the briefcase to Anson, who shook hands and opened the car door. Meadows pressed a button, and the window wound down.

"Have a good flight, old chap. You're booked first class, of course."

Ross Anson watched the Rolls-Royce purr away. He turned and walked slowly back into the terminal building with one million dollars in his hand.

"Give me that again, Taylor."

Cameron Craig leaned forward across the desk.

"I said there was a phone number in the family Bible. Someone had tried to erase it. As soon as we're finished, I'll call. . . ."

"Not that, for God's sake! Who cares about some bloody phone number." He waved his hands impatiently. "What you said before. About the friend."

Redfern squinted at his notes.

"All I said was that his mother claimed he was in Quebec City to visit a friend, and that he was an innocent victim. . . ."

"That's it!" Craig brought the palm of his hand down on the desk with a smack. "My God, Taylor, don't you see the potential story there? If she's right, then it could be that Reilly wasn't the assassin at all. Which would mean Touraine shot the wrong man and that the real killer or killers are still at large. Jesus! What a beat that would be!"

"Come on, Cam. It's pretty obvious Reilly did it. They found the murder gun in his room. His prints were all over it. Anyway, his parents were in a state of shock. That friend business sounds like a defense mechanism to me."

"Yeah. Still, it should be checked out. Maybe the so-called 'friend' was an accomplice. Get on the next plane to Quebec and do some nosing around. See if you can come up with anything."

"Okay. What about the phone number?"

"Christ, will you stop going on about that! For just once in your illustrious career will you do what your kindly editor suggests?"

Redfern shrugged. "All right, Cam. You're the boss. And you sure don't let anyone forget it."

Along Grande Allée hundreds of blue-and-white fleur-de-lis flags flapped wetly at half-mast in the northerly wind. The first snow melted as soon as it hit the ground, but it did not deter the mourners who waited patiently outside the Quebec Legislature, determined to pay their final respects to their dead Premier.

"There must be twenty thousand waiting out there. There's a great front-page pic," whispered Ed McBeam, the *Chronicle's* photographer, to Taylor Redfern. They stood at a window in the National Assembly chamber, looking down on the line of people that stretched from the legislature building down the hill to Avenue Dufferin and around the corner to Grand Allée, where it doubled back on itself. Redfern could not see the end of it from his vantage point.

Oblivious to the elements, the mourners shuffled slowly down the street and into the chamber for a quick glimpse of the closed coffin and the floral tributes from Quebec and Canada and around the world. The collective grief expressed itself in silent tears, a hand held to the mouth, and fingers closed in prayer around rosary beads. Redfern was moved by what he saw. Although he knew Quebec well, he could never have predicted the depth of feeling this tragedy had generated from the very soul of French Canada. The man who lay shattered in the coffin symbolized centuries of frustration as well as the hopes and dreams of all French Canadians. By the force of his political will, the Premier had forged a covenant with these people, and the rupturing of it had caused a national trauma as painful as the death of a beloved king. There was no parallel in Canadian history; the closest Redfern could find in his own memory was the killing of President Kennedy in 1963 and the traumatic effect it had had on the American psyche.

Two tall candles stood at the head and foot of the oak coffin, which rested on a raised dais. At each corner, a member of the Quebec Provincial Police guard of honor stood with head bowed. On top of the casket was a wreath of lilies from the Premier's family. Surrounding the dais were elaborate floral displays, arranged according to protocol. Those from heads of state had pride of place, followed by heads of government, then ambassadors, and so on down the line. Redfern noted with irony that wreaths from the Queen and from the Prime Minister of Canada occupied prominent positions. The Premier would have been amused by the hypocrisy of it all. Redfern felt a twinge of sadness that the Premier's mistress had not been permitted to send flowers for display. A functionary had decided it would be unseemly to call attention to her on such a solemn occasion. Other flowers—from the less exalted business firms, trade unions, ordinary people—were displayed in one corner. The cavernous room smelled like a greenhouse.

"Get some shots of all the wreaths and things when you get a minute, Ed," he whispered to the photographer. "We could use them as part of a center spread. Make sure you get the names in. Looks like everyone got in on the act, from the Queen down."

"Or up." McBeam grinned.

Ushers on both sides of the coffin kept the lines moving. Others policed a roped-off area for the working press which allowed reporters, photographers, and cameramen closer access to the scene than they would have had from the press gallery at the other end of the chamber. From this area, Redfern could study the faces of the people who filed past. His trip to Quebec to check whether, by some remote chance, there was any truth to Mrs. Reilly's account of her son's death had proved fruitless. The friend Kevin Reilly was supposed to have been visiting didn't exist. Redfern now had enough material on the assassin to begin writing his series, but since he was in Quebec City anyway, he decided to see the Premier's lying-in-state. And the experience suggested another story idea to him: the people's reaction to the death of their leader.

As he searched the faces in front of him, he became dimly aware that he himself was being watched. The prickling feeling in the back of his neck alerted him. He glanced quickly along the line of mourners, but their attention was fixed on the large, highly polished casket. Nor was anyone within the press area staring at him; his colleagues were all intent on the scene before them. Yet the uneasy feeling persisted. He looked up at the tall windows which filtered in the dull gray afternoon light. His eyes traveled the length of the wall to the press gallery at the far end of the room. There he caught sight of two people in the gloom, almost in shadow. A man with a camera, its telephoto lens trained in his direction, and a woman, who seemed to be pointing at him. A dark-haired woman. He felt a pang of fear pass through him, and he turned to Ed McBeam for reassurance. The photographer was putting a new roll of film into his Pentax.

"Ed, don't make it look too obvious," he said as calmly as he could, "but there's a guy with a camera in the press gallery. And a woman with him. Do you know either of them?"

McBeam turned casually and looked up.

"What's the matter? This stuff getting to you, Taylor?" he hissed. "There's no one up there."

Redfern turned and looked up again. The gallery was empty.

Cameron Craig grunted as he skimmed through Redfern's copy. The journalist had learned over the years to interpret his editor's reactions; he could tell Craig was not pleased, and he knew why. The two-part profile on Kevin Reilly was merely a reworking of the material every other newspaper already had. There was nothing new on the conspiracy theory, nothing that might have linked Reilly to an English terrorist gang, no sex, and nothing more violent than Reilly's hunting trips with his uncle.

"Taylor, frankly this is a piece of shit. What's the matter with you? That reaction story was great. Lots of response. The goddamned lines were jammed with French

Canadians sobbing their hearts out. But this . . ." He waved Redfern's article at him.

"I know. I wouldn't have given it to you, but you wanted something on Reilly before tomorrow's funeral."

"Yeah, but I could have gotten Morgan to stitch this thing together from our cuttings file."

"Everything just petered out, Cam. There's a girl in the background, but I couldn't find her and the parents are too shellshocked to give anything. At least I got to them," Redfern snapped. He had had a sleepless night after the two-and-a-half-hour drive back from Quebec. The girl and the photographer in the gallery kept coming back to him and, with their image, a tremor of anxiety passed through him.

"Well, we've got to run something, but I can't see New York picking this up. You've missed the most important thing about the man in your research."

"What the hell are you talking about? I know it's not Pulitzer Prize stuff, but at least I got a description of the parents." Redfern prided himself on the accuracy of his research, and to suggest his facts were wrong was tantamount to questioning his standing as a reporter.

"Easy, man. It's probably not your fault, but I would have thought you'd be able to dig up the one piece of information on our friend here that would blow this whole business wide open."

"What information, what are you talking about?"

Craig put his feet on the desk and locked his fingers across his stomach in a gesture of self-satisfaction.

"It seems there's an Ottawa connection here. Those missing years between school and the garage—well, I got a phone call from the Ottawa bureau. And you know what Kevin Reilly was doing for some of that time? He was in the Royal Canadian Mounted Police. That's right. Our killer's an ex-Mountie."

From his third-row pew in Quebec City's Basilica of Notre Dame, Jean-Claude Belmont, a black band on his left arm, looked up as the television crew in the rood loft turned on its lights. Two rows in front of him, in full-dress uniform, sat the Governor-General of Canada and his wife, dressed in black. Behind them sat the Lieutenant-Governor of Quebec and his family. The honorary pallbearers, of whom

Belmont was one, occupied the third row, while directly behind them sat the Prime Minister of Canada and his entourage, all steadfastly keeping their eyes on the altar. Across the aisle, the slain Premier's family filled the front pew. Several Quebec cabinet ministers, who had not been chosen as honorary pallbearers, were placed directly behind. Belmont glanced back. The ancient basilica was filled with dignitaries: the Speaker of the National Assembly, the Chief Justice of the Supreme Court of Canada, numerous ambassadors, the nine other provincial premiers, federal cabinet ministers, members of the privy council, M.P.s and M.N.A.s, civic representatives, and a few party workers. The fifteen hundred seats of the basilica were full; Belmont knew that thousands more had gathered outside in Rue de la Fabrique to hear the service over loudspeakers.

He swiveled around to check on Guy Lacroix, who was seated at the end of his pew. The two men exchanged formal nods. He thought about the bargain they had struck. As the leading honorary pallbearer on the route through Upper Town to the basilica, Belmont had scanned the crowds on the sidewalks for evidence of demonstrations inspired by the Minister of Social Affairs. But there was nothing, no placards, no agitation, no shouting. Just a sea of somber faces concentrating on the horse-drawn hearse bearing the coffin draped with a fleur-de-lis flag. At least Lacroix had kept his word.

The service began; it would be a long ritual, lasting about an hour. Belmont closed his eyes as the voice of the Archbishop of Quebec floated sonorously to the stone vaulting above, like a hot-air balloon. The camera lights added to the heat, and Belmont allowed his mind to disengage. He recalled his first meeting with the Premier. They had been on opposing sides of a debate at the University of Montreal law school. . . .

A jab in the ribs and a hoarse whisper from Gilbert St. Cyr, the Minister of Lands and Forests, brought him back to the present.

"For God's sake, Jean-Claude, the TV cameras. If they get a shot of you dozing, you can kiss the leadership good-by."

Belmont pulled himself upright. His colleague was right. He wondered how long he had been dreaming. He busied himself by studying the printed order of service. The eulogy was next.

The debate over who would deliver the eulogy had sparked off another cabinet row. In order that no one might make political capital out of the oration, the honor would fall not to the Premier's political associates but to the Archbishop of Quebec, a man known for his scrupulous integrity, and his monumental ignorance of political realities. His remarks would be brief and bland—the cabinet had already studied the text and emasculated it of any reference which might favor either faction. The congregation waited as the Archbishop moved slowly from the altar to the pulpit steps.

Belmont did not even hear Lacroix leave his seat. He was aware of the Minister of Social Affairs only as he strode purposefully toward the pulpit. He felt the blood rise in his neck.

"What the hell is he doing?" St. Cyr's whisper sounded more like a scream in his ear. Jean-Claude Belmont knew exactly what his rival was doing, and he cursed him for his opportunism.

Lacroix's occupation of the pulpit happened so quickly that there was no time for anyone to react. He exchanged a few words with the Archbishop, who appeared to shake his head, but, guided by a gentle but firm pressure on his elbow, the man of God abandoned the pulpit to the young cabinet minister. A low buzz of anticipation rose from the congregation. Belmont dug his fingers into his thighs to contain his anger. He had suspected that Lacroix would do something, but not in the basilica, not before the most influential men in Canada.

"My dear friends . . ."

Belmont leaned over to St. Cyr as Lacroix began to speak. "See if you can get the power to the television cameras cut off."

St. Cyr slithered out of his pew and ducked around the line of columns in the nave.

". . . I must apologize to the Archbishop and to you all for these unscheduled words. But sitting down there among you and seeing the coffin of my dead leader . . ."

Belmont looked back at the Prime Minister, who sat stony-faced. His bodyguard had caught his eye and made an imperceptible gesture, but the Prime Minister shook his head.

". . . I could not suppress my grief or my anger." Lacroix had gambled everything, and he had won. He had the eyes of the nation on him; the congregation sat in stunned silence, unable, and unwilling, to stop him. "Our murdered leader dedicated his life to the freedom of Quebec. And here we are, two years after his succession to the leadership mourning his loss, a loss we feel the more keenly since his goal of independence was within his grasp. Only the obstinacy of Ottawa now stands between the people of Quebec . . ." (he paused long enough for the cameras to take a reaction shot of the glowering Prime Minister) ". . . and the liberty that this man . . ." (another pause as he pointed toward the coffin) ". . . this martyr—for that is indeed what he is—had sought for them. We who are left must take up his banner and fearlessly march with it until his ideals have triumphed.

"Many of those who stand blocking the path of history are in this holy place now, going through the motions of mourning the death of this great leader while in their hearts they rejoice in his passing. I do not have to name them. The people of Quebec know who they are, and the people will not be deceived."

Isolated voices in the basilica began to call out to have Lacroix removed. The Prime Minister and his staff were on their feet and moving angrily along their aisle. Lacroix's supporters urged him to continue, chanting, "Speak, speak." The television cameras panned across the faces of the mourners.

Lacroix raised his voice in exhortation over the swelling babel from the pews. Pointing directly at the departing Prime Minister, he shouted, "But there is more. These men have not confined their opposition to the political arena. They knew they were losing the battle. So they resorted to desperate measures. They had our leader murdered by a man trained in killing by the RCMP."

As Lacroix's voice reached its crescendo of accusation, the basilica was plunged into sudden darkness. St. Cyr had found the master switch. The noise in the pews redoubled as the crowds outside burst through the west door to add their voices to the chaos. In the panic-charged darkness, Lacroix's voice, now raised to a scream, cut through the sea-like roar: "From this holy ground I pledge that their terrible plan will not succeed. The people will triumph. Quebec will be free. *Vive le Québec Libre.*"

"Bienvenue à Trois-Rivières," the sign read in French. *"Vitesse 50 km."*

Monique Gravelle did not bother to slow down. The Quebec police were rarely on the lookout for speedsters these days, and besides, they would hardly ticket an attractive girl driving a TR8 with the top down in the rain. Her black hair hung lankly down her face and spilled over the collar of her sheepskin coat. She turned off the ramp leading down from the Laviolette Bridge and followed the signs to the town center. The radio switched from music to the six o'clock news. The lead item, as it had been all day, was Guy Lacroix's outburst at the funeral that morning. The story was augmented now by reactions from provincial premiers, outraged to a man. The announcer described how the federal delegation had walked out of the basilica. The Prime Minister had flown back to Ottawa, where he issued a blistering statement denouncing the Quebec Minister of Social Affairs and categorically denying any federal complicity in the assassination. In Quebec City, Lacroix's office was reportedly inundated with telephone calls and telegrams which, according to his staff, were running four to one in favor of his performance.

With a cynical shrug Monique twisted the dial. "I bet damn few came from here," she said to the empty passenger seat. Trois Rivières was the home of Jean-Claude Belmont, and he had represented the riding in Quebec since 1972. From her research she knew the city to be deeply conservative, with a proud political heritage. Maurice Duplessis, for whom Quebec had been a personal fiefdom during his years as Premier from the mid-1940s until his death in 1959, called Trois-Rivières home. So had a phalanx of federal and provincial ministers before and since.

Monique's first impression of the place was hardly favorable. Even the dampening rain could not disguise the pungent smell of sulphur that hung like a foretaste of hell over the town—a perpetual reminder of the pulp and paper mills to which the community owed its undisciplined growth. The local industry had spewed its grime over the lines of small, unprepossessing houses, many of them shingled with asphalt. Everything about the place seemed mean and ugly.

She turned into Rue Royale, one of the main commercial streets, looking for her motel. The tawdry store windows began to depress her. "And I've got to spend a month in this hole," she muttered.

Her motel was close to the town center, off Rue des Forges. A huge neon sign winked lasciviously at her. At first sight the motel seemed passable, the one-story units set in a semicircle around the parking lot. She took her suitcase from the trunk, zipped the protective leather cover over the cockpit of the car, and hurried to the reception desk. She signed the register, paid a week in advance, and took her key.

Her room smelled damp; the iron bedstead creaked as she threw her case on the mattress. The furniture looked as if it had been refused by the Salvation Army. The dresser was chipped and pitted with cigarette burns. The mirror was cracked. The only chair in the room had a vinyl covering which had been slashed by a previous occupant. The floor lamp beside it lacked a bulb, and the curtains—originally floral-patterned, now sunbleached beyond redemption—refused to meet across the grubby windows. Monique Gravelle surveyed the room in disgust. Next door, someone flushed the toilet.

She checked the bathroom. A cigarette butt floated in the toilet bowl. Tiles around the bathtub were missing. There was no soap in the basin, and the maid, if there was one, had forgotten to provide fresh towels.

Still, she had put up with worse. She shrugged, put in a call to the reception desk for soap and linen, and set about unpacking. There was one thing more she had to do before she went in search of dinner. She slid the Trois-

Rivières telephone directory out from beneath the room phone and thumbed through the pages until she came to the B's. She had no difficulty in finding Belmont's office, printed as it was in bold typeface. She jotted the number down on the pad beside the phone. In the morning she would call the office and offer her services to Jean-Claude Belmont and his as-yet-undeclared campaign for the leadership of the Parti Québécois.

The traffic swirled around l'Étoile in a dizzying blur. A black Citroën taxi jockied for position, the curses of the driver punctuating the animated monologue he kept up for the benefit of his aristocratic-looking passenger.

"I have a friend in the Gendarmerie and he tells me there are fifty accidents a day here, monsieur. And by God, I think he's underestimating."

Antoine de Luzt glanced out of the window at the honking madness around him. "One day I would like to drive a Leopard tank around l'Étoile," he said, and the driver laughed. But de Luzt was serious. The taxi edged out of the traffic whirlpool and headed down Avenue de la Grande Armée. The driver breathed a sigh of relief, and de Luzt leaned back in his seat.

The evening until now had been a feast for his senses. Dinner at La Tour d'Argent in the company of Thérèse St. Rémy, whose coffee-colored body had been set off by a simple white gown. She was not only beautiful but as exciting in bed as any woman he had known. After the meal, they had returned to his apartment overlooking the Seine for brandy and coffee. He had undressed her on the glassed-in balcony and tilted his brandy glass over her breasts; he watched the amber liquid flow over her erect nipples, and she shivered as his tongue licked the alcohol from her body. She held his head to her stomach as his teeth sank into her flesh. She moaned as he carried her to the king-size bed, which was covered with an enormous otter-fur rug. Nor did she resist when he pulled her arms above her head and clamped leather cuffs about her wrists. She looked at him through half-closed eyes, swaying her hips back and forth on the silky animal hide. When de Luzt had secured the girl's legs in similar fashion to each of the brass posts, he felt under the bed for the tightly plaited silk whip. Then he sat himself astride her as if she were a horse and began to flick at her thighs with the whip, rocking on his knees so that his penis rubbed against her stomach. The girl's eyes shone and she stiffened with each touch of the whip. As he approached his climax, de Luzt suddenly leaped up and, standing at the bedside, began to thrash wildly at the girl's breasts and genitals. She cried out in pain, and her cries aroused him to a frenzy. Her body arched in orgasm. Her legs were wet and she was whimpering with pain and pleasure. She fell back exhausted, and de Luzt threw himself upon her, pressing himself deep into her, his hands under her buttocks. . . .

The memory of those moments stirred in his loins. A pity he had been called away; there were more games they could have played until dawn. But there was no mistaking the urgency of the summons.

The taxi entered La Défense, on the city's western limits, a sprawling cluster of high-rises and barren plazas that were the architectural legacy of de Gaulle and Pompidou. The Paris of the twenty-first century, it had been called. De Luzt grimaced at the concrete-and-glass jungle about him. The streets were deserted. The driver dropped him outside a high-rise; de Luzt paid the fare and the driver sped away as if he were impatient to return to the real Paris. De Luzt hesitated a moment and checked his watch: five minutes after midnight. The elevator whisked him to the nineteenth floor. He walked along the carpeted corridor until he found the number he was looking for. He glanced around him before he rang the bell.

He heard a movement at the peephole and then a pause before the door was opened to him. Before him stood Hilaire Noel, a man in his late sixties. He was fully dressed and freshly shaved, as if he were just starting the day instead of ending it. The odor of leaves and blossoms wafted out from the apartment, a damp, sweet smell that reminded de Luzt of the woman he had left behind in his bed.

"Forgive me for dragging you here at such an hour, my dear Antoine. Necessity dictates, however. I trust I have not taken you away from anything important?"

"No," replied de Luzt, as he made his way past potted plants and ferns. "The pleasures of the flesh are transient."

"Ah," replied the man, with a wave of the hand. "Happily one forgets pain, too. Please, do be seated."

The living-room furniture was lost in an undergrowth of exotic vegetation. "What will you have for company?" asked the older man, motioning toward the chairs. "A Venus's flytrap or an orange tree?"

"I'll live dangerously," replied de Luzt, seating himself beside the fleshy tendrils of the flytrap. "This place looks more like Borneo every time I come."

His host laughed a silvery laugh.

"On a civil servant's pension one cannot retire to the Côte d'Azur, so one brings the subtropics to Paris. Plants are more obedient than pets and better listeners than one's lovers. Some coffee, Antoine?"

"By all means." As Hilaire Noel clattered about his tiny kitchen, grinding beans and boiling water, de Luzt played with the spider plant on the coffee table in front of him. Had he not known the influence this odd little man still possessed in the corridors of power, he might have dismissed him as a dotty eccentric. But Hilaire Noel had made good use of his years in the Elysée Palace. As executive secretary to the President he had become privy to many high-level secrets, and his instinct for the backstairs kept him informed of happenings at every level of government. He had used his information wisely and disbursed his favors with discretion, all of which made him a man who could be trusted and one whose usefulness to the state did not end with his retirement from government service. The French President had enough regard for him to entrust him with matters too delicate to be furthered through official channels. As a result, de Luzt was a more than occasional visitor to the small apartment.

Noel returned from the kitchen with a tiny tray on which were set two demi-tasses and a small pot of coffee. He set it down in front of de Luzt.

"I asked you to come tonight because we have just received new intelligence concerning the situation in Quebec."

The use of the term "we" alerted de Luzt to the fact that the ex-civil servant had begun his briefing. His whole manner became crisper, and the affectations of speech and movement dropped away like a dead skin.

"First, the leadership convention. No date has been officially set, but our information indicates that it will take place on February seventeenth in Quebec City. We expect to have confirmation of this within a week."

De Luzt nodded and took a sip of coffee.

"As I've indicated to you, the future security and economic well-being of France is bound up with the future of Quebec. In fact, it rests on the shoulders of Guy Lacroix. I cannot stress this too highly, Antoine: if Lacroix is not elected on February seventeenth, it could doom France to the role of a second-rate power for generations."

De Luzt was about to interrupt, but the older man ignored him.

"Until today, we did not anticipate a great deal of difficulty in achieving this. However, the Quai d'Orsay has this very evening received a coded dispatch from our embassy in Washington which could alter the balance. The American President, according to our information, has begun to busy himself with Quebec. On his instructions, the CIA has sent operatives into the province to ensure that Monsieur Lacroix is defeated and the leadership passes to Jean-Claude Belmont. Should the Americans succeed in this, it would be disastrous for the interests of France."

De Luzt frowned. He knew the CIA of old. He had worked for them and against them. He admired the resources they had at their disposal, but he knew they would be at a disadvantage in Quebec unless they had carefully built up a network in the province over the years—which he doubted. Quebec was like a small town, and strangers were viewed with suspicion. It would be virtually impossible to go in cold in a situation like this and be effective.

"I need more information, Hilaire," he said. "I can see why the Americans might be nervous, given their proximity to Quebec. But what would they hope to gain by sending in the CIA? I still don't understand why it is so important for France. Why would we risk an open confrontation with the United States over Quebec? What makes the stakes so high?" De Luzt waited, but the old man said nothing. "You're holding something back. In the past, you've always given me full background on an assignment."

"Don't you adore these maidenhair ferns, so ethereal," said Noel, reverting to his pose as an effete old ditherer. De Luzt was one of his most efficient operatives, but one whose loyalty was to himself and then to the highest bidder. Therefore he remained a security risk. He was well paid for his services, but the Americans had fiscal persuasion of their own.

"I am truly sorry, my dear Antoine. I can tell you no more at this time. I must ask you to take my word. But I do have something to offer you. Because of this new intelligence about our American friends, I have been authorized to make available to you any additional resources you might require for the completion of your assignment."

"If I didn't know you, Hilaire, I would say that you are trying to buy my loyalty." The anger de Luzt felt expressed itself in sarcasm. Hilaire Noel would tell him no more than he already had.

"Loyalty is not a word in my vocabulary, Antoine. Only commitment."

"Let me think about it. If I need anything, I'll let you know in the usual way."

The meeting was over. De Luzt drained the last of his coffee while Noel phoned for a taxi. On the elevator down, de Luzt pondered the information. The presence of the CIA in Quebec added a new and potentially dangerous element to the situation. Why were they there? And why was the survival of France riding on the outcome? He had no answers, and he didn't like operating in the dark. He would make it his business to find out exactly what was going on.

The town of Pointe Claire, a dormitory suburb of Montreal, is a middle-class English enclave fifteen miles west of the city center. Like other English communities in and around Montreal its trim lawns had mushroomed with "For Sale" signs following the first Parti Québécois victory in 1976. Many of these signs stood peeling and rotting now, as there were no buyers even at depressed prices. The province's sagging economy frightened off investment and with the flight of businesses and businessmen to other parts of Canada there were no rising executives to buy property.

At a "good-by party" for their dentist neighbor and his family, Taylor Redfern and his wife, Lois, had joked grimly about ending up one day as the only people on the block. The prospect loomed closer as the houses on both sides of them were now vacant: the dentist was moving to Boston, leaving his unsold house in the hands of real-estate brokers with instructions to get what they could for it.

Redfern began to spend more time at home as Lois felt increasingly isolated with the departure of neighbors and friends. He had fixed up a small office in the basement, away from the children, so that he could work there free from the distractions of the *Chronicle's* newsroom.

He had been in the basement room all afternoon, trying to write the story of Kevin Reilly's RCMP connection; the balls of paper at his feet testified to the difficulty he was having in pinning it down for his readers. Cameron Craig was convinced that this link was the key to the conspiracy theory.

For four days, Redfern had shuttled between Montreal and Ottawa, trying to substantiate Guy Lacroix's accusations against the federal government. The facts that he had uncovered regarding a possible federal tie-in could be interpreted either way. He tore another sheet of paper out of the typewriter, wadded it up, and hurled it at the floor. He got up and crossed the room to a dartboard on the wall and pulled out the darts by their feathered flights. He stood back and aimed. He concentrated on the flight of the dart to try to relax.

"So this is how the gentlemen of the press spend their afternoons." Lois Redfern stood at the door with a cup of coffee in her hand. She had a moon-shaped face and large brown eyes that seemed to register constant surprise.

"Thanks," he said, taking the cup from her. "It's just not working."

"Can I help?"

"Well, maybe I've missed something. I'll go over it again. Sit down. Now. Fact: Reilly did a stint with the Mounties. I've got a photostat of his resignation card. He joined up a year and a half after high school, as soon as he turned nineteen. He completed the six-month program at the RCMP's Recruit Training School in Regina. Fact: Reilly was a top marksman. He received the crossed pistols with crown—that means he shot a perfect score. One of his group told me that he could strip and reassemble his weapon faster than anyone in his class. Assumption: he knew exactly what he was doing when he shot one or perhaps two bullets at the Premier."

"Okay," Lois shrugged. "Seems logical so far."

"Now according to his file he resigned from the RCMP after only fourteen months. A mutual parting of the ways, as far as I could gather. He just didn't have the right temperament for the force. I talked to the staffing officer who interviewed him. He said Reilly couldn't take the discipline. Assumption: suppose Reilly's resignation was a front to allow him to go under cover."

"You mean he got kicked out, but he was really still one of their agents?"

"Exactly. If Reilly was still working for the RCMP at the time of the assassination, then it could just be that there was federal involvement."

"You mean the Prime Minister . . . ?"

"Not necessarily the Prime Minister. But the hell of it is, it's only a guess. The Mounties deny it, of course. Not that they'd admit it if it were true. But Reilly didn't keep up with any of his old group after he resigned, which could add weight to the undercover theory. A man doesn't usually cut himself off from everybody like that. But that's all I have to go on. I don't even know if I believe it myself. That's why it's so damned hard to write this story."

"Well, why don't you leave it for a while? Maybe if you don't think about it, the answer will come."

"Craig is going to love you for that. He needs this for the big Saturday feature. Still, maybe I could try another tack. I should be following up on Sergeant Touraine."

"Mommy, when am I going to have my supper?" Five-year-old Jenny stood in the doorway holding her stomach to dramatize her need.

"Oh darling, I forgot all about you. Daddy and I were talking. Come on, we'll get something right away, you and me. We won't even wait for Petey to come home from Cubs. How about a pizza?"

The little girl's face lit up. Lois shooed her daughter out of the office, winked solemnly at her husband, and closed the door. Redfern smiled to himself. He threw the other two darts at the board and sat down at his desk again. From the filing drawer, he drew a manila envelope with the name "Touraine" written large in felt-tip pen.

There was something odd there, too. The Premier's

bodyguard was being held incommunicado under police guard in a Quebec City hotel room, although he had been accused of no crime. Requests for interviews were met with the same response: "Sergeant Touraine is still in a state of emotional shock as a result of the Premier's death." If that were the case, why was he not in a hospital, or at least on leave in his own home? Redfern had tried to interview Touraine's wife but there was no one in their east-end Montreal bungalow. The phone went unanswered. It seemed that someone had built a wall around Touraine and his family. But why?

As Redfern browsed through the notes, he heard a clumping down the basement steps. His nine-year-old son, Pete, still in Cub Scout uniform, rushed self-importantly into the room.

"Dad, Dad," he gasped, breathless from running. "This man . . . at the bus stop . . . he was waiting for me . . . told me to give you this." From under his sweater he drew a long brown envelope.

"Pete, calm down. A man, you say. Did you know him?"

"No, Dad. Aren't you going to open it?"

Redfern felt that same tremor of fear he had experienced in the National Assembly chamber, catching sight of the man with the camera and the pointing woman. A man who knew his son by sight, who knew his movements . . .

"Have you ever seen this man before? Anywhere?"

"No."

"What did he look like?"

"He was wearing a hat. He just gave it to me and walked off."

Redfern looked at the envelope. There was no name written on it. Gingerly, he ran his fingertips over it. There was no point in taking any chances with Pete in the room.

"I want you to go upstairs and have your supper right away."

"Aw, Dad."

"You heard me." The threatening edge in his voice was enough. Pete shuffled out of the office. When Redfern was alone, he closed the door and took the envelope to the hanging lamp in the center of the room. He held it up close to the bulb. But the envelope was too thick.

Then, quickly averting his face, he tore a strip down the side. Nothing happened. He drew out a single sheet of paper. On it was an unsigned message typewritten in capital letters:

> *FORGET ABOUT THE RCMP. TALK TO THE WOMAN AT 455 AVE. DES ORMES, CARTIERVILLE.*

Redfern's first instinct was to jump in the car and drive to Cartierville, but he checked himself. An anonymous tip from someone who knew exactly what he was doing suggested a more cautious approach. He spent the rest of the evening finding out about 455 Avenue des Ormes. The municipal directory at the office listed the occupants as a Mme. F. X. Aubin. The name meant nothing to him, nor to anyone in the newsroom. There was nothing on her in the library files. There was no answer when he called the listed phone number.

He spent a sleepless night, dozing fitfully and dreaming of Touraine and Reilly and the crowds of mourners. Could the note be a prank by the newsdesk? Or was it a trap of some kind? Was he getting too close to something or somebody? Again the specter of the couple in the press gallery rose before him. Perhaps there was someone at 455 Avenue des Ormes who could help him.

He wrote down the address and phone number on a piece of paper and handed it to his wife as he left the house next morning.

"This is where I'll be if you need me," he said casually.

He speculated about whom he would find at the house as he joined the rush-hour traffic on the Decarie Expressway and turned onto Laurentian Boulevard. Perhaps it's Reilly's girl friend. Now, she could probably tell him a lot. Or maybe it was one of Reilly's old teachers. Or the elusive Mme. Touraine. Or the black-haired woman in the press gallery. Or none of them.

Avenue des Ormes turned out to be a shabby street of semidetached houses hard against cracking sidewalks. Number 455 was as undistinguished as the rest: a redbrick, two-story home with curtains tightly drawn and the morning paper lying on the warped wooden porch. He scrutinized it from the safety of his car. There seemed to be no sign of life. He opened the car door, walked up the steps, and rang the bell. There was no response. He waited a couple of minutes and rapped on the door. He thought he could hear movement inside the house so he rang again. The door opened sufficiently to reveal a large woman in a flannel robe, her blond hair in a net.

"*Oui?*" She scowled at him.

"Excuse me, I'm Taylor Redfern of the *Montreal Chronicle*. I was led to believe there's someone at this address who wishes to speak to me."

"What? What are you talking about?" The woman was angry and her face began to redden.

"Are you Madame Aubin?"

"What of it? I never asked to talk to you or anybody else from the newspaper." She tried to close the door, but Redfern placed his palm against the handle.

"No, wait a minute, please. This is important." As he leaned forward with his shoulder, he caught a glimpse of a second woman standing on the stairs, her hand clutching her robe to her throat. She was older than the heavy blonde at the door.

"I have nothing more to say to you," said Mme. Aubin, applying greater pressure from her side. "Leave or I shall call the police."

With a sudden inspiration the journalist called out to the woman on the stairs, "Madame Touraine! Please, I must talk to you about your husband."

The blonde turned away from the door. Redfern felt the pressure subside.

"It's all right, Lise," said the older woman. "Let him come in."

He entered the darkened hall and was assailed by the smell of stale beer from an empty crate by the coat rack.

"You must forgive my sister, she does not think I should talk to strangers now. Will you sit down, please." She led him into the front room. In the light Redfern studied her features. The woman was in her mid-forties, probably attractive once but now gone to fat. The care-lined face contrasted strangely with the youthful, slim hands that grasped the frothy nylon nightgown at her neck. She gave him the impression of having reached for the Scotch bottle when she awoke; her face was bloated and her eyes red-rimmed.

Mme. Aubin hovered in the doorway like a Wagnerian heroine, plainly unhappy with his presence.

"You said you wanted to talk about my husband, Mr. . . . ?"

"Redfern. Yes."

"How did you find me? No one is supposed to know where I am."

"Madame Touraine," he began, brushing aside her question, "I had to talk to you because there's something going on and maybe you can help me. Ever since the assassination, no one has been able to talk to your husband. They say he had a nervous breakdown."

"No, that's not true," she replied quickly.

"Has he been in touch with you?"

She shook her head and looked at the floor.

"The other rumors are that he's under house arrest in Quebec and that he's been flown out of the country somewhere. Now I've got to know the truth."

Mme. Touraine let out a sigh that seemed to express the hopelessness of her life.

"I can't tell you anything. They won't tell *me* anything." Her voice began to break. "They say he's all right, but they won't let me talk to him. I don't even know if he's still alive."

She was weeping openly now. Her sister rushed to comfort her.

"See what you've done," she said angrily. "Now you've upset her. I want you out."

"No, let him stay." Marie Touraine dabbed her eyes with the sleeve of her nightgown. "I have to talk to someone."

"Who won't let you see him, Madame Touraine?"

"I don't know. I get phone calls from his captain saying he's all right. I shouldn't worry. I should stay with family or friends till it's all over."

"Until what's over?"

The woman shook her head in tearful bewilderment. "I don't understand anything. They should be treating him like a hero. After all, he shot the man who killed the Premier. And then they hide him away like this."

"Do you know where he is?"

"No. They didn't tell me. Lise, can you get me a glass of water, please?"

The younger sister looked at Redfern, reluctant to leave the distraught woman alone with him.

"Please."

"Madame Touraine, I'd like to write a story about your husband. Tell people what kind of man he really is. To a lot of people he's a hero. Can you tell me about him, anything you like. About your life together, your children, his hobbies, his work, his favorite beer, anything that comes to mind."

Lise came back with the glass of water. Marie Touraine took a sip and handed the glass back to her.

She embarked upon the story of her life with Auguste Touraine, the man she called Gus and had married twenty-three years ago. It was a life of quiet desperation, of missed opportunities and unrealized dreams. After half an hour of listening Redfern wished he hadn't asked.

Things had begun to go wrong when Touraine had been singled out to be the Premier's bodyguard, chosen, she said proudly, because of his discretion and loyalty. She admired loyalty. As bodyguard to the leader of the province, Touraine became the Premier's shadow. He spent little time at home, and she felt him drifting away from her; her own sense of loneliness and isolation fed upon itself until she found consolation in alcohol. She became agitated as she confessed to it.

"I drank because he was turning away from me, Mr. Redfern. I had nowhere to go. It got worse, you see. There was another woman."

"Marie," cautioned Lise.

"No, it doesn't matter. I know there was. After all those years. A friend of mine who served behind the bar on St. Hubert Street saw them together. He was in Montreal with another woman instead of me. You know, he even took her to Plattsburgh. That's how much I know. I took his suit to the cleaners and there was a receipt in the pocket. The Holiday Inn, Plattsburgh. He took her there, the dirty pig. And he never once took me to the States." Her shoulders shook with the pain of it. She bit her lip to stop herself from crying.

"Twenty-three years and this is what I get. I don't care what happens to him. I don't care." She buried her face in her hands and gave way to the tears that had threatened throughout her monologue.

"I think you better go now," said Lise Aubin firmly. "No more questions."

Redfern nodded. There was no point in going on. Mme. Touraine had been more helpful than she realized.

"I'm sorry," he said, "very sorry." But there was no reply from the bowed head of Marie Touraine.

Raymond Mercier, Belmont's campaign manager, escorted Monique Gravelle to the dinner table. He ate at Le Cheval Blanc in Trois-Rivières only when he was on expenses, and tonight he felt light of heart in the company of such a tantalizing young woman. Should his wife inquire about his guest, he could assure her that, as was his custom, he ate at such an expensive restaurant only when the party was footing the bill, and that they would do so only in the line of business. The auditors were very sharp on that.

Mercier treated the young woman with the exaggerated courtliness which he believed was the proper demeanor to adopt when one wasn't sure how to behave with a member of the opposite sex a generation his junior. He thought perhaps he might feel more relaxed with a drink or two.

"Of course it was a scandal, that Lacroix business at the funeral. You know there are people in this province who are actually applauding him for what he did?"

"Mmm, terrible," murmured Monique, sipping her Dubonnet.

"Sometimes I wonder what the voters have between their ears."

"It doesn't really matter, does it, as long as there are enough of them and they're with us? *La revanche du berceau,* I mean. The revenge of the cradle."

"Quite. . . . I don't know if I told you, Ma'amselle Gravelle, but I have known Jean-Claude Belmont for more years than I care to remember. We began in law practice together before you were born. As Jean-Claude's campaign director, chief fund raiser, and office manager, I enjoy his complete confidence. We are also very old friends. You know, he once told a reporter that, without Raymond Mercier, he'd have no portfolio, no seat, no money—and worst of all—in his old age, no one to confide in."

"That's quite a testimonial." Monique smiled.

"Yes. That is why I have a heavy responsibility toward him. So, I am delighted that you called. I remembered your name immediately—no, I did. It was you who handled the publicity when Jean-Claude was given the education portfolio. A splendid job. I understand the value of publicity, and that is why I am delighted to have you with us. You are an asset indeed."

Before Mercier could pursue his heavy-handed flattery, the waiter interrupted to take their orders.

"Why don't you order for both of us, Raymond. Oh, I hope you don't mind me calling you Raymond?"

"No, no, of course not," replied the flustered Mercier. "We are nothing if not democratic in our office. What would you like? Oh, you wanted me to order. Yes, let's see."

Monique Gravelle stifled a yawn behind her menu. It was going to be a long evening. She needed something to buoy her up. There was a vial of pills in her purse.

"Would you excuse me for a moment, Raymond? I'm just going to powder my nose."

Mercier stood up as she left the table. He took off his glasses and wiped them on his napkin. He could hardly believe what was happening to him. This young girl who was the center of attention for every man in the room had virtually asked him to take her to dinner. She wanted to work for him, to join the crusade. He tried to picture her in the ladies' room, drawing a comb through that lustrous black hair, applying lipstick to the full lips. The dark eyes and the pale skin and the scent of apples about her. You don't meet women like that in Trois-Rivières, he said to himself. If you do, they're on their way to somewhere else. Her very proximity aroused him and frightened him at the same time.

"Hello again." She was back. He jumped up quickly and held her chair while she seated herself.

Raymond Mercier couldn't remember what he ate. All he knew was that the dinner went very quickly. He had little memory of ordering the second bottle of champagne, but there it was on the bill. They had talked of Belmont's chances in the leadership race. Monique had been optimistic: Lacroix would overreach himself and alienate the convention delegates, she predicted. He was too overbearing, too much the firebrand. French Canadians were basically conservative; in Belmont, they would recognize the calm and stability they craved.

Over coffee they discussed Monique's role in the campaign.

"As a publicist I have excellent contacts with the media, both French and English. But I've learned a great deal about party organization and fund raising in the past three years. I might be helpful to you in those areas, if you need me."

Mercier nodded vigorously, forgetting about his double chin. He could imagine how this woman's presence would loosen the purse strings when he called on business friends for campaign contributions.

"You realize I probably could not pay you as much as your job at headquarters, much as I would like to. We'd have to see how the fund raising went."

"I'd work as a volunteer if necessary." She smiled. "I have a little money saved. I just feel very strongly about it. Monsieur Belmont has to win."

"My dear, I too feel very strongly about it," said Mercier gruffly. He reached over the table to pat her hand for emphasis. He was mildly surprised when she made no move to draw it away. Their hands remained together on the table and he found his eyes locked with hers.

It was he who broke the moment by motioning in confusion to the waiter to ask for the bill.

"I'm sorry," he said, turning to Monique, "did you want another cup of coffee?"

"Not right now, thanks. But I've got an idea. Why don't we go back to my motel and have a cup there. I've been working on some publicity ideas for the campaign and they should be started as soon as possible for maximum effect . . . that is, if you have the time?"

"Time?" He hesitated for a moment. He had told his wife he would be home by ten; it was already quarter past. Still, this was business. The campaign came first. "Yes, of course I have the time."

Raymond Mercier began to perspire in the car; there was an unaccountable ringing in his ears. One part of him told him that she really did want his views on her publicity campaign. But another voice in his blood heard her message, was appalled by it, and yet could not say no. They drove in silence to the motel. He took the key from her to open the door and fumbled with it for what seemed a full minute before he could insert it.

"Let me take your coat," she said, once they were inside. "I must apologize for the room. At such short notice, I couldn't find anything else."

"It's f-fine," he stammered, trying to keep his eyes off the bed, which occupied half the room. She was behind him, helping him remove his overcoat. He pulled his arms out of the sleeves and pretended to inspect the view through the windows, although there was nothing to see.

"Do you mind closing the drapes?" asked Monique. "I always get the feeling someone's lurking out there."

Mercier struggled to pull the drapes together, but they refused to meet. There was a frantic quality to his movements; the girl's every gesture, every word was an invitation. He could feel the pulse in his forehead throbbing with excitement.

"Now, you sit there for a second and I'll get down my files." She dragged a chair to the closet and climbed onto it, reaching upward for her case, which rested on the top shelf. The action caused her skirt to ride up her thighs. Mercier could see the roundness of the flesh pressing against the material of her clothes.

"Here, let me help you," he said, as she continued to stretch upward, manipulating the case so that she could open it.

"If you wouldn't mind just holding the chair . . ." Monique stood on tiptoe, which caused her skirt to rise higher up her thighs. Mercier could smell her perfume and his eyes were on the level of her buttocks. He reached out and touched her knee. She appeared not to notice.

"These cases, they make the locks so stiff," she said, seemingly to herself. Emboldened by the lack of reaction, he allowed his hand to slide gently up the inside of her legs. Immediately, she clamped her knees together and trapped his hand.

"Raymond!" She pushed his hand away and pulled at the hem of her skirt. She could see his chest was heaving as he stared fixedly at her legs. She hopped down from the chair and straightened her clothes with elaborate gestures.

"Monique," he said softly and tried to pull her toward

him; but she half turned away and he buried his lips in her hair.

"We came here to work, Raymond. If I'm going to help you and Monsieur Belmont, let's not get sidetracked. This isn't the time."

"I'm sorry," said the crestfallen Mercier, whose wine-befuddled mind was trying desperately to reinterpret the evening's signals.

"Now can I trust you to get that suitcase down while I order coffee?"

Taylor Redfern pulled aside the curtain of his room in the Plattsburgh Holiday Inn and looked out on the main street. He could have been in any small American town. His view encompassed the supermarket, the hardware store, a sporting-goods shop, two banks, a movie theater, and a church.

He had wasted no time getting there; a quick phone call to his editor and his wife after his meeting with Marie Touraine and he was heading out across the Champlain Bridge and Highway 9 to the American border. As he drove south, he wondered why Touraine had chosen Plattsburgh for his affair. He could have lost himself in Montreal without any trouble. It wasn't as if his face were well known. These thoughts were reinforced when Redfern arrived. Downtown Plattsburgh was hardly the most romantic setting. Was this to be another dead end?

His initial inquiries among the staff at the Holiday Inn elicited little information. A picture of Sergeant Touraine out of uniform jogged a few memories and a proffered ten-dollar bill added a few scraps of information. He had stayed over one night around the middle of October. A bell boy remembered that he had carried his own luggage.

"He wouldn't put them bags down, even in the room. Just stood there lookin' at me while I was standin' around for my tip. So I stuffed his key in his top pocket and let him get on with it."

The night room-service steward recalled Touraine ordering a bottle of whisky at midnight. No, he hadn't asked for two glasses. A woman? No. The bellboy couldn't remember a woman either.

If he was alone, then obviously Touraine hadn't come to Plattsburgh to have an affair. So what was the purpose of the trip? And why had he used a false name? The hotel register showed only one French Canadian name around the middle of October. A Paul Paquet. His car bore a Quebec registration; the others on the page, before and after, were all American plates.

Redfern stared out of the window, watching pieces of newspaper blowing down the street. How did it all fit together? Touraine drove alone, presumably, from Montreal on October 12 to spend one night in the middle of the week at a motel in Plattsburgh under an assumed name. He had breakfast in the coffee shop next morning at around 8:30 and then checked out. What was he doing here? And what conection did it have with the assassination, if any? The bellboy said he had two pieces of luggage. For one night? For one person?

When the answer came to him it seemed so obvious he wondered why he hadn't thought of it sooner. He concentrated on the main street again, looking intently at the buildings. Then he took out the phone book and began thumbing through it. He had his answer on the second call. Banks in New York State were as casual as those in Canada about divulging confidential information to strangers on the telephone; someday he would have to write a series on the subject.

"... So I told them I was a Montreal car dealer and I had a check signed by a Mr. Paul Paquet for five thousand dollars drawn on their bank. I was phoning to verify whether it was good before releasing the automobile. And you know what the girl said? Mr. Paquet didn't have sufficient funds in his checking account to cover it, but I should put it through anyway and they'd transfer the money from his savings account! Can you imagine? All that over the phone?"

Cameron Craig shook his head. "My father was a banker; he'd be turning in his grave."

"That old embezzler. I never did know how you managed to escape from his vaults."

"Talent, pure talent. Anyway, this is a real can of worms."

"Yeah, we've got a hell of a story now. We know Touraine made a secret trip across the border less than a month before the Premier was shot. We know that he took a large sum of money with him in a small suitcase which he refused to let out of his sight. That he used a fictitious name and he opened two accounts in an American bank in that name. You know what that means, don't you, Cam?"

"Now don't go jumping to conclusions."

"Oh, come on. Touraine is up to his neck in it. He's part of the whole rotten business. Touraine shot Reilly three times, remember. He hit him with all three shots. He murdered him."

"Now wait. You write one word of that and we're up to our ass in libel suits."

Craig was on his feet and moving quickly to shut his office door.

"You *know* I'm right, Cam."

"I didn't say you weren't, but that's a hell of a long way from being able to prove it. I agree it reeks of conspiracy. A big payoff."

"Yeah, and Touraine bottled up somewhere."

"But as a responsible newspaper we can only print facts. Let the readers draw their own conclusions."

"You're sitting on the biggest story this city's ever seen, goddammit, and you're preaching caution. What's the matter with you, Cam?"

"Listen, Redfern, one successful libel action against this newspaper, and we can all say good-by Charlie. We're operating on a knife edge. We can just about afford paper and ink."

"We're talking about a man's life, Cam!"

"The man is dead, and if we go off half-cocked so are we!" shouted Craig.

Redfern flopped down in the chair and rubbed his tired eyes.

"Okay, how do you want to handle it?"

The afternoon edition of the *Montreal Chronicle* hit the streets at two. It caused an international sensation. The eight-column headline read: "Slain Premier's Bodyguard Linked to Payoff."

The six-hundred-word story that followed under Taylor Redfern's byline was straightforward and factual. He made no accusations but so cleverly had he constructed the piece that, while the paper was legally in the clear, the reader could not help but draw the conclusion that Sergeant Touraine was involved in the plot to asassinate the

Premier. By six o'clock that evening the story was the lead item on every radio and television news broadcast in North America.

"Oh Mommy, not oatmeal again!" Young Pete made a face and beat on the table with his spoon .

"Petey, you eat your breakfast this instant and not another word. Really, Taylor," said Lois, "all that child does these days is complain. He won't eat a thing I put in front of him. Are you listening to me?"

"Mmmm? In a minute, dear. Look at this, the *Tribune*'s picked up my story and run it word for word. You'd think they'd have the decency to rewrite it. They even copied the typo. All they left off was my byline. He tossed the rival Montreal paper on the table. "What a way to run a railroad."

He sipped his orange juice. Lois jiggled the eggs in the pan.

"Reach over and turn on the news, love," he said. "See if they give me credit."

". . . and the barometer is falling. High today zero and low tonight minus five. And now the World at Eight. Good morning, I'm Howard North. One story dominates the national news today—a dramatic new development in the case of Sergeant Auguste Touraine, bodyguard to the recently assassinated Premier of Quebec. Provincial Police have just confirmed that Sergeant Touraine disappeared last night from the Quebec hotel where he has been under police protection since the assassination. . . ."

"Oh my God," murmured Redfern.

"A search is under way for the missing Touraine, who only yesterday was linked by a Montreal newspaper story to an alleged payoff made shortly before the assassination. It is not known at this time whether he left the hotel willingly, slipping past the police guard, or whether he was abducted. We will bring you further details as soon as they become available.

"In other news this morning, the political crisis in Britain has worsened. . . ."

Redfern switched the radio off and pulled on his jacket.

"I've got to get to the office. There's something going on. This thing is going to break wide open."

He grabbed his coat from the closet and headed for the door. Behind him, he could hear Pete shouting that he hated eggs.

The cold air stunned him momentarily, and he had to catch the banister to prevent himself from slipping on a patch of ice on the steps. He made a mental note to buy some rock salt on the weekend. He bent to lift the garage door and found it slightly ajar. Strange, he thought, I'm sure I closed it last night. Maybe it was the raccoons rummaging in the garbage cans again. He groped his way along the car, careful not to let his coat brush against the dusty paintwork. He opened the door and as the overhead light went on, he saw a man apparently asleep in the passenger seat. At first, he thought it was a drunk who had escaped from the cold to sleep the night, but as his eyes became accustomed to the gloom, he realized the man's head was lolling at an impossible angle. He lifted the hat and recognized the gray features of Auguste Touraine. His throat had been cut.

There were no lights on in the Oval Office except for the one on the President's desk. Its bulb illuminated the inkstand with its impressive Presidential seal but left everything else in shadow.

Warren Cummings, the director of the CIA, could not see the expression on the President's face. He was left in no doubt, however, of the Presidential mood when a fist came out of the darkness and banged hard on the desk top.

"For God's sake, Warren, it's over a month since the Quebec assassination and you have the temerity to sit there and tell me your people haven't delivered the goods yet?"

"You must understand, sir, the circumstances surrounding—"

"Don't equivocate, man. I don't need your excuses. Wilde gave the agency a simple assignment: find out who hired the gunman and why. And what have you come up with? Next to nothing. Perhaps you're waiting for the KGB to tell you."

Warren Cummings winced under the President's sarcasm. He had tried to explain to the President that there were a number of complicating factors. Internal cooperation, for instance. The RCMP was cooperative enough in its dealings with the CIA operatives in Canada but tardy in coming forward with requested information.

The Quebec Provincial Police were downright obstructionist: the head of the Sûreté was a closet separatist, placed in the office by the Parti Québécois government for obvious reasons. His orders had been explicit—any CIA agent found operating in Quebec was to be exposed. There was to be no outside interference with the shaping of the new state. When this edict came down, Cummings had been forced to pull out two experienced agents whose identities were known to the QPP.

Another problem was the penetration of key organizations in the province. The men and women running the party, the unions, the media, and the universities were all known to each other, either from college days or from political activity in their youth. And they were suspicious to the point of paranoia about outsiders. Many of them had been members during the 1960s of the separatist organizations that had been infiltrated by RCMP agents. They were determined not to repeat their mistakes; as a result, rigorous screening procedures had been adopted for applicants to key jobs. The CIA had found it impossible to penetrate these. And as far as buying agents was concerned, the CIA had encountered a deep-seated and widespread antipathy toward the United States by likely candidates in the province—members of the Union Nationale and the fragmented Liberal Party, as well as disaffected PQ supporters. Cummings had even tried shipping in a top Belgian operative, but three days after he arrived the man was on the plane back to Brussels. He could not grasp *joual,* the Quebec street dialect.

"You're absolutely right, Mr. President, we'll just have to try harder. In the meantime, we have isolated a number of probable scenarios for the Quebec assassination which are now being investigated. Would you like me to run them past you?"

"Sounds like a waste of time," rumbled the voice in the darkness, "but let me hear them."

"There are five scenarios, each highly plausible given the political climate in Quebec. I should add that we are now convinced there was a conspiracy. The murder of the Premier's bodyguard has confirmed that. We also believe the bodyguard was involved in the plot on the basis of evidence accumulated to date."

Cummings heard the scratch of a match, and suddenly the President's face was visible, wreathed in a cloud of blue smoke as he drew on a cigar.

"Only damn thing we got out of re-establishing diplomatic links with Cuba. I can now smoke their cigars without feeling guilty about it. Go on, Warren."

"Scenario One: The assassination was carried out by

a terrorist organization of English-speaking Quebeckers.
Motive: to keep Quebec in Canada. Because of the background of the assassin, we worked on this one first. On
the surface it seems plausible, but our sources among the
English community have found no evidence of organized
terror. It's all on the level of excrement through the mails.
There are a few fringe nuts collecting weapons and playing around with homemade bombs—one blew himself up
in a Westmount garage a year or so back—but there's
nothing organized, nothing to suggest a group dedicated
and disciplined enough to carry through something like
this. So we are de-emphasizing this possibility."

"Couldn't that guy have planned the killing with one
of these groups? Maybe he got the weapon through them?"
interjected the President.

"It's possible, sir, which is why we are not discount-
ing the terrorist theory entirely. But our information suggests that since Sergeant Touraine could hardly speak
English, it would have been difficult for an English group
to recruit him."

"Okay, so it's not an English group." The President
was impatient to hear more.

"Scenario Two: The assassination was engineered by
the federal government, through the agency of the RCMP."
The President let out a low whistle.

"Motive: to eliminate the strong man of the Parti
Québécois; the result, the party breaks up into warring
factions and is severely weakened for the next provincial
election. Machiavellian but politically plausible, sir."

"Too subtle. I don't buy it," grunted the President.

"Well, sir, remember the gunman had been RCMP
trained."

"This myth of the Mounties, they're about as effective
as Nelson Eddy and Jeanette MacDonald." Warren Cummings smiled diplomatically.

"Scenario Three: The killing was arranged by international business interests."

The President snorted.

"It's not as farfetched as it sounds, sir. There's a lot
of capital, especially Wall Street money, invested in Quebec. And the Parti Québécois has been giving business a
rough ride. Their economic policies have been going more
and more socialistic. First, there was the partial national-

ization of the asbestos industry a couple of years ago, and lately the word is they want to grab the aluminum industry. Add to that the pro-union legislation they've enacted and the government's negative impact on the economic climate of Quebec as a whole, and there's enough motive for any one of a dozen conglomerates."

"Next." The President owed his election to massive backing by big business. He did not even want to entertain the possibility that a multinational was behind the assassination.

"Scenario Four: The whole thing was planned by one of the Premier's political opponents within the province. Perhaps a rival inside the Parti Québécois. We're paying close attention to this one. You remember the man who made that outburst at the funeral? Guy Lacroix? Well, he's the radical who's running for the leadership."

"Yes, yes, I know all about that. Wilde briefed me weeks ago."

"Well, he was very quick to capitalize on the situation for his own political ends. He's ruthless enough to do it and his supporters are almost as fanatical in their loyalty to him. We've done a psychological profile on him, and he spits nails. We've come up with something that ties in; it seems that Sergeant Touraine owed his appointment as the Premier's bodyguard to the director of the Quebec Provincial Police. A certain Yvon Taschereau. And he was the best man at Guy Lacroix's wedding and godfather to his son."

"Interesting." In the gloom Cummings could see the President writing something. "If we can finger Lacroix, then the ball game's ours. Work on that one; that has definite possibilities."

"There's one more, Mr. President. Scenario Five. The assassination was arranged by a foreign power."

"A government, you mean?"

"Yes."

"Look, Warren, I don't want this thing hashed out in the Security Council. Let's try to keep it in the family. Who's on your list?"

"The Soviet Union is an obvious candidate. They've got the motive. To encourage political tension between NATO allies, that's us and Canada. To divert our attention from Europe so they can move in force into the Mediterranean."

The President rose from his chair and walked over to the window. He looked down on the White House lawn, quilted with an unusually early snow.

"Any evidence?"

"Nothing we could take up with them."

"You realize that if the Russians are involved, they're deliberately challenging me. The new leadership in the Kremlin want to flex their muscles."

"Yes, sir, that's why we have to be positive before we go pointing any fingers."

"They've kept strangely quiet about the whole damned business. I wouldn't put it past them."

"There's one more candidate. France."

The President turned, his cigar poised an inch from his lips.

"France?"

"Yes, sir. The French, as you know, have long been supporters of Quebec independence. You will recall President de Gaulle's speech in Montreal in 1967. That was the first formal expression of support for a Quebec state. But it goes back long before that. The French have a variety of motives, none that strong by itself, but taken together they just might light a fuse. France would like to regain an influential foothold on this continent, and Quebec is their only steppingstone. They'd like to develop a closer economic tie with the province, perhaps as a common market of Francophones. Ever since the Common Market died, the French have been canvassing the idea of a Francophone market. They need more captive outlets for their industries. And they want unimpeded access to Quebec's minerals. And, most important, there's the energy factor."

"What's that?"

"As you know, Mr. President, the French are spending billions on the expansion of their nuclear generating capacity. They're trying to reduce their dependence on Arab oil. And they've been testing a new generation of nuclear weapons for their Mirage jets. Their problem is a steady supply of enriched uranium. For a number of years now, they've been trying to get a uranium-enrichment plant at James Bay to take advantage of the new hydroelectric development there. As you're aware, sir, the enrichment process demands a tremendous amount of electricity, and no one is prepared to use energy for that purpose today to benefit another country. So this James Bay idea has been surfacing periodically for the past ten years, but each time it's been blocked by Ottawa."

"Well, I'm glad they've had the backbone to do something positive."

"Yes, sir. But if Quebec were to become independent, the situation might change. It could be a reason for France to become involved, although it's hard to see why they would bother now. As I say, it's an old idea and their own breeder plant is just coming on stream, so there doesn't seem to be any urgency about getting into James Bay."

"Any evidence?"

"Only circumstantial. We're checking."

"Okay. Anyone else on this merry-go-round?"

"Not really. China conceivably, but they would appear to have little to gain from the Premier's death. With the Russians jumping up and down on their border again, they've got enough on their plate. Then there's Israel: the government in Quebec has been sending out top-level delegations to Kuwait and Saudi Arabia in an effort to get Arab investment in the province. But it's not enough for the Israelis to risk angering us."

"You've given me a lot of theories, Warren, but I need facts. Before I can move, we've got to pinpoint this thing once and for all. I'm holding you personally responsible for getting some results, understand?"

The President's temper was rising again. The CIA director snapped his briefcase shut and stood up.

"Sir, we'll get you the answer. My people know how important it is. They've given it top priority."

"Then they'd better deliver," growled the President as he stubbed out his cigar, barely smoked. "A lot more than your job depends on it."

Ice was forming over the St. Lawrence River. From his office overlooking St. Helen's Island, Taylor Redfern could see the beginnings of the marblelike slabs growing out from the riverbanks. He had not answered Cameron Craig's question; he kept staring at the ice.

"I'm asking you again, Taylor. Do you want off the story? Jesus, there's no disgrace."

The ice reminded him of the color of Sergeant Touraine's face.

"You did the right thing sending Lois and the kids to Vancouver. They'll be safe with her parents. So why the hell don't you join them?"

Redfern found himself perspiring again; for no reason at all he began sweating in the coldest rooms these days.

"For God's sake, say something, Taylor. Do you want to spend Christmas here by yourself?"

"I've got to see it through, Cam," he said quietly, more to himself than to his editor.

He thought of Lois and the children safe behind the Rockies, of his house in Pointe Claire, shut up now, and of the tiny two-room apartment he had rented above a delicatessen on Rue de la Montagne, right in the heart of downtown Montreal. He felt safer there at the hub of the city's activities. Yet he had had an extra lock put on the door, and he started at every sound in the hall. The first night he awoke at 3:15 A.M. imagining there was someone in his room. He slept the rest of the night with all the lights on. He took taxis to avoid having to use the apartment building's underground car park, and when he was on the street, he carried a sheath knife in his coat pocket.

"I can't guarantee your safety, dammit!" Cameron Craig shouted in frustration.

"It's no use my going to the police, I know that."

"Haven't you had enough hints? This isn't some genteel game where you pick up your marbles and go home afterward."

"Don't you think I know that!" Redfern swiveled around quickly in his chair. Craig could see the bags under his red eyes. "Look at these." He held his hands out in front of him. They were trembling. "I haven't been able to control them since I found . . . Touraine."

"All right. I'm sorry. You've got my pity. Now, give up."

Redfern turned away and stared out the window again.

"You see that ice out there? It's going to join across that channel soon. The water's doing its damnedest to keep the two sides apart. But it's inexorable. The ice is going to win. And by Christ, I'm going to win!"

There was something obsessive in the journalist's manner that brooked no argument. Craig realized that anything he might say would only exacerbate Redfern's mood.

"There's something pretty rotten going on here, and somebody's got to do something about it, Cam. And I just elected myself."

"Okay. All right. Just calm down."

"Don't you see what's happening here? The police don't give a damn. They're more than happy to point the finger at the English and leave it at that. The RCMP is a joke in the province. So who's going to do anything?"

"A policeman's been killed. They won't let that go by."

"What do you mean? It's not just a cop. This is political. Everything is falling into Lacroix's lap, and his friend who sits on top of the heap in the QPP isn't going to do a thing to compromise that."

"All right, Taylor. I've done my best to dissuade you. Nobody's going to think badly of you for leaving town."

"I don't give a fart what people think!"

"Well, if you're going to stay with the story, there's something you should know. Someone pretty high up has been leaning on the publisher to have you reined in. So far he's resisted the pressures, but there's big money involved."

"Any idea who?"

"No. But it's there."

"One of our advertisers?"

"I told you I don't know."

"Like hell."

"Don't you trust anyone anymore?"

Redfern didn't answer.

The frozen silence was interrupted by Winslow Phelps, the business editor, who barged in without knocking.

"Say, Taylor—" He spotted Cameron Craig and

stopped short. "Oh, sorry. Didn't know there was someone with you." He started to withdraw.

"It's all right, Wins. Cam and I didn't have much more to say to each other anyway. What is it?"

The business editor looked uncertainly at Craig. The editor waved his hand vaguely.

"Well, it's just that I was up at SoMin this morning. Just got back. There's been a rumor around that they've found something big in northern Quebec. I asked Ross Anson about it . . ."

"Did he tell you anything?" Craig was suddenly interested.

"No. He hedged, you know him. He should have been a diplomat." The editor went back into his sulk.

"But the thing I wanted to tell you, Taylor, is that while I was waiting to see Anson I saw Rodrique Barré come out of his office."

"You're kidding! Are you sure it was him?"

"Damn right. I've met him several times. He even recognized me, seemed embarrassed, and left in a hurry."

"Jesus. That's somthing."

"What the hell's this all about?" Cameron Craig demanded. "Who's Rodrique Barré?"

"He's Guy Lacroix's bagman, Cam," Redfern said. "The guy who makes all the collections and raises the dough for the campaign. But why the blazes would he be calling on Ross Anson? The corporations hate his guts; he's buddy-buddy with the union leaders."

"Maybe they figure the companies will kick in now that Lacroix's got a shot at the leadership," Phelps suggested.

"Could be. But it seems to me Lacroix would be smart enough to send someone else if that were the case," Redfern said. "I'm hearing bells ringing all over the place. Hang on, Cam, I want to check something. Thanks for the tip, Wins."

Redfern rushed out of the office and a moment later barged into Ed McBeam's darkroom.

"Hey, man, you could have ruined the whole roll," protested the photographer.

"Ed, listen, the shots you took at the Premier's lying-in-state. Where are they?"

"In a folder in my desk, why?"

"Thanks!" Redfern dashed out again and hurried to the photographer's desk. He took out a file and began to riffle through the 8 x 10 prints. "That's it," he exclaimed and withdrew a photo of a huge floral tribute; emblazoned across it in silk was a message proclaiming "Deepest sympathy to the Premier's family from the chairman and board of directors of IntCon."

He ran back into his office and handed it to Craig. "A wreath from IntCom! I knew I'd seen the name before."

"Where are they located, their headquarters?"

Redfern took down a copy of *Moody's Industrial Manual* from his bookshelf. No listing there. He had better luck with *Jane's Major Companies of Europe.*

"Headquarters in London. Chairman, Holbrook Meadows."

"Well, maybe you should take a few days to root around London," suggested Craig gently. "It might be just what's needed right now."

But Taylor Redfern had not heard him. He was reading the IntCon entry, and as he came to the end he let out a low whistle.

"I think I'd better go to London, Cam," he said. "I'm beginning to see daylight."

Antoine de Luzt sat in Café Victor on Boulevard St. Michel, a Pernod untasted on the zinc-topped table in front of him. The charivari of pimps, drug pushers, prostitutes, tourists, Moroccan rug sellers, and derelicts passed before his eyes along the winter street outside the window. He took in the familiar scene, but its constantly changing kaleidoscope of faces and incidents failed to move him. He was troubled by the intelligence Hilaire Noel had passed on to him: the CIA's interest in Quebec. A bad sign. The presence of the CIA was like a dog in a bowling alley—you never knew when they would break their cover and destroy everything for everyone. Worse, they were dangerous enough to put his own people in jeopardy. So for his own security, he had alerted trusted informants in Paris to find out what Hilaire Noel had not told him. The future of France. What could be so important in Quebec?

Through the window he saw the man he had been

waiting for running across the street, dodging through the honking traffic. Roger Quesnel had served under him in the bitter days of Algeria. De Luzt had taught him the subtle arts of interrogation, and the younger man had learned quickly.

De Luzt watched him dart in front of the passing cars. A true survivor, he thought. A man like Quesnel has to risk himself every minute of the day. How sorry Quesnel had been to leave Algeria! His aggression had been well harnessed by de Luzt in several covert enterprises on behalf of the French government, and now he was an excellent and highly trained operative.

The two men greeted each other casually, and de Luzt motioned for the younger man to sit. He ordered a *café filtre.*

"Any joy?"

Quesnel shook his head. "It's tighter than a drum. You mention Quebec around La Piscine and they look at you as if you've got gonorrhea." De Luzt grasped the reference immediately. La Piscine was the nickname for SDECE—*Service de Documentation Extérieur et de Contre-Espionnage*—France's equivalent of the CIA.

"We have to find out what's happening, Roger. Our people are at risk."

"The only thing I've come up with is this." Quesnel pulled out a folded piece of foolscap from his jacket pocket. "I lifted it off a desk at the Western Hemisphere bureau. It's a photostat of a decoded message from the French consulate in Quebec. I just saw the word Quebec, so I liberated it. I don't know if it has any bearing."

De Luzt studied the message. It gave details of a major uranium strike in northern Quebec by IntCon.

"That's interesting," murmured de Luzt.

"Who are IntCon?" asked Quesnel.

"They're a large British consortium. The find must be important if it's reported back to La Piscine. But France has got sufficient uranium. The new breeder reactors will give the government more than enough enriched fuel for our nuclear plants."

"Maybe I could find out something if you sent me to Quebec," prompted Quesnel.

"You never change, do you, Roger? Our people there can tell us all we need to know. But I want you to keep on this one. Why is an independent Quebec so necessary to France? I have to have the answer to that soon. You keep in touch, eh? And Roger, don't play in the traffic. You're getting too old."

"La-croix, La-croix, La-croix, La-croix . . ." The crowd in the school hall in Percé chanted in unison and clapped to the cadence as the Minister of Social Affairs made his way down the aisle to the flag-festooned stage. As he went, smiling and waving, he shook the hands thrust at him from the cheering, stomping crowd. A full hall and the TV cameras in attendance, he noted with satisfaction as his retinue reached the stage and began to mount the steps. Guy Lacroix, once on stage, turned to his audience and raised his hands, clenching them above his head in a gesture of triumph and defiance. He flicked the lock of black hair from his eyes. The crowd responded with a roar. He savored the moment before joining his colleagues on the platform. The same scene had been repeated in town after town throughout the Gaspé during his pre-Christmas tour. Some of his aides had advised against it: "No one is interested in politics in December," they had said. Lacroix had insisted: he had to capitalize on the positive public reaction to his basilica address and to keep building up the momentum that would carry him on a tidal wave of public approbation into the February convention in Quebec City. The strategy was simple enough and it appeared to be working.

As the intensity of the cheering abated he extended his arms and motioned the audience to silence. He sat down, and the mayor of the town bobbed up and tapped the microphone with his fingers.

"*Mesdames et messieurs* . . . is it working? . . . good . . . good evening, ladies and gentlemen. We are honored to pay host tonight to a man . . ."

Lacroix's mind wandered. The speech he would deliver was the same he had used in the last town and the one he would use in the next. Unemployment was the issue, and the blame was Ottawa's. He had chosen his route carefully; selecting only those rural towns where his support was guaranteed. He had made no sorties into potentially hostile territory. The Quebec hinterland was Jean-Claude Belmont's natural constituency, but there were areas, such as this, where Lacroix could expect to do well.

He saw the white, upturned faces; they appeared to hunger for him; thin, haggard men and tired-looking women, old before their time. They probably had little to smile about, he thought. He had seen the same looks in halls up and down the province.

"Thank you, Monsieur le Maire, for your presence here tonight . . ."

Yves Pelletier, the local party organizer, was on his feet and about to introduce Lacroix.

Yes, things were going extremely well. The public-opinion poll run by *Le Devoir* immediately after Lacroix's outburst at the funeral indicated a sixty-seven per cent positive response among French Quebeckers. What did he care about the rest of Canada as long as his own people believed that Ottawa, the old enemy, was somehow instrumental in the death of the Premier? The battle was being fought in Quebec towns like this one, and he knew his constituency. As long as Ottawa could not disprove the conspiracy theory, he could continue to make political capital out of it. The fact that the Quebec Provincial Police were in no hurry to close their file on the assassination—thanks to his friend at their head—could only strengthen his hand.

Guy Lacroix had the field to himself. Belmont hadn't even begun his campaign. He had watched the Minister of Education in a recent television interview; why, Belmont was asked, had he not started campaigning, since his rival was already on the road? "The body of my friend is not yet cold," he had said. The poor fool, it would be January before he could start now, and by that time the nomination would be sewn up.

It was hot in the hall. Lacroix could feel drops of sweat running from his armpits. For some reason, Quebeckers always insisted on treating their visiting politicians like orchids and heating their halls in winter to jungle temperatures. Now, with the television lights on, the heat became intolerable. Yves Pelletier was winding up his introduction. Lacroix cleared his throat and turned his head to cough.

"Ladies and gentlemen, I give you Guy Lacroix, the next Premier of Quebec!"

The crowd roared and Guy Lacroix began to rise. His

face was in profile to his audience, because in the wings at stage left his eyes had locked on to the figure of a man in an overcoat pointing a revolver at him. His shout of "No" and the fizz of a silenced .38 were drowned out in the jubilant cheer of the audience.

The Church of St. Mary-le-Bow chimed the noon hour. The sound of the ancient bell echoed around the modern glass towers of the City of London. Taylor Redfern sat in the reception area of IntCon's head office and ostentatiously checked his watch. He had telexed a request for an appointment to see Holbrook Meadows at 10:30 A.M. The receptionist studiously ignored him.

"Will he be long, do you think?" inquired Redfern.

The woman continued to busy herself with nothing in particular. "Mr. Meadows said he will see you when he can. If you would like a copy of the *Economist* to read . . . ?" The offer was left vague. Redfern hummed softly to himself. The Brits sure know how to live. He wouldn't have minded furniture like this in the *Chronicle*'s offices in Montreal. And hard-edged paintings by the latest fashionable artist adorned every inch of wall space.

The moment his plane had taken off from Montreal's Mirabel Airport, Redfern had felt a weight of anxiety lifted from him. The fear he had experienced over the weeks since the Premier's assassination, and especially since the murder of Sergent Touraine, seemed like a thing of the past, forgotten paranoia. He was almost enjoying the enforced wait to see the chairman of IntCon. Whenever he sensed the possibility of an exclusive story, he felt a tingling in the small of his back. He was convinced that IntCon was somehow tied into the events in Quebec. His hunch had been reinforced by the inarticulate embarrassment of Ross Anson in Montreal during an interview. And if he needed more circumstantial proof, *Jane's* had supplied the missing link: one of IntCon's wholly owned subsidiaries was a Belgian company called d'Aston Ltée., Western Europe's second-largest armaments manufacturer. D'Aston had developed the sophisticated infrared night-sight that Redfern had spotted on the televised photo of the murder weapon. The name of the munitions firm in the reference book had jogged his memory. The night-sight had been demonstrated to a group of Canadian reporters covering a NATO exercise in West Germany two years before. The ordnance officer briefing the journalists had described it as the most spectacular advance in night weaponry since the Very pistol. The NATO command was proud of the little gadget, which had been issued to all combat troops.

Redfern had checked with the Department of National Defence in Ottawa. They had confirmed the nightsight was still on the classified list and was unavailable to nonmilitary personnel. It would have been impossible for Reilly to get hold of one—unless IntCon had supplied him.

The buzzer sounded on the receptionist's desk. She picked up the phone. "Certainly, Mr. Meadows." Redfern raised himself out of his chair, but the woman shook her head and dialed a number. "Mr. Meadows will not be dining tonight. Thank you," was all she said, and hung up.

"Will you tell him I'm still waiting out here?"

"I did tell him. I'm sure he's well aware of it," retorted the woman.

"For the sake of Commonwealth relations why don't you just remind him."

She picked up her receiver and pressed a button.

"Excuse me, Mr. Meadows, Mr.—uh—Redfern of the *Montreal Chronicle* is still with us."

Redfern strained to hear the reply.

"That Canadian journalist fellow, eh, Mrs. Marston? Has he got checkered trousers by any chance?"

"No, sir."

"Humph, they usually do. And their wives wear mapleleaf pins. I suppose he'll camp on our doorstep till I see him. Better wheel him in."

Holbrook Meadows affected a jocular mood, but Redfern's sudden arrival had troubled him. At all costs, IntCon's name had to be kept out of the Quebec situation. As soon as the telex had arrived, Meadows had called Ross Anson. Anson had briefed him about the journalist's visit to him at SoMin. "Why couldn't you satisfy him there?" Meadows had asked. "Why is he here? He must be suspicious." Meadows had allowed well over an hour to elapse before admitting Redfern, on the premise that angry men get to the point very quickly.

Mrs. Marston invited Redfern to step into the office

of Mr. Meadows's secretary. From there he was conducted into the chairman's presence. Redfern was amused by the feudal chain of command, but he was not prepared for Meadows's office. In contrast to the muted elegance of the reception area, Holbrook Meadows's inner sanctum looked like a petrified zoo. The walls were covered with stuffed animal heads—the booty of many safaris—and in pride of place was a Thomson's gazelle, retaining in death the expression of elegant surprise it must have had when the bullet struck. Mounted on the wall was a gunrack housing a handsome display of heavy-duty hunting rifles.

In the midst of the trophies—his back to the window —sat Holbrook Meadows, framed by a spectacular view of St. Paul's. Approaching him from a standing position, it seemed to Redfern that the large head, worthy of taxidermy itself, was crowned by the dome of the cathedral. In his unnatural habitat, Holbrook Meadows was an imposing and somewhat forbidding quarry.

"Mr. Redburn."

"Redfern, with an 'f.' "

"Ah, yes, forgive me, Redfern. Do have a seat. I must say that I'm flattered you should fly all this way to talk to me. I can't imagine why I merit the attentions of the Montreal press."

"Let's just say Quebec is very much in the news," said Redfern, sitting in the black leather sofa opposite Meadows's desk.

"The world has gone mad, Mr. Redfern. Things were so much simpler when I was your age. The Hun was the enemy. Clear and simple."

"You have holdings in Quebec, Mr. Meadows," began Redfern, getting quickly to the point.

"The company does, yes. That is common knowledge. Our subsidiary is quoted on the Montreal and Toronto exchanges."

"Let me put it another way then."

"I wish you would, my dear fellow. I do have a rather busy schedule."

"Okay. I'm busy too, so I won't pussyfoot. I've been working on the assassination story and I have learned certain things which I believe have put my life in danger."

"Perhaps you should choose a less hazardous occupation, Mr. Redfern."

"What I have found leads me to IntCon," said Redfern, ignoring the remark. "I believe that IntCon is somehow involved in what is happening in Quebec."

"To what exactly are you referring?"

"The assassination of the Premier."

"Let me understand you correctly. Are you saying that this company is involved in a political murder?"

"If that's what you choose to call it."

"Do you realize that we have laws of slander in this country? To say nothing of libel should you print such accusations."

"That's why I'm here. I'm not going to print anything until I have some answers from you. First of all, why would a multinational company like IntCon send a wreath to the Premier's funeral? The Quebec business community hated the man. And your company had more cause than most to hate him. He stood in the way of your mineral-development rights."

Holbrook Meadows leaned back in his chair; his heavy jowls seemed to puff out, giving him the appearance of an outraged hamster.

"What in God's name are you talking about? Funeral wreaths? Corporations do that all the time. Call us hypocrites if you like, but it's a fact of business life. Every business in the province that ever had a crack at a government contract sent a wreath, you mark my words."

Redfern could feel the blood rising in his cheeks. He tried another tack.

"All right, let's forget that for a moment. Let's talk about why your man in Montreal has suddenly become very chummy with Guy Lacroix's bagman."

"Bagman?"

"His campaign treasurer, if you like." The sparring was exasperating Redfern.

"I imagine they've been discussing our donation to his political campaign," Meadows said airily, watching Redfern closely.

"But why Lacroix? Why not Belmont?"

"As far as I know, he didn't ask for one. But you can rest assured that he will be receiving a substantial financial donation as well. We have to hedge our bets, Mr. Redfern. That's sensible business practice. A corporation of our importance has to be behind the winning man."

Redfern felt his case crumbling. He switched his attack again.

"How did Kevin Reilly get hold of your infrared night-sight then?"

"Who?"

"Surely the name is not unknown to you."

"A footballer is he? Or a singer?"

"He's the man who shot the Premier, Mr. Meadows. Using one of your night-sights."

"What you are saying is that the killer's rifle was fitted with a night-sight manufactured by our subsidiary, d'Aston, in Belgium?"

"Exactly."

Meadows heaved himself out of his chair, tugged at his vest, and took a small key out of the pocket. He crossed the deep pile carpet to the gun cabinet and unlocked the glass door. From it he lifted out a 30/30 lever-action Winchester.

"Is this the sight you're referring to?"

Redfern joined him at the cabinet.

"Yes, I guess so."

Meadows replaced the rifle in the rack and locked it away, having dusted the barrel with his silk handkerchief.

"I saw it field-tested two years ago during NATO exercises. It's still classified," added Redfern.

"A remarkable piece of engineering. I bagged that antelope with it in Tsavo Park—that's in Kenya. Got it just at sundown."

"How come Reilly had one?" Redfern would not be sidetracked.

"When you say that it is still classified, you're only partly right. D'Aston has made a couple of refinements and the new model is a great improvement over this one. Perhaps there's a story for you."

"I'm more interested in how Reilly came to have that sight on his rifle."

"You are persistent, Mr. Redfern. This particular model is about to be declassified, and we happen to think that it has considerable commercial possibilities. Several hundred, I don't know the exact figure, but several hundred units are currently being tested on both sides of the Atlantic. Your killer could have obtained one from one of our field testers. Or it could even have been stolen."

Redfern's theory had been exploded. Every prop had been kicked away, and the hypothesis he had painstakingly built up crumbled around him.

"Well, um, thank you for clearing up those points," he mumbled.

Holbrook Meadows, sensing the change of mood, moved in for the *coup de grâce*.

"I think we have exhausted this subject now, Mr. Redfern. I am extremely busy. But before you leave, let me give you a piece of advice. I will not tolerate any attempts to besmirch the good name of this company. If you print a single suggestion or innuendo that IntCon was or is in any way connected with the grotesque goings-on in Quebec, I will sue your newspaper and you personally for every devalued cent you have. Do I make myself crystal clear? Good day."

Redfern left the office thoroughly dispirited. The theory had seemed so right when he formulated it. Now that it had been demolished he felt suddenly very demoralized and very tired. The weeks of tension and fear had taken their toll.

When he reached the street, his head ached and the rush of lunchtime traffic through the narrow canyons of London's financial district confused him. He was nearly knocked down trying to hail a taxi, and he didn't even notice the noon edition of the *Evening Standard* displayed on a news vendor's kiosk. The front page carried a huge picture of Guy Lacroix.

Taylor Redfern wandered moodily through the City, oblivious to the light drizzle. He kept turning over the facts in his mind. In spite of Holbrook Meadows's unhesitating rebuttal of all the evidence, he was convinced that somehow IntCon was tied into the conspiracy surrounding the Premier's death. Yet he had no proof. So why had Cameron Craig allowed him to fly the Atlantic, to spend valuable time on what the editor must have recognized as a wild-goose chase? Surely Craig must have been aware how flimsy the evidence was. He normally doled out the expense money as if it were his own, but he had knowingly sent Redfern off on the basis of a weak theory. Was his editor bowing to pressure to have him taken off the story, and was this his response? Damn it, Redfern said to himself, who can I trust?

He thought of Lois and the children, and his sense of isolation grew. Perhaps a drink would cheer him up. He hated drinking alone, but he headed for the nearest pub and ordered himself a large Scotch. The alcohol warmed him, and he ordered another. If Craig wants me to spend a few days chasing phantoms at the *Chronicle*'s expense, then at least I can enjoy myself doing it, he thought. He took out his book of contacts and turned to the page marked "London, Eng." One name leaped out at him: Brian Windsor, All-Canada News Service. Brian and he had worked together in Quebec for a time. Redfern had not seen him for four years, since his London posting.

He left his drink on the bar and crossed to the phone booth in the corner.

"All-Canada News Service. Madge Tillwood speaking." He was amused by the flat London accent.

"Hello. Is Brian Windsor there, please?"

"I'm afraid he may have left for lunch. Hold on a minute if you would . . . no, he's here. He's just coming."

"Hello, Brian Windsor here."

"Brian, hi! It's Taylor Redfern."

"Taylor! How the hell are you!"

The taxi driver had never heard of All-Canada News Service, but he agreed to drop Redfern at the corner of Fleet Street and Bouverie Street, from where he could find the building himself. Redfern settled back against the leather seat, feeling unaccountably happy.

The cab moved slowly down Threadneedle Street, past the Bank of England and the Royal Exchange and along toward St. Paul's. Once past Wren's cathedral the traffic filtered down Ludgate Hill into Ludgate Circus, and Redfern became aware of a low roar like the sound of an angry sea in the distance.

"What's that?" he asked the driver, leaning forward to talk through the glass partition.

"Search me, guv," replied the cabbie. "Probably some march down Fleet Street. Happens all the time these days."

Before the driver had completed his remark, the taxi was suddenly surrounded by a band of screaming, brawling youths. A rock hit the side window and shattered it into opaque fragments.

"What the hell's going on?" yelled Redfern. Through the windshield, he caught sight of a man with a placard, swinging it above his head like an axe. As the driver attempted to accelerate to safety, he brought it down with a crash on the hood of the cab.

"Lock your doors, mate, and get your head down," warned the driver. His voice betrayed the fear he felt. From the comparative safety of the cab, Redfern could see men running in all directions and flailing out at each other. A face covered with blood rose up at the window and then disappeared as hands tore at the doors and rocked the cab from side to side. Police in riot gear brandished night sticks and transparent plastic shields; they formed a human wedge and drove into the crowd of rioters, beating heads indiscriminately.

The taxi rocked and jolted as the driver threw his gear shift into reverse, narrowly missing the car behind. Rocks bounced off the roof like hailstones.

"What in God's name is happening?" screamed Redfern.

The driver was too intent on extricating his precious taxi from the riot to answer. He wove his way back to safety and pulled to a halt. He mopped his sweating forehead.

"I remember now. The Commies had planned a march from Fleet Street to Number Ten Downing Street today. Looks like the National Front tried to break it up."

"The National Front?"

"Yeah, you probably saw their armbands. England for the English, that's what they believe in. Repatriate the blacks, get rid of the Jews and the Commies. I'm sorry you had to see this."

Redfern could still see the bloody battle raging in Fleet Street as men with staves swept across the roadway and then surged back again under a barrage of stones and bottles. Police with bull horns were shouting instructions as individual troublemakers were isolated from the mob and dragged off to waiting Black Marias. Redfern could see a phalanx of mounted police lined up in Ludgate Circus. The horses walked steadily forward into the melee in tight formation, clearing a path through the jeering mob. The worst of the riot appeared to be over.

"I don't know what's happening to this country, guv. The government don't count for nothing no more. It's the Commies and the Front and they're fighting it out between them. Just like in Germany in the 1930s. I'm sorry, but this is as far as I go. Wouldn't go down there if I was you. Least not till the police get control."

"How much do I owe you?"

"Nothing, this one's on me, guv."

Brian Windsor ordered a round of Scotches at the Press Club—the only place in Fleet Street where journalists could continue drinking between pub hours. Taylor Redfern had arrived at the All-Canada News Service office pale and trembling. Madge Tillwood, an attractive redhead, had given him a medicinal whisky, and they had waited until the police had finished clearing the street before venturing out. While the three of them sat in the tiny, cluttered office sipping Scotch out of paper cups, Windsor talked about the National Front and their burgeoning political fortunes. He drew a parallel to Hitler's National Socialist Party in the early 1930s. Like Germany then, the poisonous bloom of fascism in Britain fed on fifteen years of economic crisis. As the country's financial health deteriorated, so the National Front grew and its party candidates enjoyed by-election victories in working-class constituencies. The party leader had vowed that he would be the Prime Minister of Britain within two years.

"My God, it's enough to turn anyone to drink," said Madge, and the three of them decided that the situation called for that very remedy.

The Scotch they had been drinking was now supplemented with beer chasers at the Press Club. The conversation had turned to Quebec, and Redfern drunkenly recounted the events that had led him to London and IntCon.

"Fascinating, fascinating," mumbled Windsor, punctuating Redfern's monologue with the odd remark to show that he was still listening, although his eyes were closed.

"That chap Lacroix nearly got his though, didn't he," added Madge.

"Whassat? What did she say?" asked Redfern.

Madge smiled muzzily at him, and he felt her hand reach out under the table and begin stroking his thigh.

Taylor Redfern awoke with a parched throat and a rasping pain in his eyes. He had fallen asleep still wearing his contact lenses, something his optometrist had repeatedly warned him against. God, they hurt! He focused on the plaster rosette in the center of the ceiling, trying to remember where he was. There was a movement in the bed next to him. Madge Tillwood's red hair spilled over the pillow like copper wire. She wore only a slip.

The events of the night before were a blur. He vaguely remembered returning to the hotel, the three of them arm in arm, singing. He raised himself on his elbows and looked around. Brian Windsor was snoring softly on the couch, one shoe on and one off. Oh my God, Redfern thought to himself, and a wave of nausea, brought on by a combination of guilt and liquor, passed through him.

He eased himself gently out of bed and felt for his pants over the back of the chair. He carried them to the bathroom and put them on, being careful not to jingle the change in his pockets. His eye drops were on the sink next to his toothbrush. He removed the contact lenses and gratefully applied the numbing solution to his irritated eyes. His mouth was parched. He filled a glass with cold tap water and drank it.

"How about one for me too, Taylor?" Madge Tillwood stood in the doorway. Her make-up was smudged about her eyes.

"What a sight," she said, combing her fingers through her hair. She took the proffered glass and smiled at him.

"I don't recall much of last night," began Redfern apologetically.

"Perhaps it's best that way," said Madge. "Now, how about rustling up some room service. And maybe we'd better give Sleeping Beauty out there a shake."

They spoke little over breakfast; no one seemed to know what to say. Redfern had had the presence of mind to order three newspapers with breakfast, so they hid their mutual embarrassment behind the newsprint.

"You were asking about Lacroix last night," said Madge, breaking the silence. "There's a story here: 'Lacroix Assailant in Hospital.' "

"What!" Redfern grabbed the paper from her.

"Bottom left-hand corner," said Madge.

The story was datelined Percé, Quebec.

Olivier Blanchette, a Montreal bank clerk, is reported to be in critical condition in Sacré Coeur Hospital following an attempt on the life of Quebec cabinet minister Guy Lacroix. A hospital spokesman says Blanchette, aged thirty-two, is suffering from multiple fractures and concussion.

Blanchette, who fired one shot at the minister during a campaign rally in a school hall here, was severely beaten by the crowd before police could take him into custody. Sources close to Mr. Lacroix say the minister was uninjured but is being treated for shock.

Doctors have refused to allow authorities to interview Blanchette and no motive has yet been established for the attack.

Mr. Lacroix told reporters that he intends to continue his campaign tour as soon as his personal physician allows him to travel. In a carefully worded statement he intimated that he believed the Canadian government was instrumental in the attempt on his life.

"Jesus Christ!" breathed Redfern. "Has everyone gone crazy?"

"You know, Taylor, I think you're better off out of it," said Brian.

"We're all in it," he replied.

It was late in the day when they arrived at Heathrow. Redfern had wanted to take a cab to the airport, but Brian and Madge had insisted on driving him there.

Redfern had made up his mind not to return to Montreal. He would fly straight to Vancouver to spend Christmas with Lois and the children. The events of the last week had exhausted his preoccupation with justice—they could go on murdering each other as far as he was concerned. He had no more stomach for the story; he was tired of the dead ends, the deceit, the intrigues, the violence. He wanted to turn his back on the whole sordid business.

At the terminal building, Brian helped him with his luggage. "Have a good flight," he said, smiling sadly at

Redfern. "And listen, if there's anything I can do at this end to help, you let me know. Okay?"

"Yeah, thanks, Brian."

Madge kissed him quickly and squeezed his hand.

"Me, too," she said. "Take care of yourself."

Redfern picked up his suitcase and his portable typewriter and gave them a final wave as he passed through the gate to the security check.

"Warren, I find this difficult to believe," the President said wearily. He stared out of the window of the Florida White House at the beach in the distance. Some kids were gathering sea shells. He wished he were with them.

Warren Cummings shifted uneasily in his chair.

"Have your people gone beserk?" the President demanded. "What the hell is going on with the CIA?"

"It's this one operative in Quebec. He seems to have acted on his own initiative. No one briefed him to—"

"A CIA man walks into a crowded hall and takes a potshot at Lacroix. What is this? *High Noon?* You're supposed to be running a highly sophisticated agency with all the latest equipment science can dream up available to you. Do you realize the implications for us if this man's link with the CIA is discovered?"

"The man was badly beaten, sir. He's still in a coma. They doubt he'll survive."

"He'd better not, for your sake. How the hell could it have happened?"

Warren Cummings sighed. The fact that the agent had acted against orders was not an excuse the President would accept. Blanchette was one of the few French Canadians the Company had been able to recruit. He had seemed a steady, reliable person. His file showed he had worked as a Parti Québécois volunteer at the riding level in Montreal. When his superiors had asked him for a report on the most effective way of deterring a Lacroix victory, the man had obviously decided he was another James Bond and hatched a scheme designed to cover himself with glory.

"Your man Blanchette must not talk to the police," the President was saying. "We cannot take the chance of his recovering. There's too much at stake. See to it. Do you understand?"

"Yes, sir. I understand."

"Good. Thank you, Warren."

The President went back to staring at the sea. The kids were gone. There were storm clouds building up far out over the Gulf. It would be a wet night.

Cameron Craig was in the *Chronicle* wire room when the bell on the Canadian Press ticker rang five times, indicating a flash. He tore the item off and read it quickly.

Percé, Quebec—(CP)—Olivier Blanchette, the man accused of firing a shot at the Social Affairs Minister Guy Lacroix, died early this morning in Sacré Coeur Hospital without regaining consciousness.

Following an immediate autopsy a hospital spokesman announced that Blanchette, a thirty-two-year-old Montreal bank clerk, had died from injuries sustained as the result of a beating by angry Lacroix supporters during a campaign rally. Police had been waiting to interview Blanchette in connection with the assassination attempt.

Craig took the story into the newsroom and tossed it onto the news editor's desk.

"There's your lead for this afternoon, Jim. Get rewrite to tart it up with some background and have it set fast. We've got twenty-five minutes to deadline."

The only suggestion of Christmas in the Prime Minister's office was a tiny silver tree that stood on his desk. Instead of colored balls and sugar canes its branches were hung with minute rubber frogs, and on the top was a paper fleur-de-lis. It was a joke-gift from Doris Faber and despite its bad taste, the P.M. had allowed himself a smile when she presented it to him earlier in the day. He reminded himself to take it home before some reporter got wind of it. The press could be counted on to turn it into a mini-scandal.

"Excuse me, sir." Doris Faber put her head around the door.

"Yes, Doris, what is it?"

"This has just come, hand-delivered from Montreal. It's the results of the latest Gallup Poll in Quebec."

"Oh? How does it look?"

"I'm not going to be the one to spoil your Christmas, sir. You'd better see it for yourself."

He opened the file and began to read. Doris Faber stood expectantly in front of his desk.

"Yes, Doris, anything else?" A tinge of annoyance colored his voice.

"I just wondered if you needed me any more this evening. It's Christmas Eve. . . ."

"Good heavens, so it is. You should be with your family and so should I. Go, by all means, Doris . . . and Merry Christmas."

An hour and a half later, the Prime Minister wished that he had tossed the file in the basket and left with Doris. The news from Quebec was all bad. Lacroix's popularity had rocketed since the attempt on his life. Gallup gave the Minister of Social Affairs a twenty-nine per cent lead over Belmont as the people's choice for the next Premier of Quebec. That figure included English-speaking Quebeckers. Among French Canadians the poll was running three to one in Lacroix's favor. The popular choice would not necessarily be that of the convention delegates, as the Prime Minister knew, but in a two-man race it would weigh heavily on the final outcome.

Maybe the guy who had tried to kill Lacroix had had the right idea, he mused. It began to look as if that were the only way to stop the man. He speculated idly on who might have been behind the assassination attempt. The fact that Blanchette had died without regaining consciousness seemed altogether too convenient. Perhaps the nomination for Premier would be decided by a shootout in front of the Quebec Legislature, the way things were going.

The Prime Minister picked up a paper knife and amused himself by prodding the tiny rubber frogs until they danced up and down on their silver branches.

The Belmont campaign office two hundred miles away was more festive in mood and decoration. Sprigs of holly adorned the walls, and the ceilings were hung with paper streamers. The air was redolent of cigarette smoke and the smell of whisky as the campaign staff celebrated the season of peace and good will.

"Come on, Monique. We're all leaving now. Get your coat." Raymond Mercier, glassy-eyed with drink, stood in the doorway of her office, supporting himself with both hands on the door frame. The rest of the party was preparing to adjourn to the Hôtel Faisan d'Or down the street to continue the celebrations.

"I'm sorry, Raymond, I can't make it. Truly. There's simply too much to be left till after the holiday." Monique Gravelle gestured at the mound of paper on her desk. "You go ahead, I'll catch up with you in a little while."

"Monique . . ." Mercier weaved his way over to her. "Come along, my little . . ." She could smell the whisky on his breath as he planted a kiss on her cheek.

"Raymond. Someone will see. Now stop it."

"Only if you promise to come right now."

"Hey, what's going on in here?" Denise Carrier, Mercier's secretary, stuck her head in the door. "Let's go, you two; everybody's on their way."

"Take Mr. Mercier with you, will you, Denise," Monique called out to the retreating blonde. "I've got some work that must be finished."

The secretary reappeared and exchanged a knowing look with Monique.

"Sure," she said. She grabbed Mercier firmly by the arm and steered him to the door. "Let's go, boss, tonight you're mine."

Mercier giggled and allowed himself to be led away. Monique listened as they made their way through the reception area and joined the larger group out in the snowy night. From the window she watched them all move into the street; they were singing Christmas carols.

She checked her watch and waited for a few minutes before making a tour of the premises. The offices were all empty, as were both bathrooms. She bolted the front door and put the night latch on. Then she returned to her own office, pulled the blinds, and cleared off her desk.

She took a flashlight from her purse and followed its beam down the corridor to Raymond Mercier's office. She checked to see if the blinds were drawn. When she was satisfied that no one could see in, she crossed into the inner office where he kept the safe with the campaign funds. To her surprise the door to the room was unlocked. She would have no need of the key she had had made. She ignored the safe but concentrated on the filing cabinet next to it, which was always kept locked. The cabinet had a complicated combination mechanism, but she had seen Mercier open it on several occasions and had memorized the numbers.

She punched in the combination code as she remembered it. There was no soft click to indicate that the lock had tripped. She couldn't understand it. She tried again. Still no telltale click. What was wrong? Had she made a mistake? Again she failed. Beads of perspiration began to stand out on her forehead. In her frustration she pulled at one of the steel drawers, and it rolled out smoothly on its ballbearings. Mercier, the drunken fool, had forgotten to lock the filing cabinet as well. It's a wonder he didn't leave the campaign money lying on his desk for the cleaners to pick up, she thought.

The bottom drawer contained what she was looking for— the ledgers. She lifted them carefully out. Recorded in them was all the financial information relating to the Belmont campaign—contributions, expenditures, bank accounts, staff salaries, everything. There were three heavy tomes, and she carried them one by one back to her own desk. When that was done, she locked herself in her office.

Slowly and methodically she went through each page. All the bookkeeping entries had been made by hand with a thin-nibbed cartridge pen which Mercier kept in the marble stand on his desk. With that same pen Monique Gravelle skillfully altered several of the figures. Fives became threes, sevens became ones, nines became eights. At one point she began to feel tired. She took two pills from her purse and swallowed them quickly without the aid of water. A few minutes later she was working at peak efficiency again.

The job took a couple of hours of meticulous work. When she finally replaced the ledgers in the filing cabinet, she debated whether to lock it or not. She decided to do so on the assumption that Mercier would never believe or admit that he had left it open. What a fool the man was.

The snow on her face felt cold and refreshing as she stepped outside. Merry Christmas, Monsieur Belmont, she said to herself as she walked slowly to the Faisan d'Or. There was only one thing left to do to complete the plan.

When she entered the hotel bar, she found Mercier and three of the campaign workers still drinking, their arms around each other in maudlin camaraderie, singing carols.

"Monique, Monique," shouted Mercier when he caught sight of her. "You came. Come and have a cup of Christmas cheer." He was very drunk; there were wet stains on his shirt and tie where he had slopped his whisky.

"I think it's time I got you home, Raymond."

"Another drink, a drink for everyone." He made an expansive sweep with his arm, a gesture which knocked a glass from the table into the lap of Denise Carrier. The girl watched the wet dark patch spread over her skirt and giggled helplessly.

"Sorry, sorry," mumbled Mercier, and he mopped clumsily at the stain with his handkerchief.

"Come along, Raymond, you've had enough. Time to get you back to your family." Monique gave a conspiratorial wink to the rest of the party. Without further protest, Mercier rose unsteadily and allowed himself to be led off. Monique put one arm around him and steered him out of the hotel bar into the cold night air. Mercier weaved along the snow-covered sidewalk. Monique supported him until they reached her car. He sang happily to himself as she propped him up against the hood in order to brush off the windows and put the top down; it was the only way she could get him into the passenger seat. The rush of cold air revived Mercier somewhat as they sped through the deserted streets of Trois-Rivières.

"This isn't home," said Mercier as they pulled up in front of Monique's motel.

"No," she replied. "But I have a Christmas present for you. Come on, let's get you out." She heaved him bodily out of the car and guided him toward her room. Once inside, Mercier flopped unceremoniously down on the bed and closed his eyes. His mouth was open and he snorted as he breathed.

"Damn you," said Monique, "you're not going to sleep." She unlaced his shoes and slipped them off. Then she unbuttoned his coat and jacket and pulled them off together.

"I'm awake," mumbled Mercier, although his eyes were closed.

Very deliberately, she unzipped his trousers and

reached into his pants. She began to squeeze his flaccid member.

"Get hard, Raymond, concentrate."

Mercier's eyes opened in astonishment.

"Do you know what's happening to you?" she whispered, as she rubbed his penis to erection. He said nothing but stared at her with a foolish grin on his face. Slowly she undid her skirt and let it fall to the ground. With one hand she rolled down her tights and pulled them off and then stepped out of her panties. She squatted over him on the bed and inserted his penis into her. Slowly, she began to move up and down.

"Remember what we're doing," she kept repeating in an urgent whisper, "remember what we're doing." Gradually she increased the rhythm until his body arched backward in a rush of pleasure and he lay back with a sigh on the pillows.

Thérèse St. Rémy read the entry in the *Guide Michelin* again. Les Trois Frères, Malville, twenty kilometers northeast of N-75 Grenoble to Bourg. Surely this wasn't it? She frowned as she surveyed what looked like a two-story cottage with a red tile roof.

"Les Trois Frères is reputedly one of the twelve finest restaurants in France," said Antoine de Luzt, bringing the Peugeot to a halt in the snow-covered parking lot.

"I hope you didn't drag me a hundred kilometers out of our way to have lunch in some peasant's kitchen," grumbled the woman.

"Paris has spoiled you, my dear," he said, holding the door open for her.

De Luzt had invited Thérèse to accompany him on a business trip to Liechtenstein to look after the affairs of his company there, followed by a week's skiing over New Year's at Chamonix. On the drive back to Paris, he had had the sudden inspiration to detour south for lunch at Les Trois Frères, which had recently received a third star from the Michelin inspectors.

Like its exterior, the restaurant was unprepossessing. The tables were grouped about an old millstone in the center of the low-ceilinged room. The whitewashed walls threw into sharp contrast the age-blackened beams and the rough hardwood floors. A few potted plants added the only color to the room. De Luzt noted with some surprise that none of the tables was occupied, although it was one o'clock.

A portly man with a walrus mustache and a glistening bald head emerged from the kitchen.

"*Ah, bonjour. Monsieur de Luzt, n'est ce pas? We*

have a table by the window for you and your charming lady." He picked up two handwritten menus and escorted them to their chairs. The absence of a cold table aroused de Luzt's curiosity.

"Business is slow, monsieur?"

The fat man shrugged. "Midweek, you know, January. It is better in the evening. Would madame care for an aperitif?"

He took the drinks order and bustled away. De Luzt studied the menu; he wondered what had motivated the *Guide Michelin* to bestow its highest and most coveted honor on this establishment.

"Doesn't look very thrilling," remarked Thérèse. "Grilled chicken, grilled steak, grilled *noisette de veau.* Are you sure this is the right place?"

The waiter returned with the drinks.

De Luzt pushed his chair away from the table. "Surely a three-star restaurant has more to offer than this?"

The man's mustache seemed to droop in utter defeat. "*Je suis désolé, monsieur.* That is the only selection."

"Where is the proprietor? I would like a word with him."

"Monsieur, I am the proprietor."

"But where are your staff, your waiters?" De Luzt made a gesture with his arm that embraced the entire establishment.

The fat man looked heavenward as if some kindly fate would deliver him.

"There are only my wife and I. She does the cooking and the washing. I wait at table. You are right, monsieur, business is slow."

"Slow, I've seen more action in a morgue," said Thérèse.

"You should be turning them away now. Three stars is money in the bank."

"Yes, monsieur, it was until two months ago. Since then times have been bad. My two brothers have left to work in hotels in Lyon. I have had to let the rest of the staff go."

"What happened?"

"The economy, monsieur," the fat man began, waving his hands vaguely.

"There are always people who eat well, even in a depression," replied de Luzt. "What's the real reason?"

"Monsieur, we have been told to say nothing . . ."

"Told? By whom?"

"The men from the government, monsieur. They came and told the farmers around here to plow under all their crops. Now we have no fresh vegetables."

"You were told to plow under all your crops?"

"Yes, and we had to kill all the livestock, cows, horses, pigs. They compensated the farmers for them at market prices, but how can you run a restaurant without fresh meat and vegetables? Everything in the local stores is frozen. Terrible. The government has ruined my business."

"Why haven't we heard of this in Paris?" asked de Luzt.

"We were ordered to keep silent, monsieur. That was the condition of the compensation payment. But who compensates me for the loss of my reputation?"

"Why did they have to shoot all the animals?" asked Thérèse.

The man became evasive again; he realized he had said more than he should have.

"The order came from Paris, you say? How large an area is involved?" asked de Luzt.

"For twenty miles around, monsieur. Some people say it's the Super Phénix."

Super Phénix. The name rang a bell. De Luzt excused himself and asked the proprietor if he could borrow his phone for a reverse-charge call. In a room off the kitchen where in more prosperous times the proprietor had kept the books and reservation charts, de Luzt placed a call to Roger Quesnel in Paris.

"Roger, de Luzt here. Listen, the Super Phénix. Isn't that the government's fast-neutron plant? The prototype of the breeders we were discussing the other day?"

"Yes, it's the first of the reactors they're setting up to manufacture plutonium fuel from uranium waste. I have the locations of all the plants for you. I was waiting for your arrival."

"Is Super Phénix near Malville?"

"Where?"

"Malville, it's off N-75, near the Rhône River."

"There's one about sixty kilometers east of Lyon."

"Fine. I'll call you when I get to Paris, Roger. In the meantime, find out what you can on the project."

De Luzt returned to the table in better humor.

"I ordered two *noisettes de veau*," said Thérèse.

"Splendid," said de Luzt, but his mind was elsewhere. The Super Phénix plant was the linchpin in France's crash program to convert its domestic energy-generating capacity from conventional fuel to nuclear-based. The former President, Valéry Giscard d'Estaing, had made a speech a few years ago saying that nuclear energy was the double helix of France's future independence—independence for the country's defense systems and independence for her energy requirements. Since then the country had been spending billions of francs on the construction of more than forty nuclear-power plants, which the government claimed would cut the country's imported energy bill by seventy-five per cent. The whole project depended on the success of Super Phénix, however. The problem had been uranium supplies. Australia was insisting on monitoring the uses to which its exported uranium was put—a condition France could not accept. South African supplies were held largely for domestic use, and what they exported was hardly enough to keep one French generator working at capacity. Neither the United States nor the U.S.S.R. would sell to France. And repeated attempts to gain access to Canadian supplies, and to use the massive power generated by the James Bay project in Quebec to produce enriched uranium, had been blocked by Ottawa.

So France had gambled on Super Phénix, a highly controversial breeder reactor which employed a still unproven sodium system operating at dangerously high temperatures. If Super Phénix worked, then the other breeders in the chain could produce all the nuclear fuel France needed.

The meal arrived and de Luzt pushed it around his plate reflectively. Perhaps this was the reason Hilaire Noel had been so secretive. And now it looked as if there had been a leak at Super Phénix. Nuclear waste had contaminated the area, and the government had tried to hush the affair. A scandal by environmentalists would endanger France's nuclear capacity, and the government could not afford that.

The proprietor reappeared to inquire if the meal was to their satisfaction.

"Tell me something," said de Luzt. "Did the government people inoculate you?"

"Yes, monsieur." He pulled up his sleeve to show the mark. "They did everyone. Even the babies. Enjoy your meal, monsieur."

Antoine de Luzt forgot the food in front of him and stared out the window over the snow-covered fields.

"What's that you are always telling me?" said Thérèse. "A girl who likes her food is good in bed."

The motel room in Trois-Rivères had over the weeks become a loathsome place for Monique Gravelle. She longed to be free of it. Lying in bed smoking and staring at the ceiling with Raymond Mercier asleep at her side, she thought of quitting, of flying to Hawaii and basking on white sandy beaches. The intermittent light from the motel sign illuminated the sleeping naked body of Mercier next to her; stretched out on top of the sheet, he reminded her of a giant jellyfish she had once found washed up on a beach. She felt like carving notches on the bedpost each time she suffered the inept sexual attentions of her employer. How many times since Christmas? Five, six? She'd lost count.

She stubbed out the cigarette in the ashtray. Mercier had the annoying habit of falling asleep as soon as he had been satisfied. But that wouldn't do tonight. She had some questions she wanted answered.

Monique got out of bed and noisily hung her clothes on the wire hangers, but even this did not disturb Mercier. She lit another cigarette and sat on the bed beside him. Impulsively, she thrust it between his lips and held it there until he awoke coughing.

"What? What is it? Monique?"

"I thought you might like a cigarette, *chéri*," she said, smiling. "You usually do, you know . . . afterward."

Mercier sat up. The hot ash fell on his stomach and he brushed it off, trying not to appear comical in front of this extraordinary woman.

Monique picked up the glass from the bedside table.

"Another one?"

"What time is it?"

"Why do you always ask what time it is? You're always worried about her."

"No, it's not that," lied Mercier. "My wife knows I have to work late."

"Have another drink then."

"All right. If you have one with me. I've got to leave soon."

He watched her rise from the bed and cross to the bottles on the dresser. The light etched the soft curve of her breast and the line of her stomach. He felt the urge coming on him again.

"I hear the results of the latest poll aren't so hot," she said casually, pouring a large measure of Scotch into his glass.

"Where did you hear that?"

"Oh, I have my sources."

"Well, keep it to yourself, my dear. I've been trying not to let anything affect the morale of the office. I don't want it to get out."

"How bad is it?" she asked, handing him the glass and expertly avoiding his groping hand as she did so. She seated herself in the torn vinyl chair.

Mercier leaned back on the pillow and sighed. "Not good. It's not so much the figures, they're pretty bad, but in delegate strength Lacroix is ahead about three to two. A lot of delegates from rural ridings are still being selected. That's where our strength lies. They're very conservative, the country folk. They aren't likely to vote for a radical like Lacroix. It's not over by any means, not by a long shot. But it's going to get rougher. My guess is that it will all be decided on the convention floor."

"Can I quote you on that?"

"Certainly, my dear."

"Raymond," began Monique softly, "if I am to be of any use to you and Monsieur Belmont, you have to keep me informed. If I don't know what's in your mind, I'm hardly able to orchestrate the press properly. Where do we go from here?"

"Well, it's a question of hard work. Making sure that our people get chosen at the delegate-selection meetings coming up. Keeping Jean-Claude in front of the public as acting Premier, you know, the heir-apparent. And I've got a couple of ideas too."

"Like what?"

"You're too curious. I haven't worked them out fully yet."

"Oh, Raymond, I'm here to help you." She pouted.

He put the glass on the bedside table and heaved himself out of bed. Before she could take evasive action, he had surrounded the chair in which she sat in his jellyfish way.

"Anyway, I've got some good news for you," he whispered as he nuzzled her neck.

"What's that?" She tried to twist away, but both his hands were firmly planted on the arms of the chair and his knees worked between her legs, prising them apart.

"We're moving the campaign headquarters to Quebec City next week. It's closer to the center of the action. You'll be living in the Quebec Hilton. No more cheap motels."

The full weight of his body descended upon her. She let herself go limp.

In Roger Quesnel's darkroom the photographs in the developing tank began to show through on the paper. Antoine de Luzt concentrated on the darkening images.

"*Voilà!* There you have it, Antoine. The whole story."

"Well done, Roger, I knew you'd come through."

"Once you put me onto Super Phénix, the rest was easy." Quesnel pulled the sheet out of the developing solution with a pair of tongs and hung it up to dry. "There it is. The top-secret report on the SP disaster. It even names the men who died. Seven casualties and nine hospitalized with radiation burns."

"What was the story?"

"It seems the reactor was about to come on stream when they discovered a small leak of radioactive fumes. Enough to contaminate a twenty-mile radius. The government, bless its heart, clamped an immediate news blackout on the story and sent in security people to kill off all the livestock in the area and destroy the crops."

"Well, at least they are effective in some things," noted de Luzt. "There's been no wind of it."

"Here you see the inspectors' recommendations," said Quesnel, pointing at a second photograph. "The breeder program must be suspended indefinitely."

"That means the whole network of France's nuclear-generating stations will be hungry for fuel. We can't manufacture it domestically, so we'll have to go looking for it on the world market. And that would compromise the entire energy program as well as an independent nuclear-defense system. No wonder Hilaire Noel was being so mysterious."

"That rumor about the English company, IntCon, their big uranium strike in Quebec. It begins to make sense now," said Quesnel. "They say it may be the biggest uranium-ore strike ever."

De Luzt gave a low whistle. The pieces began to fit. Quebec uranium, James Bay hydroelectricity to provide power for the enrichment process—all at a time when France had a sudden, desperate need for unlimited supplies. And only Ottawa stood in the way. He understood now how high the stakes were in the deadly game being played between so-called friendly nations.

He placed the damp photographs between the pages of his newspaper and slipped it into his briefcase.

"I want to borrow your flat for an hour or two," he said. "Go out and have a drink, will you, Roger. And stay on this. Let me know if you come up with anything else."

When he was alone, de Luzt made two phone calls. The first was to his lawyer in Liechtenstein, who acted for his small holding company, Les Enterprises de Luzt, Ltée. The conversation was short and to the point: buy every IntCon share that comes on the market.

The second call was to Canada. The conversation lasted for over an hour.

From his bedroom window Taylor Redfern looked out over the majestic sweep of the city of Vancouver. Below him stood a cluster of white apartment buildings that seemed to float on the edge of the blue waters of the harbor. In the distance he could see the sensuous curve of the Lion's Gate Bridge and beyond it the chain of small, green islands. The city was enclosed on three sides by the Coast Range, like a protective hand of stone. Behind these mountains rose the mighty granite of the Rockies.

The scene was spectacular in all weathers, but in the early morning sun on a crisp January day the view was bathed in burnished gold.

"Admiring my city again, I see." Lois came into the bedroom behind him and handed him a glass of freshly squeezed orange juice. Redfern put his arm around her waist and pulled her close to him.

"Your parents are lucky to wake up to this every morning. You always said it was like this, but I never believed you. Just as you'd never believe me about the Laurentians in October."

"Can't stop thinking of Quebec, can you, Taylor?"

It was the first time he had mentioned Quebec since his arrival to spend Christmas with the family. The visit had become the occasion for a mental and physical regeneration. He had not realized just how exhausted he was. Working on the assassination story had steadily drained him of his energy, and the interview with Holbrook Meadows in London had undermined his morale to a point where he had lost confidence in his own judgment. He had called Cameron Craig in Montreal and told him he was taking two weeks' holiday. That done, he put the whole business out of his mind, the killings, the conspiracies, the politics; he finally let go and allowed himself to be nursed back to full strength by his wife and mother-in-law.

It had been a good holiday. Christmas morning with his excited children; delightful dinners in the colorful restaurants of Vancouver's Gastown and Chinatown; long, lazy mornings of sleeping late and awakening to the panorama outside his window; getting high on fine champagne at the family's New Year's Eve party—it was exactly what he had needed to restore body and soul. Even the weather had cooperated—the sun had shone almost every day.

"Taylor?"

"Hmmm?"

"Have you given any more thought to Dad's suggestion?"

Lois's father wanted him to move the family out to Vancouver. He owned some land up the street and he had said that Taylor could have it if he built a home there. Lois was excited about the idea and urged her husband to accept. Redfern knew that although she had never mentioned it, the house in Pointe Claire had become tainted since the discovery of Touraine's body in the garage. She had no desire to go back there.

"I don't know, Lois. It's very tempting. But my roots

are in Quebec. I was born there. My whole experience is there. I'd be a stranger anywhere else."

He could feel her disappointment, although she said nothing.

"Look, I tell you what. I have to go back to Montreal and follow up one more possibility on this conspiracy thing. . . ."

"Oh, Taylor, enough is enough. It's too dangerous."

"No, honey, I have to. For my own peace of mind. Listen to me. I promise—no, really—if it turns out to be another dead end, which it probably will, that's it. No more. I'll get Cam to take me off the story. I'll take a sabbatical, and I'll come back out here and look around. Okay? Deal?"

She looked up at him slightly sideways.

"You're serious? You'll give Vancouver a chance?"

"I said so, didn't I?"

"Okay then, deal." She stood on tiptoes and kissed him.

The bedroom door opened behind them.

"Oh, excuse me." It was Lois's father. "Taylor, there's a long-distance call for you. From Montreal. Take it in the den, you'll be more private there."

Taylor threw on his robe and followed his father-in-law down the hall.

"Taylor! Cam Craig. According to my calendar your two weeks' vacation is up."

"Hi, Cam. You know something? I didn't miss you one bit. And I didn't even send a post card."

"Very funny. You get your ass on the next plane. I've got no one here. The leadership campaign's in full swing, Britain's going down the drain, Ottawa and Quebec are slinging mud at each other, and all I've got is Morgan. Would you believe everyone else has got the flu or is on vacation. I've got to sub the copy myself."

"Do you good."

"I'll remember that."

"Okay, Cam, I was going to call you today. I have a flight on Saturday. I'll see you in the office bright-eyed and bushy-tailed on Monday."

"Good. You can take over obits from Morgan. I can't stand it. I think it's getting to the kid. He touches a file and the guy dies. He should have been an undertaker, not a journalist."

"Well, don't let him work on mine. I'll see you Monday."

"Just a minute. Once piece of news might interest you. Your buddies at Int Con."

"Yeah?"

"I just got a memo from our financial department. It seems their stock is going crazy on the Zurich and London exchanges. Somebody's buying up everything going. No one here can figure out why all the action. Mean anything to you?"

"Uh-uh. Don't the wires have anything?"

"No."

"Keep an eye on it for me, will you?"

"Okay, and stop jabbering, you're costing me money. G'by."

" 'By, Cam."

"This isn't very solid." Secretary of State Lawrence Wilde, his feet on the desk, held up a two-page report between thumb and forefinger as if it were a piece of dirty laundry. The young attaché from the U.S. embassy in Paris who had helped compile the document and flown with it to Washington shifted uncomfortably in his seat. "What did you say your name was?"

"Grogan, sir. Frederick O. Grogan. The Third."

"Well, Frederick O. Grogan the Third. Am I expected to recommend to the President of the United States a policy based on press reports and cocktail-party gossip?"

"Sir, Ambassador Dunford anticipated a possible ambivalent reaction. He intimated to me that I should brief you on the extreme security blackout on all Quebec-related operations perpetrated by the French government."

"Grogan, what the hell are you talking about?"

"Sir?"

"You mean the French have put the lid on it."

"Yes, sir."

"Nobody's talking? Not even for Lincolns and Washingtons?"

"Sir?"

"Money, Grogan."

"No, sir."

The Secretary of State nodded. He knew Dunford personally; they had been junior partners in the same law firm and played squash together. If anyone could get the information the U.S. government needed, it was he. Washington had to know what France was up to in Quebec, and why. Wilde picked up the report again and reread it.

> To: Secretary of State Lawrence Wilde
> From: Ambassador Milton Dunford
> Further to your request for information re French involvement in Quebec in the light of current events, there appears to be no evidence of any overt French action. On the diplomatic level the government professes ignorance of developments within the province, and our contacts have nothing to add to this on the unofficial level. The only recent public statement on the subject came during the President's New Year's press conference. In response to a direct question from a Canadian journalist (English) as to which candidate France favored for the Quebec leadership, the President replied, "We do not involve ourselves in the internal affairs of other countries."
>
> However, there are some indications that the French government is quietly supporting Guy Lacroix. The French television network, ORTF, which is, as you know, state-controlled, recently ran a documentary on Quebec which included lengthy footage about Lacroix at the expense of his rival. (This program was well reviewed in Le Monde.) The evening paper, France-Soir, whose editor is known to have the ear of the Elysée Palace, recently ran an editorial (see attached) stating that Quebec is at a turning point in its history and that the province must make the right political choices now if it is to fulfill its destiny. (It does not say what its destiny ought to be, however.) While not overtly supporting Lacroix, the editorial is couched in such terms as to suggest support, relying heavily as it does on the kind of rhetoric Lacroix favors in his public pronouncements.
>
> There is some talk on the diplomatic cocktail

circuit as well, for what it's worth. A number of lower-echelon French officials have been drawn into discussions on Quebec by our people and the consensus is that Lacroix is the choice here. But, I emphasize, these are not decision-makers talking.

In summation, the French are being uncharacteristically discreet about this, which in itself makes me suspicious. As you are aware, French policy has long tended to support Quebec independence. At times this support has been muted for political considerations. My own assessment of the situation is that this underlying policy remains the same: the French are backing the candidate for leadership who can deliver independence soonest. That, by all appearances, would be Lacroix. This is mere conjecture unsupported by corroborative facts. I will keep you informed.

Good old Milton, thought Wilde, first and always the cautious advocate. He tossed the report on his desk.

"All right, Grogan. I want you to get back to Paris immediately. Give the ambassador my personal regards and have him advise me of any developments, no matter how insignificant they may seem."

"Yes, sir." The attaché rose to go.

"Oh, and Grogan."

"Sir?"

"A piece of advice. If you want to go anywhere in the diplomatic service, drop 'the Third.' It might make the natives restless."

Taylor Redfern surveyed the clientele of Le Coq d'Or Tavern in Point St. Charles. A warm, damp fog made visible by cigarette smoke seemed to rise out of the concrete floor. The acrid smell of stale beer, dank clothing, and tobacco assailed his nostrils. In one corner, a jukebox throbbed the latest hit songs while in another, high up on a shelf, a color television competed more successfully for the attention of the lonely men who sat hunched over glasses of beer at the tables. Although they sat in twos and threes as well as singly, there seemed to be no conversation. The eyes were turned to the television and the ears absorbed the pounding music. Surely, Kevin Reilly would never have brought a woman to a place like this? But Redfern had to check out all the bars in the neighborhood. He unbuttoned his coat and crossed over to the barman, who was washing glasses in desultory fashion. It took little time to go through the ritual—the photograph of Reilly, a few questions, the predictable shake of the head. He was used to it now; this was the eleventh place on his list. Two minutes later he was outside again, in the snow-covered street, breathing the icy air that was preferable to the stale, stagnant atmosphere inside the bar.

He stopped under a street lamp, removed a glove and withdrew the list from his pocket. He crossed off Le Coq d'Or. The next bar was three blocks away. There was no point in taking a cab, even if he could find one. He dug his hands into his pockets and crunched through the newly fallen snow. How many times had he dragged around the bars of Montreal to research his stories? For four nights now, he had toured the Point St. Charles restaurants and taverns trying to find someone who remembered Reilly and the girl he had been seen with. That was his only chance now to break the story wide open. Someone had to remember them together. But the more places he stopped, the more he realized that interest in the Premier's assassination was fading away; no one cared any longer. Those he questioned were only concerned with the leadership battle between Lacroix and Belmont.

He listened to the sound of his overshoes packing the snow beneath his feet; the brittle crunching sound echoed down the deserted street. He paused at the corner and looked up at the street sign to take his bearings. He thought he sensed movement behind him, but when he looked there was no one, only the long silent shadows cast by the street lights across the snow dimpled only by his footprints.

He turned the corner, looking for the sign of Le Chantecler, his next port of call. He was amused that all the bars seemed to choose the names of animals and birds as if to invest their establishments with an aura of country freshness. Once again, he sensed the presence of someone behind him, but when he stopped to listen all he could hear was the muted hum of the city and the distant whine of an ambulance far off. The old fear returned. Images of Touraine with his slit throat and the man with the camera and the pointing woman rose up at him from the snowbanks He quickened his pace. The noise of his own steps sounded in his ears, compounding his sense of fear. He looked wildly about him, convinced now that he was being followed. But each time he glanced behind there was only his shadow pursuing him. He broke into a run, and he could feel the sweat drying on his forehead.

The snow seemed to suck at his feet and slow him down. All the while, the crunching rhythm of feet and the beat of his heart rang in his head. Oh my God, I'm going mad, he thought. He looked around for the reassuring sight of a bus or a crowded restaurant, but all he saw were faceless gray buildings. The dummies in the shop windows began to take on a sinister appearance as the sound of his footsteps grew louder. The freezing air entered his lungs like barbed wire, and his heart was pounding painfully. He no longer looked behind him but ran stumbling toward the lights ahead, to the main artery where there would be people. He saw a bus draw into the curb, and he sprinted after it. It pulled away as he arrived. He hammered on the side, yelling to the driver to let him on, but the bus moved slowly, inexorably away on the icy pavement. In desperation, he grabbed onto the rear bumper and allowed himself to be pulled along, skating over the frozen tarmac behind the slow-moving vehicle. He held on grimly, congratulating himself on his deliverance from the unidentified menace that pursued him. He averted his face from the gray plume of the exhaust, and when the bus stopped he quickly boarded it, safe in the knowledge that he had shaken off whoever it was following him. He stayed long enough to catch his breath and then darted off the bus and took the Metro, changing trains twice before he emerged at the Peel and St. Catherine. Safe at the hub of the city, he walked the few blocks to his apartment on Rue de la Montagne.

He breathed a sigh of relief when he entered the building and walked up the stairs. He felt very tired, but he promised himself a stiff Scotch before he turned in. Happy to be back on familiar ground, he pressed the key into the lock and opened the door.

"Don't switch on the light, Mr. Redfern." The voice pierced him like an arrow. "There's a gun pointed at your belly, so just come and sit down here. We have a lot to talk about."

Salon des Portraits (Québec) Ltée. read the sign on the door. The polished-apple faces of young brides and grinning children stared out at Raymond Mercier as he peered in at the window. He ignored the *"Fermé"* sign on the door and turned the handle. The place was unlocked, as he had been assured it would be. The studio in darkness smelled of dust and chemicals. He glanced behind him through the window to ensure he had not been followed. There was no reason to believe he might be, but Monsieur Mercier was a cautious man. He had had the taxi drop him off two blocks from the studio, and he had taken a circuitous route to it, strolling through the ancient streets of Quebec's lower town as if he were a tourist. One could not be too careful.

A line of light under a door at the rear of the studio signified that he was expected. He opened the door onto a larger studio filled with photographic paraphernalia: cameras on tripods, klieg lights, rolls of paper suspended from brackets on the ceiling, backdrop curtains, and coils of wire and cables snaking across the floor. There was no one in the studio, but a red light above a second door leading from it warned him that the darkroom was in use. He knocked on the door and announced his presence. A high-pitched voice acknowledged him and asked him to wait for a moment. Mercier sat down and lit a cigarette. He felt ill at ease. In all his years of political activity, he had never done anything for which he would not hold himself publicly accountable. But desperate times called for desperate measures, he told himself, and he seemed to take comfort from the phrase. Jean-Claude Belmont must win, and any means to accomplish that end would be for the greater good. And if Belmont won, he, Raymond Mercier, would be the right-hand man of the Premier of Quebec.

The red light went off and the dark room door opened. Mercier rose from his chair to greet the dapper little man with the shiny black hair and pencil mustache who emerged with a wad of photographs.

"Emile, how did it work?"

The photographer evaded the advancing embrace and fussed with the photos he was carrying.

"Fine, fine."

"How are you? And how's the family?" Mercier boomed.

Emile Doucette concentrated on the job at hand, spreading out the shots for inspection. "Well, thank you. And how is my sister?"

"Oh, she's just fine, sends her love," Mercier lied. His wife did not know he was seeing her brother. No point in having her ask a lot of questions. He glanced at the pictures Doucette was carefully laying out on the green baize table.

"Are those . . . ?"

Doucette nodded and Mercier moved in closer to look.

"They're absolutely fantastic. Emile, I must congratulate you. How did you manage it? If I didn't know, I'd swear . . ."

The photographer gave a nonchalant shrug.

"A simple job, for a professional. Did you bring the money?"

"Yes, of course." Mercier fumbled in his pocket and withdrew an envelope. He handed it to Doucette, who tore it open and counted the bills. Mercier had never liked his brother-in-law, and this demonstrable lack of trust underlined his feelings toward the man. "I think you'll find it's all there."

Doucette sucked in through his teeth as he counted each bill with deliberation.

Mercier studied the photos again.

"Remarkable. I wouldn't have believed it was possible," he said. There was no doubt in his mind that his plan would succeed.

"Yes, it's all here," said Doucette, placing the elastic band which had bound the notes around his wrist and pocketing the wad. He scooped up the photographs and slid them into a plain brown envelope.

"There you are, Raymond. I have no wish to know what you will do with them. If there are any repercussions I shall, of course, deny any involvement. If we didn't need the money, I would never have agreed."

"Yes, yes, of course. It is just between us."

"Now, if you will excuse me, I have my work to do."

Mercier slid the envelope into his coat and nodded to his brother-in-law.

"Good night, Emile," he said, "and please give my love to Hortense."

The intermittent pulses of the neon sign outside Taylor Redfern's apartment illuminated a man in a heavy overcoat. Its garish light reflected off a snub-nosed .38. The man motioned Redfern to sit. He obeyed, his heart pounding. As his eyes became accustomed to the dark, he saw that the man was not looking at him at all. He seemed to be waiting.

"Are we just going to sit here?" asked Redfern. "If so, can I get the cards?"

"Mr. Redfern, we are not in a joking mood. Perhaps we can talk now without you running off like a jack rabbit." He placed the revolver in a shoulder holster and switched on the light.

"Am I allowed to know whom I'm entertaining?"

"Just be patient." The bedroom door opened and a second man came into the room. Behind him, Redfern could see his clothes hanging over the opened drawers of his dresser.

"Come in, make yourself at home," said Redfern in disgust.

"Let me introduce myself," said the first man. "Lieutenant Charles Watson, RCMP. My colleague here is Frank Stubbs of the CIA."

Redfern felt the fear start to ebb away.

"I'd like to see your identification." Both men reached into their inside pockets and produced cards in plastic holders. Redfern leaned forward. They seemed genuine.

"You know you guys gave me a hell of a scare. I thought you were trying to kill me, for God's sake."

"Relax, Mr. Redfern," said the American.

"Relax! You bust into my apartment, you pull guns on me, and you tell me to relax."

"I have an authorized warrant, Mr. Redfern, if you'd care to look at it," replied Watson. Redfern shook his head.

"I'm sure you do. What do you want with me, anyway?"

"Information," said Stubbs. "We've been keeping an eye on you for some time. For your own protection."

"It seems you know more about what's going on here than anyone else," said Watson. His tone became friendly, almost confidential.

"That's really funny," replied Redfern. "I thought you guys were the professionals."

"It would make things easier if you trusted us, Mr. Redfern," Watson said patiently. "I'm going to be honest with you."

"He's Frank and you'll be honest," quipped Redfern. The two men exchanged glances.

"We're operating at a great disadvantage here," continued Watson. "The Quebec Provincial Police have, shall we say, been uncooperative."

"You mean obstructive," broke in Stubbs.

"Let me tell him, Frank. The RCMP has been denied access to any information relating to the murder of the Premier. The Provincials are dragging their feet, and we know for a fact that the top people there are keeping the lid on under orders from the PQ cabinet. Specifically, the Lacroix faction. If we don't solve that murder, Lacroix can keep slinging mud at Ottawa, and that's just fine by him."

"Okay, I understand all that. But what do you expect me to do?"

"We want you to tell us all you know about the affair. About Touraine and the payoff, about IntCon. About Reilly. Anything else that comes to mind. Then we want you to get your ass back to Vancouver—otherwise, my friend, you're likely to end up in the city morgue."

"Or in someone's garage, like Touraine?"

"We had nothing to do with Touraine," interjected Stubbs. "That's not our style."

"What's the CIA doing here anyway?" said Redfern, changing the subject. "This is a Canadian affair."

Lieutenant Watson sighed. "In matters of mutual concern we work closely with the CIA and the FBI."

"Yeah, and this is of mutual concern," added Stubbs.

"You want me to give you my sources, is that it? Fat chance."

"Listen, fella . . ." Frank Stubbs took one step forward. Watson held up his hand.

"Look, Taylor, you may not realize it, but the fact you're still alive has a lot to do with us. And a lot of the stuff you got was because we put it your way. How do you think your newspaper got wind of Reilly's RCMP background? And who d'you think tipped you off about Mrs. Touraine?"

"You gave my son the envelope?"

Watson nodded. "We found her, but we couldn't approach her. The Provincials would have screamed bloody murder, and our nuts would be in the wringer for interfering in Quebec's internal affairs. Like it or not, you were our best route to her."

"Jesus." Redfern tried to think back. "Were you guys at the Premier's lying-in-state, taking pictures?"

"Why do you ask?"

"Nothing. And what about Touraine?"

"It's a pity about Touraine," said Stubbs. "He could have told us who was behind the assassination. You did us a disservice, Taylor, breaking that story about the payoff. They got to him before we could talk to him."

"My God, then who *is* behind it?"

"That's what we're trying to find out. That's why we need your help," said Watson.

Redfern lay back in the chair. He was beginning to feel hot. He shut his eyes but made no move to take off his coat. He tried to make some sense of his position. It would be better to have these guys for him rather than against him. He had to feed them just enough information to satisfy them without giving enough for them to shut him out of the case.

"All right," he said finally, "what do you want to know?"

For the next two hours, he was subjected to a barrage of questions skillfully framed to elicit new facts about the assassination and its widening ramifications. Redfern tried to appear cool and responsive, giving away only what he guessed the two men already knew. They had come to the end of their cross-examination.

"What were you doing touring the Point St. Charles bars?" asked Watson.

"Reilly had a cousin or an uncle he used to hunt with when he was at school. I was trying to find him. He might have been able to tell me something."

"You spent a hell of a lot of time trying to find a guy who might have been able to tell you something," said Stubbs, sitting down on the arm of Redfern's chair.

"The man probably taught Reilly how to handle a gun," he said, looking up at Stubbs's round, red face. He looks like a diabetic, thought Redfern. "Sure, it's not much to go on, but there isn't much left."

The two agents glanced at each other, and Watson shrugged.

"Okay, Taylor," said Watson, rising. "Now I want you to take my advice. Drop the story and get out of Montreal."

"Is that an order?"

"Just say it's a friendly tip," said Stubbs, patting him ironically on the shoulder.

"And if I don't?"

Watson smiled, the first time he had done so all evening. He took out a piece of paper and wrote a telephone number on it.

"Give me a call at this number if you come up with anything you think we ought to know." He looked around the apartment. "Sorry about the mess. We'd help you clear it up but my time is paid by the taxpayers."

The two agents left, and Redfern bolted the door behind them. He took out a bottle of Scotch from the cabinet and poured a full glass. He was pleased with himself. They knew nothing about the girl. He was still far ahead of them.

In recognition of his wife's ability as a political hostess, Lawrence Wilde had ordered a cake made in the shape of the Capitol building. Across the dome in pink icing was the legend "Happy Birthday, Madeleine." One candle burned diplomatically where the flag would be. The cake, in the center of the hors d'oeuvres table, was the conversational point of the party. Wilde, long skilled in the subtle rhythm of such diplomatic social functions, knew that if his guests had nothing else in common, at least they could talk about the cake, and its presence afforded him the opportunity of an epigram or two.

The Secretary of State was in his element as he moved from group to group, exchanging anecdotes and gossip, flirting with some of the diplomatic wives, and generally making sure that the Washington power brokers met the trade commissioners and senior diplomats whose friendship could further American interests around the world.

The party was turning out to be a great success; he could see the Israeli first secretary in decorous conversation with the Syrian commercial attaché by the buffet. Maybe some progress was finally being made there.

He moved toward the bar to refill his glass, shaking hands and welcoming late-comers as he went. He noticed the Iranian ambassador and made a mental note to speak to him later. And there at the door, handing his top hat and cape to the butler, was Maurice de Couvelles, the ambassador from France. The lady in sable whom he escorted was not his wife, but then the French could carry these things off so much better than the Americans, he thought. He would catch up with de Couvelles later, after the party began to wind down. It was imperative they speak tonight.

As the black barman poured him a malt whisky, Wilde surveyed the room. Close to three hundred guests, including all the senior diplomats in Washington, had been invited to Madeleine's fortieth birthday party and very few had declined. The satisfaction this gave him was mingled with pride in his wife's achievement as a hostess. He caught a glimpse of her across the crowded room, deep in animated conversation with the wife of the Italian ambassador—probably practicing her execrable Italian, he thought.

"Another social triumph for Maddy, eh, Larry?" David Dwyer, the Australian ambassador and a long-time personal friend, was standing next to him, handing his champagne glass to the barman.

"Looks like. How she manages to get them out in their fine feathers in mid-January to watch her blow out her candles beats me."

"She's a very persuasive woman," the Australian diplomat replied. "You should know that by now."

Lawrence Wilde smiled. He did know it. Only too well.

"Say, are you going to get down to Nassau next month for our annual golfing weekend?"

Wilde shook his head.

"Can't say yet, Dave. Things are coming to a head in Canada and Britain. I may not be able to get away this year. That's what happens when you get your handicap down to two."

"What do you mean? It's not two."

"Sure. Canada and Britain."

"Oh. Right. Well, too bad," the Australian smiled. The golfing weekends with Wilde were not only enormous fun but also provided him with an annual updating on the latest thinking in U.S. foreign policy. "Well, if you can make it, let me know. By the way, I have something which may be of interest to you."

"Oh?"

"It seems the French have been sniffing around. What chances of our easing our export controls on uranium? They're interested in a long-term supply contract."

"Is that so?"

"It's all hush-hush at this stage, of course, but they seem serious. The word I get from home is that they haven't got a snowball's chance in hell. But they're making noises about butter and lamb import tariffs."

The Secretary of State frowned. "France hasn't bought uranium on the international market for years. Apart from spot buys. What do you think's going on, Dave?"

"Search me. I just thought you'd find the information interesting."

"I do, Dave. Thanks. I'll let you know about Nassau."

The two men moved away and mingled with the guests.

It was well past midnight before Lawrence Wilde was able to invite Maurice de Couvelles to join him in the upstairs library for a cognac.

"I bought a Matisse ink drawing at Parke-Bernet in New York and I'd like your opinion of it," he said to the French ambassador by way of explanation, edging the older man away from two soviet diplomats. He took de Couvelles by the arm and led him upstairs.

"Your knowledge for fine art preceded your appointment here, m'sieur," said Wilde flatteringly.

The old diplomat smiled warily. "When an American alludes to my reputation as an art connoisseur, I can only fear the worst."

The library was a quiet refuge from the music and talk below. The butler had lit a fire and placed a decanter of Courvoisier V.S.O.P. with two balloon snifters on a silver tray on the coffee table. Wilde poured generous measures into the glasses while de Couvelles tactfully inspected the drawing, which had been hung in pride of place over the mantelpiece.

"Very fine," he nodded approvingly as Wilde handed him a glass. "May I be so rude as to ask you how much you paid for it?"

"Seventeen thousand dollars."

"A bargain, you did very well. You have a good eye, Lawrence."

The French ambassador turned to face him. He looked every one of his seventy-two years, Wilde thought. The face was etched with the ambiguity of his calling. Lines of mockery played about his mouth, but his eyes were solemn. He carried himself with a bearing that suggested his aristocratic antecedents, although he no longer used his title. In deference, he always said, to emergent African countries.

"Your Matisse is most charming, but I am long past the age when I can be seduced away from a party to see etchings. What is on your mind?" His English was flawless, and he spoke without the trace of an accent.

The Secretary of State waited for the older man to sit.

"As perceptive as usual, Maurice. All right, to the point. The President has expressed his concern to me about your government's interference in the Quebec situation. No, let me finish. I didn't want to call you in for a formal discussion on this matter. I hoped that we could resolve it before it became—well, let's just say the lady in question is just a little pregnant."

De Couvelles raised an eyebrow but did not interrupt.

"You must know that the President feels very strongly about this, and he has directed me to ensure that the French government is made aware of his concern."

The French ambassador's face wore a quizzical expression, and had Wilde not known the man's remarkable ability to mask his emotions, he would have sworn that de Couvelles had no idea what he was talking about.

"Forgive me, Lawrence, but I am not sure that I understand you. Of course, France is interested in Quebec. Our historical ties go back four hundred years. We share the same cultural heritage, but it is the stated policy of my government that we will not interfere in the internal affairs of Canada, as I believe it is your government's policy also. I assure you that we have done nothing to compromise that position."

The Secretary of State swirled the cognac in his glass and stared into the fire. This was going to be harder than he had thought.

"Maurice, we've known each other for a long time. We both know the rules of the game. But this matter is no game. The President is in deadly earnest over the Quebec problem. My department has done a thorough analysis based on Quebec independence and its implications for the United States, both in economic terms and strategic terms vis à vis this continent and Europe. On the basis of that study, I have recommended to the President that the United States cannot tolerate such a development."

"I see," replied de Couvelles, rocking slowly as he swirled the brandy round his glass.

"We have also done a comparative study of the effect of independence for Quebec on your country. You would benefit in a number of ways—a new market would open up to you for your manufactured goods, you would have access to a rich source of raw materials, including iron ore, asbestos, copper . . . and uranium."

"Uranium?"

"Maurice, please, no games. We know about that Int-Con uranium strike on Hudson's Bay just as well as you do. But let me finish. An independent Quebec would also give France tremendous political leverage in North America for the first time since the early nineteenth century, and God knows it might even give Louisiana some ideas. The United States government would look with disfavor on such influence. Do you understand me?"

"You are making yourself perfectly clear."

"I told you I was going to be candid with you, Maurice. Intelligence reaching us from Quebec suggests that if Guy Lacroix wins the leadership of the Parti Québécois at the convention next month, a unilateral declaration of independence would follow within weeks. We cannot accept that. Nor will we accept any interference by an outside power to further that end. Am I coming through loud and clear?"

"Mr. Secretary, you are laboring the point. But why are you telling me all this? What possible evidence could you have that my government has departed from its stated policy of nonintervention?"

Wilde pulled at his shirt collar. He could feel the heat of the fire.

"That's not the point. We have reason to believe that your people have been active in Quebec. I warn you, Maurice, we want them out of there. The United States will not accept any interference by a foreign power in Quebec. Do you want to hear it from me or the President?"

The French ambassador slowly set his untasted glass of cognac on the table.

"So. The Monroe Doctrine is reborn." His voice could not camouflage the cynicism of the remark.

"If you want to look at it that way," replied Wilde.

The ambassador rose from his chair.

"Thank you for the cognac and your hospitality, Mr. Secretary," he said formally. "I wish you joy of your Matisse. Now I must go."

The throb of the music and the flashing strobe lights seemed to vibrate through the floor and up through the feet and legs of the dancers in La Discocave. As the lights changed, turning the gyrating dancers from green to red and then to blue, Taylor Redfern pressed his way through the crowd of young French Canadians at the bar. The pall of smoke that hung over the room like early morning mist stung his eyes. He dabbed them gently with a handkerchief so as not to dislodge his contact lenses.

After the bars, he had started on the discothèques in his search for Reilly's girl friend. A friend of Reilly's in a Point St. Charles tavern recalled seeing the assassin with an attractive dark-haired girl at La Discocave on Rue St. Denis in midtown Montreal. No, he had not met the girl himself; Reilly had not introduced her. But somebody in this sweating, noise-filled *boîte* must know her. Perhaps Reilly and she had frequented the place.

Redfern reached the bar. The bartender was working at top speed filling the orders of three petulant waiters at the service bar. There were no empty stools, so Redfern wedged himself between two gum-chewing blondes, ignoring their black looks. When the bartender had satisfied the demands of the waiters, he turned his attentions to the customers at the bar. Redfern beckoned to him.

"Labatt's Fifty, please," he shouted over the din. "And some information." He handed the man a five-dollar bill.

The bartender looked at it suspiciously. Redfern pulled out a photograph from his pocket.

"This guy. You know him? Did he ever come in here? With a dark-haired girl?"

"Why do you want to know? You police?"

"No, the girl's my daughter. She's run away from home."

The bartender took the photo and held it up to the light by the cash desk.

"Yeah, I seen him somewhere. Wait a minute. Isn't that the guy who shot the Premier?"

"Yes. You know him?" Redfern experienced a surge of excitement.

The bartender tossed the photo onto the bar as if it were infected.

"Hell, no. Why should I know him? That pig." He started to move away.

"Wait a minute. Was he ever in here?" Redfern shouted after the retreating figure.

"Who knows?" The bartender waved his arms at the mass of writhing youth on the dance floor. "Who looks at faces in a place like this?"

Redfern felt as if he were drowning.

"What about the waiters? Maybe they'd remember him. Or the girl!"

The man came back, his face menacing. He leaned across the bar and put his face so close to the reporter that he could see the pores of his sallow skin.

"Listen to me, fella. You get out of here right now. I don't want anyone bothering my guys with crap like this. Understand? Now beat it."

The bartender turned away. Redfern noticed that his five dollars had vanished.

"Keep the change," he muttered as he started to push his way back toward the door. He did not see the bartender nod his head at the two hulking bouncers standing at the back of the room.

Outside in the black, freezing night Redfern breathed

deeply to clear his lungs. The bartender knew Reilly, he was sure of it. He looked around for a taxi to take him back to the *Chronicle* building. Suddenly, he became aware of a man standing behind him on the sidewalk.

"*Excusez-moi, monsieur,* you were inquiring about a Mr. Reilly and a young lady?"

Redfern studied the face of the stranger. He had to look upward at him because the man stood six-foot-two and his frame seemed to blot out the street behind him. He looked like a cartoonist's idea of a professional wrestler, broken-nosed and cauliflower-eared.

"What do you know about them?" Redfern was instantly wary, glancing around for an escape route should he need one.

"I have some information. . . . It'll cost you."

"How much?"

"Fifty dollars."

"That's a lot. Is it worth it?"

"Depends how badly you want to know."

Redfern had no option. There was nowhere else to go, and besides, if he refused, the man mountain in front of him might not remain so polite.

"All right." He took out his wallet.

"Not here," said the man fiercely. "Not under the lights. Come over here."

He motioned Redfern to an alley running behind the discothèque. The reporter hesitated a moment. Then he began to walk slowly up the alleyway into the dark shadows. He could hear his heart pounding as he approached the huge black shape in front of him.

"Holy Jesus!" Cameron Craig shouted into the phone. The early morning sun hovered above the St. Lawrence on the same level as his office window, too bright to look at.

"Two broken ribs? And how many teeth? Yeah, I understand. But he's not in any serious danger? Thank heaven for that. No, his family's in Vancouver. I'll contact them. All right. Thank you for calling." He hung up and yelled for his secretary.

"Julie, get in here. Taylor Redfern got beaten up in an alley last night. He's in Royal Victoria Hospital. They just called."

"Gee, I'm sorry, Mr. Craig."

"Yeah. He says Taylor's pretty shaken up but it's not too serious. They've checked him over and there's no internal injuries. They're going to hold him for observation for a few days."

"Shall I send him some flowers? From the office?" Julie had a soft spot for Redfern.

"This paper can't afford cut flowers in winter. He should have waited till spring."

"The least I could do is take him some magazines. I'll buy them out of my own pocket, Mr. Craig," said the girl as she turned on her heel.

"Here, you can take him this!" shouted Craig after the girl. He had picked up a French-language tabloid which he intended to read later. Julie kept on walking. He threw the paper back on his desk. His eye was caught by the front page. It was dominated by a single photo of Guy Lacroix. He was accompanied by two men, and they were boarding a Soviet Aeroflot jet. The headline was set in end-of-the-world type: *Lacroix: Agent Soviétique?*

With the aid of tweezers, Hilaire Noel dropped a dead beetle onto the leaf of the Venus's flytrap and watched it snap shut.

"There you are, my dear," he said to the plant, oblivious, it seemed, to the presence of Antoine de Luzt, who sat across the coffee table from him. "Nourishment for the winter. Enjoy." He put the tweezers down and turned to de Luzt. "Not much food around for them this time of year. I keep a special stock for this chap in the ice tray."

"Remind me never to have Scotch on the rocks in your household, Hilaire." The old man was dithering again. De Luzt had humored him for as long as his patience lasted. He had not made a special visit to Noel's hothouse of an apartment for a lecture on the care and nurturing of insectivorous plants.

"Well, can I have your answer?" De Luzt posed the question as Noel bent squinting over the table with his tweezers, looking for another newly defrosted beetle. The old civil servant leaned back in his chair with a sigh of resignation.

"Ten million dollars is a lot of money, Antoine. We agreed on a price, a gentlemen's agreement. Seven hundred and fifty thousand dollars on the successful completion of the assignment. Very generous, I would have thought. But ten million. Somewhat excessive, no?"

"Not excessive when you know what's involved in Quebec. If you'd been honest with me at the beginning, Hilaire . . . well, no matter. Now that I realize how much this means to France, I'm raising my price. Or let me put it another way—I'm taking you up on your offer to provide additional resources."

"You're already doing very well out of this enterprise, Antoine, better than you have any right to expect." Noel's demeanor had changed. He was alert now, and keen-minded. "I understand your company has bought heavily into IntCon shares. Very shrewd. If events in Quebec develop as we all hope, you stand to make a killing." He gave special emphasis to the word, as if there were a veiled threat in the way he pronounced it.

De Luzt was momentarily taken aback. The French government had obviously been doing some investigating of its own.

"Any money I make from share dealings is beside the point," he replied. "And come to think of it, it's no thanks to you. You did your damnedest to keep the information from me."

Noel looked hurt. "It had to be that way, Antoine. Security . . ."

"Security, my ass!" de Luzt exploded. "I've got people whose lives are at stake here. The least I can expect is to be fully briefed and properly compensated for the risks. Now, do I get the money or don't I? Because if I don't, then you and your friends at the Elysée Palace can sit back and watch while I make Jean-Claude Belmont the next Premier of Quebec."

"I do believe you're trying to blackmail the government." Noel dropped another beetle on the greedy plant. The fleshy leaf instantly devoured the dead insect. The older man looked up at de Luzt and smiled.

"It's a rotten game, Hilaire. The trick is to play it well. We must all look after ourselves in these inflationary times. I might have been satisfied if you'd told me about Super Phénix."

"That didn't happen until after our original agreement. No, Antoine, I swear. There were other reasons for making a move in Quebec. Super Phénix only made the operation more urgent."

"It doesn't really matter," said de Luzt. "The fact remains that the government now needs a successful operation in Quebec more than ever. My price is still ten million dollars."

Hilaire Noel closed his eyes, apparently in thought. The minutes passed in silence. De Luzt wondered if the old man had drifted off to sleep.

"Hilaire?"

"All right, Antoine, you'll get your money."

"Half now, on deposit in my Liechtenstein bank by next Wednesday. The other half when it's over."

"Very well."

"Good. Then I can get on with it." De Luzt rose and extended his hand to Hilaire Noel. The older man hesitated fractionally, then took it.

"You are a hard man, Antoine."

"Yes. That's how I stay alive," replied de Luzt.

From his bed in the apartment, Taylor Redfern could see a line of dishwater-colored sky above the buildings across the street. Each movement he made sent pains shooting up his chest and neck. It must be time for another Demerol. He picked up his watch from the bedside table. It read 8:05 A.M. He felt he had hardly slept the entire night. It had been five days since the beating in the alley, two since he had discharged himself from hospital. He should have been feeling better by now, but he still hurt all over.

He gently eased himself off the bed and crossed the apartment to the kitchen as if he were walking on eggs. He opened the refrigerator and took out a carton of orange juice. Unconsciously, his tongue probed the pulpy sockets where teeth had been knocked out. He carried the orange juice to the counter and poured a glass; then he took a pill from the bottle in the cupboard. His right side began to ache from stretching upward; he rubbed a hand over the heavily taped area. Oh God, make the pill work quickly, he thought.

Redfern could remember little of the beating in the alley behind La Discocave. As he had approached the squash-nosed man in the darkness, there had been a sudden explosion of light and he had felt the warm wetness of blood gushing from his nose over his mouth and chin. He had bounced back against a wall, and from then on he remembered nothing until he regained consciousness in the hospital.

He poured another glass of orange juice and hobbled into the living room. The doctors had told him he wasn't seriously injured. If that was the case, he told himself, I'd hate to know what real pain is like. Slowly, he put his feet up on the footstool and lay back in the chair listening to the morning traffic below his window. The Demerol was starting to take effect. The pain was receding and his eyes felt heavy.

He was just about to doze off when he was jangled into wakefulness by the telephone. He started from his chair and the pain returned. The telephone shrilled at him from the corner. He cursed it and the caller as he made his way across the room, supporting himself on the furniture as he went.

"Hello."

"Taylor, it's Cam. How are you?"

"Oh, it's you. The friendly neighborhood obscene caller." He winced with the effort of speech.

"How're you feeling?"

"Like second prize in an ugly contest, how're you?"

"Yeah, well, I just wanted to know if you were okay. I would have come to see you but I hate hospitals. They make me ill."

"It's all right. Thanks for the flowers, by the way. They tasted good."

"Don't mention it. Anything I can do for you?"

Redfern thought for a moment. The way he felt, he wasn't going to leave the apartment for a couple of days. But there was work to be done. The fact that he had been roughed up meant he was close to something.

"Cam, what I need most is some help. Another pair of legs, someone who can chase down some leads for me."

"Leads on what?"

"For crying out loud, Cam, what do you think I'm talking about? The story I've been working on for the last three months. The one that's got me beaten up. I really think I'm close to nailing it now."

There was silence at the end of the line.

"You there, Cam?"

"Yeah, I'm here. Look, Taylor, I've got to level with you. I've taken you off the story. No more investigating. This thing's gone too far."

"What's the matter, Cam? They got to you, too? They put the screws on, did they?"

"What are you talking about! It's you and your family I'm thinking of."

"But we're almost there. I can't stop now. Why do you

think I've gone through all this already? What's the point if I quit now?" Redfern's head began to pound.

"Look, no arguments. It's finished and that's final. I won't be responsible for you ending up like Touraine. You're like a son to me. I'm ordering you off for your own protection. It's just not worth dying for, Taylor. It says in the Bible: 'Thou shalt come to thy grave in full age, like a shock of corn cometh in his season.' And you're only thirty-eight, dammit."

"Come off it, Cam."

"No point in discussing it further, Taylor. Call me if you need anything." There was a click, and Redfern found himself holding a dead phone. He slammed the receiver down.

"Bloody hypocrite," Redfern yelled at the walls. "Quoting the Bible at me. He probably uses it as a doorstop." He lowered himself into a chair and pounded his fist in frustration on its leather arm. The Bible. A second after he uttered the word he realized it had a significance beyond his conversation with Cameron Craig. Where was it? In Reilly's room, the family Bible. A quotation underlined. A phone number.

Forgetting his pain, he sprang out of the chair and crossed to the card table which served as his desk. His notebooks were neatly stacked in one corner. He pushed the portable typewriter aside and began leafing through them. He found the page; the quotation was there and the phone number. He had completely forgotten about it. He made his way eagerly to the phone and dialed; it was answered on the fourth ring.

"Bellevista Apartment-Hotel, *bonjour*."

Redfern hesitated only a moment. "May I have Mr. Reilly's room, please?"

"One moment, sir." There was a long pause at the other end. "Is that R-I-L-E-Y?"

"No, R-E-I-L-L-Y."

"I'm sorry. We have no one of that name registered here."

"Miss, please, this is very urgent. Have you had anyone by that name in the past five or six months?"

"I'm very sorry, sir, I can't give out that information."

"Look, it's very important . . ."

"I'm sorry, sir, those are the rules."

Redfern knew there was no point in continuing the conversation. "All right, thank you." He hung up. There had to be a connection. Why else would Reilly have written the phone number in the margin of the family Bible?

He went back into the bedroom, moving more quickly than he had since the night of the beating. Pain or no pain, he had to find out. He took off his pajamas, tossed them onto the bed, and began to dress. "Shock of corn," he muttered to himself. "I'll give him a shock of corn."

Later in the day the clouds melted under the winter sun and the province of Quebec basked under a blue sky. It was picture-post-card weather at the ski resort of Lac Beauport, sixteen miles north of Quebec City. Monique Gravelle pushed off from the plateau by the ski lift and edged out from the main run to a trail through the pines. Raymond Mercier set off after her. The trail was too narrow for her to look back over her shoulder, but Monique was surprised that a man of his age and build could ski so expertly. Her skis cut a path through the virgin powder snow and the sun flashed in her eyes through the trees as she swept downward. She could sense rather than hear Mercier behind her. The exhilarating sensation of wind and sun on her face made her feel light and happy.

Once through the pine grove, the trail opened up on a vista of sparkling snow. Far below her, she could see the Manoir St. Castin and the village of Lac Beauport set at the edge of an ice-covered lake that was enclosed by the stubby Laurentian Mountains. What a great idea of Raymond's, to spend a weekend here before the final run-up to the convention!

On the open slope, she relaxed and allowed gravity to take over, pulling her down the mountainside in a lazy, snakelike movement. Monique felt as if she would take off like a snowy owl at any second and float above the fairytale scene.

Just at that moment her skis hit an unseen mogul and upended her in a snowbank. The fall knocked her breath out, and she lay back in the snow wondering if she had hurt herself. But the only injury was to her pride.

Mercier pulled up in a shower of powder beside her, his face a picture of concern. Monique started to laugh.

"Are you all right? You took quite a spill there. What's so funny?"

Monique's whole body shook with laughter as she lay back in the snow, her skis embedded in the drift. "I was just thinking how nice it would be to take off and fly like an owl. I guess someone heard me." She took off her goggles and shook the snow out of her hair.

Mercier chuckled. He had never seen her like this, so vulnerable, so girlish. He held out his hand. She grasped it and allowed him to pull her upright, a movement which propelled her into his arms. She pressed her red, wet cheek against his.

"This is fun, Raymond. Thanks."

"Hey, you'll get us tangled up in your skis," he protested, confident now, and in charge.

She disengaged herself. "C'mon!" she shouted. "Last one down buys the drinks." She pointed her skis directly down the gradient and bent her knees. The wind tore at her body as she gathered speed. She reached the end of the run before him.

"Slowpoke," she taunted as he pulled up beside her.

"You want another one?" he asked. "I bet I beat you."

"Sure you can manage it?" she said as they fishboned their way up the slope to the chair-lift.

"My dear, I was skiing on barrel staves before you were born."

It was nearing the end of the afternoon. The line of skiers waiting to use the lift was short, and in a few minutes they were sitting side by side in twin chairs, watching the landscape moving below them. For the first time, Monique found herself genuinely regretting what she was doing to Mercier. She quickly put the thought out of her mind; there was a job to be done and time was running short.

"Being here makes you want to forget all about leadership campaigns and everything else, doesn't it?" She gestured at the winter panorama below them. "Why don't we stay on for a few days, Raymond? That Russian business has just about finished Lacroix, hasn't it? Can't we relax for a bit?"

Raymond Mercier shook his head sadly and took her mitten-covered hand in his.

"There's nothing I'd like better than to spend the

winter here with you, *chérie*—especially the long, cold
nights. But we can't let up now. Lacroix's been hurt but
he's not out. He still has a lot of support."

"You know, Raymond, whoever got that picture into
the papers was absolutely brilliant," said Monique as they
dangled high above the mountainside. "I can't help feeling
you had something to do with it. I bet it was you."

She could feel Mercier swelling with pride. Nobody
but his brother-in-law knew about the retouched photos,
and he had every reason to keep it that way. Mercier had
not told Belmont about it, knowing how scrupulously
honest the man was—too much so for a successful politician, Mercier had always thought. But he did want to share
his triumph with someone, and he wanted to confess to
Monique most of all. Keeping his secret when she was
around was like holding his breath.

"You knew all the time it was me?" He tried to
sound casual.

"It *was* you then, Raymond? How did you do it?"

The chair-lift was approaching the mountaintop. They
held their ski tips up in readiness to disembark.

"Tell you what, Monique. That chalet at the top of
the run. They make great hot buttered rum. Why don't we
get one before we ski? I'll tell you all about it then."

They unharnessed their skis and stood them in the
snow outside the wooden shack. Inside, a number of skiers
were sitting on the floor in front of a log fire, unlacing
their boots to give tired ankles a rest. In one corner, a girl
in *habitant* costume stood behind a low bar dispensing
mugs of steaming buttered rum. A young man with long
hair lazily strummed a guitar in the corner, singing softly
to himself. The atmosphere was warm and comfortable.

"Mmm, this looks lovely," said Monique, unzipping
her ski jacket. Mercier led the way to a small pine table by
a window which looked out onto the slope. He held her
chair for her and caught the eye of the girl behind the bar,
holding up two fingers. Then he sat down opposite her and
took her hands in his. Monique waited for him to start but
he just stared smiling into her eyes until the hot rum arrived.

"You were going to tell me about Lacroix, the Russian
spy," she said jokingly when the girl had left.

"Well," he began, leaning confidentially toward her,

careful not to let anyone else hear, "I really felt we had to do something. Lacroix was scoring all the points. He was beginning to really roll, and you can't stop a bandwagon once it's gained momentum. I toyed with a number of ideas and then I remembered that Lacroix had taken a holiday in Cuba last winter—one of those package tours."

"Yes, I've always wanted to go on one of those."

"There were a few raised eyebrows at the time, but nobody at headquarters thought much about it. There were a couple of pictures in the papers, Lacroix at Havana airport, Lacroix sunning himself on the beach. That was about it. But people in Quebec still get a bit jumpy about communists, especially in the rural areas. It's probably a hangover from the time when the Church was all-powerful. It came to me like a flash. If I could link Lacroix with the communists, maybe through that Cuba trip, we could turn the entire rural vote against him."

"So what did you do?" Monique urged him on.

"I remembered we had some glossies of that Cuba trip in party files. I dug them out. There was a shot of Lacroix getting onto an Air Canada charter flight and that was perfect. All I had to do then was to get a stock shot of an Aeroflot jet."

"I don't follow."

"I have a brother-in-law in Quebec City who's in the photographic business. He's an absolute genius at retouching. He did my wedding pictures. Even managed to make my wife look exciting."

"Raymond."

"Okay. He used to retouch photos for family jokes. On April Fool's Day he did one for my wife to give me. It was my head on the body of a fish. You couldn't tell how he did it. So I took the photos to him and asked him to fix them up for me. He did a terrific job. I concocted a story about Lacroix using the Cuba trip as a cover for a secret flight to Moscow to confer with Soviet leaders. Then it was simply a matter of getting the whole package to a newspaper sympathetic to Jean-Claude. The rest you know."

"Brilliant. Absolutely brilliant," exclaimed Monique, disengaging her hands as if to clap them. She found herself wishing that Mercier hadn't told her. But now it was too late. It was done.

"I think I need some fresh air now," she said. "Shall we ski?"

The same sun that reflected off snow crystals in Quebec shone out of a cloudless sky on Secretary of State Lawrence Wilde and CIA Director Warren Cummings as they stood on the last tee of the President's nine-hole course at the Florida White House.

"Tough luck, Larry," chuckled Cummings as he watched his opponent's drive slice into a pond bordering the ninth fairway.

"A brand new Titleist, too," grumbled Wilde, audibly enough to disconcert Cummings, who was in the middle of his swing. But the gamesmanship didn't work. The CIA director drove his ball two hundred ten yards straight down the center of the fairway.

"I don't know why I play with you, Warren."

"So you can pick my brain when you're not trying to put me off my game." Cummings slid his drver back into his golf bag. "Still, I don't mind as long as I beat you."

The two men climbed into the golf cart, Cummings behind the wheel. Normally, Lawrence Wilde enjoyed playing the demanding course the President had personally designed, but today other matters preoccupied him. He and Cummings had been peremptorily summoned to Florida, where the President spent more and more time during the winter. The purpose of the summons had been to hammer out a course of action on Quebec. The President had met him the moment his helicopter had touched down on the estate. Without even welcoming the Secretary of State, he had launched into a monologue on Quebec.

"I've got Cummings down here, Larry, and he has detailed information indicating that that son of a bitch Lacroix has already drawn up plans for a Quebec UDI as soon as he's sworn in as Premier." From that point the President had proceeded with an angry diatribe against Lacroix and the Canadian government for its seeming inability to do anything to halt Quebec's slide into independence. "And that must not be allowed to happen." The President had tightened his grip on Wilde's elbow by way of emphasis as they walked toward the ranch-style house.

"You once told me you do your best thinking on the golf course, Larry. Well, I'm taking you at your word. Get out there with Warren Cummings and don't come back until you've got the answer."

As the two men were changing into their golfing clothes, the President had come into the locker room and harangued the pair of them on the subject again. "I need an answer. And for God's sake, no more bungled assassinations."

Cummings brought the golf cart to a halt on the edge of the fairway in line with where Wilde's ball had disappeared into the pond.

"You can drop it on the edge of the fairway here, Larry," he said. But the Secretary of State didn't move.

"What the hell are we going to tell him, Warren? He wants us to wave a magic wand and make it all go away."

"Frankly, I don't know. I hate to admit it, but we seem to be powerless to influence events in Quebec. Now if it were Chile . . ."

"Yeah. We all remember that." Wilde smiled.

"Whoever dreamed up that communist-smear stunt has done more to spoke Lacroix's wheel than we have. Right out of the fifties, but effective."

The midday sun brought perspiration to Wilde's forehead. He shielded his eyes as he looked out over the yellow-green expanse of the golf course, once sand dunes, now beautifully manicured turf.

"There's got to be a lever somewhere, Warren. What about this IntCon business?"

"I'm waiting for a report on it now." He glanced at his watch. "It could be there when we get back. Let's finish the hole and I'll check."

"No, I concede. Pick up your ball and let's go."

A white-coated steward was waiting with an envelope as they pulled up to the small clubhouse which had been built as part of the complex.

"Just came in, sir. I was on my way to deliver it to you."

"Thank you," said Cummings, tearing the short end off the envelope. Inside was a telexed message. He read it quickly and handed it to Wilde.

"Maybe this is the lever you were talking about."

Lawrence Wilde scanned the message quickly. He singled out one key passage, which he carefully reread.

"We have sufficient evidence to prove that IntCon has

and still is providing massive financial support to the Lacroix leadership campaign," it read. "This support appears to be linked to IntCon's recent uranium find near Hudson's Bay. It also appears, although there is no material evidence, that IntCon has been involved in secret talks with the French government concerning a long-term-supply agreement for this uranium. Word of these talks appears to have leaked, as there has been heavy buying of IntCon shares on the Zurich and London exchanges in recent weeks."

Wilde handed the paper back to Cummings. "This business of IntCon supplying financial backing to Lacroix. How solid is it?"

"I don't know. First time I've heard about it. But Anderson's a good man. He wouldn't have used the word evidence if he weren't one hundred per cent sure."

"All right. I think we've got something for the President. Warren, I want you to have your people track down who's buying IntCon shares in Europe. Somebody's benefiting from the leak. I'm going to let the President know about IntCon and give him some ideas as to how they can be neutralized. Without their money, the whole picture might change."

He swung himself out of the golf cart. "You know, Warren, if I were a betting man, I'd put my money on us. Are you flying back to Washington with me?"

Taylor Redfern was beginning to wish he'd never left the comparative comfort of his apartment. The visit to the Bellevista Apartment-Hotel was a painful ordeal, getting in and out of taxis, walking up stairs, and shuffling through revolving doors. Passersby stared at his bruised face, and he had to explain sheepishly to his taxi driver that he'd been in an accident. He sat down in the lobby of the Bellevista, trying to get his breath back. He'd had a rough few hours, and it looked like another dead end. Kevin Reilly had never been registered there; a complaint room clerk had checked back through the files for the past year. Reilly's photograph drew blank stares from the hotel staff, even with the inducement of a five-dollar bill. No one seemed to have met the man.

He waited for the head housekeeper to finish her rounds. But when the woman invited him into her tiny office and sat brooding over the photograph, he knew he had drawn another blank.

"Well, thank you, madame," he said, raising himself painfully to his feet. He was about to leave when the door of the office opened and a small black girl in a maid's uniform entered the room. She looked in confusion at Redfern's battered face and then started to back out, murmuring her apologies.

"No, wait a minute." Redfern made a move toward her, intending to show her the photograph. As he did, he saw a look of fear in the girl's eyes and she turned as if to run away.

"*Marie, reste là.*" The sharp command in the housekeeper's voice brought the girl to a stop. When she turned back Redfern could see that she was trembling.

"I'm sorry. I didn't mean to frighten you," Redfern said.

"She doesn't speak English," the housekeeper said.

"*Je m'excuse, ma'amselle, mais . . .*"

"She won't get that either. She's Haitian. They speak a dialect all their own. We've got a number of them here. They come and go." The housekeeper spoke briefly to the girl, as a warden might to a prisoner. Redfern, even with his command of French, could pick out only a word here and there.

The girl seemed to calm down, but she kept her eyes on the floor.

"I've had to pick up their patois, otherwise nothing'd get done around here," the housekeeper said by way of explanation. "They're the only ones who'll work for the wages the owners pay."

"Why is she so afraid? Ask her."

"She thought you were from Immigration. She's here illegally, like most of them. Most Haitians in Montreal have no papers. That's why the management can hire them so cheaply. They're happy for any work so long as no one asks any questions."

Redfern's disgust showed in his face, but he had other problems to solve.

"Do you mind if I show her the photo?"

"Sure, go ahead." The housekeeper spoke a few curt words to the girl, who nodded her head. Redfern handed her the photo. The maid looked at it and said something in a voice so soft Redfern could hardly hear her.

"What did she say?"

"She says she's seen the man. She says she doesn't want to talk about it."

"But she must! Why doesn't she want to talk about it?"

The housekeeper translated the question. The girl became agitated and words tumbled from her, as if to make up for her initial reticence. The housekeeper nodded with pursed lips. Redfern took out a roll of bills from his pocket and allowed the older woman to see it.

"She says it was very bad for her. She was cleaning the apartments one day, and she unlocked one she thought was empty. But it wasn't. There was a man in it."

The girl gave a little whimper and rubbed her palms up and down her thighs, turning her head slowly to left and right.

"What was the matter?"

"The man had no clothes on. She says she cannot forget him. Nothing like that has ever happened to her. They are very religious, these girls."

In his excitement, Redfern could not stifle a smile, but he covered his mouth with his fist and pretended to cough.

"It was this man she saw?" he said, holding up the photo to her. Again the girl became agitated. "Does she remember which apartment it was?"

The question was translated again. The girl replied quickly. Then the housekeeper said something, and the maid left abruptly without looking at Redfern again.

"What was the room number?"

"It's important to you, isn't it?" The woman stared at the pocket where Redfern had replaced the roll of bills.

"Oh yes, of course. I was forgetting." He took out the money and slowly began to peel off two five-dollar bills. He laid them on the desk in front of the woman. She made no move to retrieve them. He peeled off another, and another.

"The room was Sixteen-fourteen. Another one of those, and I might remember who rented it."

Redfern slid another note across the desk. The woman added it to the other four, squared them up on the desk top, and folded them before slipping them into the cleavage of her bosom.

"It was a Miss Gravelle," she murmured. "Such a lovely girl."

"I'm sorry, I cannot divulge personal information about our guests, past or present." The manager of the Bellevista, whose establishment was well known for its discretion and the fact that rooms could be rented by the hour, waved Taylor Redfern out of his office. "I do not wish to discuss the matter further. Good day to you."

The reporter didn't move from his chair. "Monsieur Ducharme, I take it if this place were to be closed down by the police you could find other employment?"

"I could have you thrown out, you know."

"I'm a persistent man, Monsieur Ducharme."

"I can see that."

"I happen to know that you employ a number of Haitian maids in this hotel at salary levels that are in direct violation of the province's minimum-wage laws. I think the authorities would be most interested in learning about that. Furthermore, one word to the Immigration Department and all your sweated labor would be repatriated to Haiti. How would you like that?"

The manager began to fidget behind his desk, arranging his pens in order on the blotting paper.

"I don't even have to tip off the Immigration people," continued Redfern. "All I have to do is write a story about a certain hotel that makes its money out of slave labor . . ."

"I don't like being pushed around, Mr. Redfern."

"I'm sure those maids of yours don't either."

"All right. But anything I tell you doesn't come from me. Do you understand?"

"My sources are inviolate, Monsieur Ducharme. Why, I'd even go to jail for you," Redfern said mockingly.

"We get some pretty important people here, you understand. That's why I don't want any trouble."

"Cross my heart."

Ducharme opened a desk drawer and drew out a gold-colored chain containing several keys. He got out of his chair and crossed the room to the filing cabinet. He fumbled for a moment with the keys; then found the correct one and unlocked the file. From the middle drawer, he removed a manila folder tied with a brown ribbon. He undid the knot and extracted several sheets of paper which he handed to Redfern. It was a six-month lease executed in the name of Monique Gravelle for Room Sixteen-fourteen. Redfern let out a low whistle. In the lease, Monique Gravelle had listed her employer as the Parti Québécois; apparently she had been working out of their Montreal headquarters. The information in the lease suggested that she had given up the apartment in mid-November, a month and a half before the six months were up. She had paid the balance owing in full. There was no forwarding address.

Redfern scanned the other papers attached. The hotel had run a routine credit check on her. Redfern noted that she had an excellent rating; she was never delinquent in her payments. He made a mental note of her bank branch.

The last sheet of paper was a personal reference written on Parti Québécois stationery. The letter was signed by the Minister of Education for the Province of Quebec, Jean-Claude Belmont.

The private dining room at the rear of the Hotel Radisson in Old Montreal was crowded with newsmen. Under the heat of television lights photographers and cameramen jostled for position. The atmosphere was one of anticipation: why had Guy Lacroix violated all the rules of media relations by summoning a major news conference on a Saturday night?

The Radisson was hardly the ideal location for such an event. The dining room was the largest public area in the hotel, but it was far too small for the scores of journalists in attendance. Moreover, the power points in the century-old building were totally inadequate for the needs of electronic journalism. But the Radisson had been Lacroix's favorite hangout in Montreal ever since his days as a firebrand union leader when he used the hotel for his periodic, sparsely attended press receptions at which he ritually denounced the capitalist traitors in Quebec City. After he became a cabinet minister, he confided to a reporter that if he switched to a tonier place like the Hotel Bonaventure or the Château Champlain he would be denounced by long-time friends and allies as *"un snob."*

So press conferences called by the Minister of Social

Affairs continued to take place at the Radisson and would likely continue to do so even if he were elected Premier.

The journalists had been invited for eight o'clock. It was now twenty minutes to nine and the television crews were fretting over making the eleven o'clock news. Lacroix waited in a nearby room, aware of his tardiness and of the need to cut his announcement short to allow enough time for film processing. He had already decided that he would permit no questions so that the TV reporters could get away as soon as he finished his statement. He glanced impatiently at his watch.

A faulty copying machine had been the cause of the delay. Lacroix paced the floor, waiting for an aide to return with the documents he needed. When the door opened and the assistant appeared, red-faced and out of breath, Lacroix grabbed the envelope from him without a word and made his way hurriedly to the improvised press room.

The chatter died away as soon as the young minister entered and seated himself behind a table at the front of the room. He cleared his throat and stared out, trying to see beyond the battery of lights. He heard the whir of the cameras as he started to speak.

"Ladies and gentlemen, thank you for coming. My apologies for taking you away from more enjoyable pursuits on a Saturday night, but what I have to say could not wait until Monday."

He paused dramatically to sense the mood of his audience; all he could hear were the cameras and the sound of pencils scribbling across notebooks.

"As you are all aware, I have been accused of being involved in a conspiracy with the leaders of the Soviet Union to hand them control of the Province of Quebec. I am old enough in the ways of the world to know that the timing of these allegations was no accident. My opponents, in their heavy-handed way, are employing the same kind of cheap smear tactics that gave politics in this province a bad name for decades. Had they been more subtle, they might have embarrassed me in my campaign for Premier. But they have failed, and I have asked you here tonight to denounce this libel once and for all."

There was a murmur of conversation around the room. Lacroix waited for it to subside.

"You have all seen the photographs which were gleefully carried by *Montréal Aujourd'hui*, a newspaper sympathetic to my opponent, and by the entire English press across Canada. I could expect such attention from the English press, of course. I have, however, concentrated on *Montréal Aujourd'hui*, and I have instructed my lawyers to institute proceedings against them for defamation . . ."

"Can you tell us, Minister . . ." called a voice from the darkness behind the lights.

"No questions, please. I am here to give you a statement and that is all. You will have the full story, believe me. As soon as those photographs appeared, I requested the Provincial Police to investigate the matter, as is the right of any citizen in my situation. I received their report today."

He held up a sheaf of paper.

"Ladies and gentlemen, as a result of this report there can be no doubt that the man responsible for perpetrating this libel against me was . . . Jean-Claude Belmont."

As the buzz of disbelief grew, Lacroix raised his voice.

"I accuse him of comspiring with his campaign manager, Raymond Mercier, to damage my reputation and turn the people against me."

"Proof, where's your proof?" called another voice.

"You don't think I would come before you without evidence, do you?" Lacroix produced the thick brown envelope his aide had given him. "I have here documentary evidence which my associates will distribute among you. You will receive a complete copy of the Provincial Police report containing details of the raid they carried out on a photographic studio in Quebec City. You will be handed copies of the negatives of the photos used to make the composite pictures which appeared in the press. And you will receive what the police so colorfully call a dope sheet on the man who runs the photo studio in question. This man, by sheer coincidence, just happens to be the brother-in-law of Raymond Mercier."

The buzz of conversation rose to a crescendo of questions and exclamations. Some reporters grabbed copies of the documents and headed for the door. Lacroix raised his hand for silence.

"One moment, please. In the light of these findings, I would like to say to the people of Quebec through your good selves that Jean-Claude Belmont has shown himself unworthy of their trust and esteem. He has shown himself to be unfit to be Premier of our incipient new state. I therefore call upon him to withdraw from the leadership race immediately and if he has any conscience, to release those delegates already pledged to him. Thank you very much for your indulgence, ladies and gentlemen."

Lacroix was on his feet and heading for the door to avoid the rush of reporters. The room had exploded in an uproar, but Lacroix, having raised the whirlwind, was no longer there to face it.

Monique Gravelle scanned the newspaper for any reference to Belmont. She heard her office door close, but she didn't look up. Raymond Mercier stood in front of her desk with a face like thunder. When she did not acknowledge his presence, he pulled the newspaper out of her hands.

"The story about the photographs is out," he said in a thick voice, fighting for control.

"Oh dear, Raymond. That means trouble, I suppose," she said.

"Don't come the innocent miss with me. You're the only person who knew, apart from my brother-in-law and me. I didn't even tell Jean-Claude. You told Lacroix, didn't you?"

Monique shrugged and ironed out the crumpled pages with the flat of her hand.

"Why did you tell him? What possible good? You want my job, that's it. Well, you're not going to get it, you ambitious little bitch."

"Raymond, if you don't mind, I've got work to do."

"Don't you 'Raymond' me, you two-faced little whore. You've sunk me all right, but by God I'll make sure you sink too, my fine friend!"

"You're shouting. Do you want everyone in the office to know your business?"

"I'm warning you, Monique, you're finished here. Finished."

"You're threatening me, Raymond."

"It's no threat, it's a promise. You won't get my job, because I'm going straight to Jean-Claude and tell him it was you who took the story to Lacroix."

"It was you who discredited him. And yourself."

"You, you're sick. But you're finished, Monique, all your games, your scheming, you're finished."

"You're not going to say a word to anyone, Raymond," replied Monique sweetly.

"Oh yes, my pretty miss, don't underestimate me."

"You're not going to speak to Monsieur Belmont, or anyone else, for that matter, because all I have to do is to pick up this phone, call your wife, and tell her about the Christmas present I gave you. To say nothing of all the times since."

"You can't blackmail me," blustered Mercier. "She won't believe you."

"All I need tell her is that you have a kidney-shaped birthmark on your left buttock. She'd get the message. Then your career *and* your marriage would be on the rocks. Two catastrophes in one day."

"She wouldn't believe a slut like you," hissed Mercier.

"Shall we find out?" Monique picked up the receiver and began to dial. Before she could complete this call, Mercier's hand clamped down on the phone, cutting the line.

"Don't ever call my bluff, Raymond," said Monique, her voice suddenly cold and venomous. "And now get out of here. I can't stand the smell of fear."

"Carnaval du Québec—Bienvenue." The huge welcoming sign at Quebec City's Ancienne Lorette airport was hung with icicles. The small terminal building was thronged with holiday-makers being greeted by a larger-than-life snowman, Bonhomme Carnaval, the symbol of the winter festivities. Pretty girls in white dresses were passing out free cups of caribou, an intoxicating mixture of red wine and grain alcohol, in flagrant violation of Department of Transport regulations.

Taylor Redfern ignored the cheerful hubbub and pushed his way through the jostling crowd to the taxi stand. As the cab careened out of the airport, sliding over the icy road at each turn of the wheel, he settled back in his seat. Although his body still ached from the beating, he felt a kind of grim satisfaction in knowing he was close to solving the riddle of the Premier's assassination.

"Lots of people in the city?" he asked, leaning forward to the driver.

"Very much people, yes." The driver grinned at him

in the mirror. *"Carnaval,* she start tomorrow. Big parade, boat race, many parties. Lots of people."

Thank God for the *Chronicle*'s permanent room at the Château Frontenac, thought Redfern. During the carnival, it was impossible to find a room anywhere in the city. A quick phone call from Montreal had confirmed that no one would be using the newspaper's room for the next few days.

The taxi turned onto an expressway and headed toward the center of the city. In front of him Redfern could see a pair of giant snowblowers sending up a solid arc onto the mountainous drifts that made the road seem like a river of ice between the walls of a snow canyon. Everything seemed exaggerated in Quebec: winter was colder and longer, the snow more abundant. What was the old Gilles Vigneault song? "My country is not a country at all, it's winter."

The taxi exited from the expressway and threaded through the traffic of Lower Town. Redfern contemplated his next move. He had established that the mysterious Monique Gravelle had been employed by the Parti Québécois in Montreal as a public-relations officer. A receptionist at party headquarters informed him that she had taken a leave of absence for three months in order to work for Belmont's campaign. She had been in Trois-Rivières for a while, but the campaign headquarters had now been moved to Quebec City to prepare for the convention, to be held in Quebec Coliseum.

Redfern had decided that, pain or no pain, the answer to all his questions could be found in the provincial capital. He had thrown some clothes into a bag, shut up his apartment, and headed for the airport. As he waited for his plane, he debated whether he should telephone Cameron Craig but decided against it. As far as Craig was concerned, he had been taken off the story.

The taxi's progress was slowed by milling crowds in the street, admiring the ice sculptures outside the slum dwellings of Lower Town. The dreams and aspirations of the families who inhabited these hovels seemed to be embodied in the lovingly carved pieces, some as high as the houses themselves. Giant animals reared up over the street in frozen menace, vying with each other for the attentions of the celebrants who handed flasks of caribou to total strangers and invited them to drink the health of Bonhomme Carnaval. The taxi edged past sleighs filled with tourists. The drivers, old men in raccoon coats and furry ear muffs, their noses red with winter and alcohol, made sucking noises through their teeth to encourage their blanketed horses to move along the street. Strung between the lamp posts, the ubiquitous symbol of the snowman with his red tuque and sash presided over the revels.

Redfern was impatient to get through the crowd. Eventually, the taxi drew up at what appeared to be a vacated store in the commercial heart of Lower Town. Above the door in faded letters was the legend *"Meubles —Furniture."*

"Here it is, monsieur, the office of Monsieur Belmont."

There was no mistaking the campaign headquarters. Every inch of window space was plastered with benign posters of Belmont, pipe in hand, with the exhortation *"Jean-Claude Belmont, l'homme pour Québec."* Redfern could feel his heart pounding as he handed the driver a ten-dollar bill; he waved away the change and, grabbing his suitcase, stepped out into the bitter February cold. The taxi spun its wheels on the ice and moved away, its back wheels at an angle. Redfern realized that, in his haste, he had forgotten his gloves.

Inside the Belmont campaign headquarters, the sound of typewriters and jangling phones bounced off the ceiling. The floor space had been divided into cubicles by temporary partitions. Redfern had the impression of an army of worker ants completely preoccupied by their various tasks. Over the noise of two copying machines vomiting campaign literature, he shouted at a girl wearing a *"Votez Belmont"* button.

"Where can I find Monique Gravelle, please?"

"At the back there. Behind the coffee machine. In Monsieur Mercier's old office," he replied, without really looking at him.

Redfern picked his way through the partitions. Mercier had resigned immediately after the Lacroix press conference. It appeared Monique Gravelle had taken his place.

The office was empty. Redfern looked around for assistance.

"Monsieur Redfern! I'm delighted to see you again." Jean-Claude Belmont was standing in the corridor, as benign as his photograph in the window. "To what do I owe the pleasure of your company?" He said it without a hint of irony. Redfern had interviewed him on several occasions.

"Actually, I was looking for one of your campaign people. Monique Gravelle."

"Monique? A splendid worker. She's been a godsend, I don't mind admitting. Took over completely when Raymond left us. Unfortunate, that. Can't imagine what possessed him." He shook his head as if to dispel the whole affair. "You know, Mr. Redfern, all these years you think you know a man and suddenly . . . poof. He does a stupid thing like that. It hurt me, of course."

"Yeah."

"No, I mean personally. I trusted him. When it came out, he took the blame. But mud sticks."

"Well, these things happen in politics." Redfern was eager to end the conversation.

"From your tone I suspect you think I had prior knowledge of the plan. I assure you I didn't. For what it's worth."

"I believe you. Miss Gravelle, where is she now?"

"Oh, yes. She's away for the rest of the day. I'm not altogether sure where. I told her to take the afternoon off. She's been working too hard."

"Do you know where she's staying?"

"At the Quebec Hilton. Most of us are there."

"Thanks. I'll try to reach her there." He shook hands quickly with Belmont.

"Here, Mr. Redfern, a keepsake for you," said Belmont, reaching into his pocket. He handed the journalist a campaign button. *"Votez Belmont,"* it said. "Wear it, it's good advice, Mr. Redfern."

He needs all the help he can get, thought Redfern as he pinned the button to the lapel of his coat and made his way through the noisy office to the street.

The Prime Minister of Canada sat at the head of a long, baize-covered cabinet table, absently twisting the ring on his finger. He waited for the scuffling of chairs to stop and for the tardy André Lafontaine to scurry to his place. On either side of him, his ministers sat in descending order of seniority. Their eyes were fixed on him, waiting for him to begin. In front of him was a file labeled "Emergency Cabinet Meeting." It was one of the few such meetings he had been forced to call since taking office. He had cautioned his ministers to secrecy, since the faintest whisper of such a meeting would be immediately blown up by the press into a national crisis—which, God knows, it was. Yet the tight-lipped denials had been in vain. The press had somehow got wind of the secret session and the television cameras had been waiting at the Cabinet Room door when he had arrived. The Prime Minister had been cheerfully noncommittal in his comments to reporters, but, like beagles on the scent, they seemed to be salivating with anticipation out there. Whatever the reporters might be thinking, it could not be as unspeakable as the reality set out in the file before him, he thought.

Three hours earlier he had been handed a formal message from the President of the United States, delivered personally by Ralston Bishop, the American ambassador. As the Prime Minister read the message in the ambassador's presence—a man he had known for many years—he needed no further proof that the President was not bluffing and that he himself was facing the gravest crisis of his career. In fact, he would look back on it in his memoirs as being the gravest crisis in the history of Canada.

"I appreciate your attendance at such short notice. I assure you, I'm not crying wolf," he began. There was an air of tension in the room. Busy ministers had been called away from their desks with no explanation.

"I have here a letter from the President of the United States. I shall read it to you." He withdrew the letter from the file folder and read the contents aloud.

> *'Dear Prime Minister:*
>
> *'I must express to you and your government my deepest concern over the evolution of events in the Province of Quebec. My senior advisors and I, having given careful study to the matter, believe that a situation is developing there which threatens the peace and stability of this entire continent and, as such, gravely affects the national interests of the United States.*
>
> *'We have in our possession incontrovertible evidence that one of the candidates for the lead-*

ership of Quebec, Mr. Guy Lacroix, has prepared a comprehensive plan for a unilateral declaration of independence, the announcement of which would be made immediately following a successful bid for the leadership of the Parti Québécois at the forthcoming convention.

'We understand that the program envisaged by Mr. Lacroix contains several points that give us cause for concern. In broad outline, these are:

'One: The severing of economic ties with the rest of Canada.

'Two: A tacit invitation to France to enhance its presence and to increase its political and cultural influence in North America.

'Three: An attempt to coerce the United States government into quick recognition of an independent Quebec by exerting economic pressure on this country's substantial investments in the province, and by regulating passage through the St. Lawrence Seaway.

'Four: An appeal to France and the Soviet Union to act as joint guarantors of the sovereignty of the new state.

'I am sure you will understand, my dear Prime Minister, that the United States cannot tolerate such a situation. I am therefore writing to request, in the strongest possible terms, that your government embark upon a strategy of intervention to negate such a threat to an ally, a major trading partner and a military colleague. In doing so you will have any support, moral or material, from the United States government and its agencies as you might consider helpful in the implementation of such a strategy.

'I have no doubt that you and your ministers will appreciate the urgency of the situation and will act accordingly. It should be clearly understood, however, that if your government for any reason decides against intervention to prevent Mr. Lacroix from declaring UDI, it will become the prerogative of the United States to

*take those measures it deems necessary to protect
its interests. I am, yours very truly, etc. etc.'*

During the stunned silence that immediately followed
the reading of the President's letter, the Prime Minister
ran his fingertips over the heavily embossed letterhead like
a blind man trying to find some comfort in words that
held only threats.

Bill McVee, the Nova Scotia fisherman, broke the
silence.

"The bastard wants us to go in there and bomb the
frogs into submission. Christ, we can't do that, whatever
we think of them." He became aware of the glares from
French Canadians at the table. "I'm sorry, but you know
what I mean, sir."

"What you say, Bill, is in essence correct. The President is telling us to step in, politically if we can, by force
if we can't, to stop Lacroix. And if we don't do it, he will.
And that, in the proverbial nutshell, is it, my friends. What
are we to do?"

"Political intervention of this kind would be unprecedented in Canadian history," said André Lafontaine. "Legally we would have to suspend the provincial government
on some pretext and place Quebec under federal trustee-
ship, much as the British did in Northern Ireland in nineteen seventy-two. But under our constitution, I don't think
we have that option."

"What are the chances of Lacroix losing? Where does
Belmont stand now?" asked Avery Walton.

"Lacroix is so far ahead he's almost home," said Lafontaine. "That smear tactic that backfired hurt Belmont badly.
Lacroix is stumping the province, denouncing him as a
crook. And people are listening to him."

"Is there any political action we can take, André?"
asked the P.M.

Lafontaine shook his head. "There's nothing I can see.
Not before the convention, anyway. I think we have to let
events take their course and then move to isolate Lacroix
and try to force an early election in Quebec which could
knock him out of office."

"Any other thoughts on the political front?" The
Prime Minister looked from face to face down the table. In

the expressions of his ministers he read the anger and frustration born in impotence.

"All right. It seems that immediate political action on our part is out. Let's think the unthinkable for a moment. What about military intervention—proclamation of the War Measures Act as a result of an apprehended insurrection in Quebec? Trudeau got away with it during the FLQ terrorist crisis in nineteen-seventy."

The ministers around the table stared glumly at the ceiling, at the table, at the windows, anywhere but at the Prime Minister.

Jim Hanson, the ebullient Minister of National Defence, finally spoke.

"It's a nonstarter, Mr. Prime Minister."

"Why?"

"This isn't nineteen-seventy. The situation has changed. We had enough trouble then keeping some of the French Canadian troops in line. They were occupying their own province. They didn't like that. This time we'd be faced with open rebellion, and I sure as hell am not going to order anyone shot for desertion. The armed forces are now over twenty-five per cent French Canadian. Most of them are concentrated in bases in Quebec. A large proportion of the key tactical units that would be essential in such an operation are Quebec-based. Mobile Command has its headquarters at St. Hubert, outside Montreal. It controls all our ground forces. The Brigade Group is based at Valcartier, near Quebec City. Bagotville is our main eastern military air base. They're all strategically vital, they're all staffed mainly by French Canadians, and there's a hell of a lot of Parti Québécois sympathy there. Frankly, sir, I couldn't guarantee the loyalty of these men under circumstances such as we're discussing. There'd be a real danger of civil war. We have to face that."

The Prime Minister suddenly felt very tired. Control of the situation seemed to be slipping away from him like mercury through his fingers. There was nothing the government in Ottawa could do to ameliorate matters. A passage from a book he was reading came back to him—about history as a series of waves, rhythmic, inexorable; he felt caught up on one now, waiting to be dashed against the rocks.

"Any other comments?"

The room remained quiet.

"All right. To sum up, then. Military action, according to Jim, is too perilous to contemplate. I'd like to add another reason to what has already been said on that score. Soundings we have taken on the subject suggest that such a course would not have support in the rest of Canada. Our people do not have the will to take up arms to keep Quebec within Confederation. The attitude seems to be let them go, if that's what they want.

"Political intervention at this late stage would be worse than useless. But what we can concentrate on is the formulation of policies for the longer term if events do go sour on us. Is that acceptable?"

"We seem to have run out of options," commented John Penny gloomily.

"What about the President?" asked Avery Walton. "Can we sell it to him?"

"I really don't know," the Prime Minister answered. "All I can do is try. One thing I can promise you—I will not go down in history as the man who led this country into a bloody civil war. Abraham Lincoln has never been one of my heroes."

The elevator in the Quebec Hilton was jammed with brightly dressed Carnaval revelers. Taylor Redfern took a deep breath and pressed himself inside. In a curious way, he felt as lighthearted as these laughing, jostling, slightly drunk people pushing against him. He alighted on the fourteenth floor and scanned the doors for the number of Monique Gravelle's room. He had thought of calling from the lobby but had decided against it. It might frighten her off. He found the room and knocked softly, as a maid would who had come to turn down the bed. He waited. There was no reply. He returned to the elevator and descended to the lobby again.

Once more, he was thrown in with a crowd of carnival celebrants breathing alcohol over each other and singing traditional French songs. He sat down in the lobby to wait. The ceiling above him was hung with red and white banners which were set in motion by the constant swirl of people in traditional carnival dress: tuques, bright red flannel shirts with a Bonhomme crest, and gaudy red and white sashes tied round the waist pirate-fashion. Free drinks in tiny paper cups were carried about the lobby on large trays by the hotel staff. Amid all this confusion Taylor Redfern sat, thinking how best to approach Monique Gravelle. Until her arrival, he decided he could utilize his time in finding out what he could about the girl. He crossed to the cashier's counter and waited for the woman clerk to raise her head from a list of figures.

"Excuse me. I'm from Monsieur Belmont's campaign headquarters. You have one of our staff staying in Room Fourteen-ten, Mademoiselle Monique Gravelle. Unfortunately, she has been unexpectedly called back to Montreal. I've been authorized to settle her account. Could I see it, please?"

"Just a minute." The woman looked at the Belmont button on Redfern's lapel and turned to the computer beside her. She entered a few digits and the machine uttered the bill. The woman slid it across the counter to him. "Will that be cash or charge?"

"Charge," he replied quickly, as he studied the figures. Room charges, tax, several meals, beauty shop—all expected. What startled him was the unusual number of very expensive long-distance calls. Two of them were for more than one hundred dollars.

"Excuse me. These telephone charges. Mademoiselle told me she made only one long-distance call. There are several here. Could you check on them, please? Would you have the dockets to confirm them?"

"I'll have to speak to the operators. Could you wait just a moment, sir." The woman disappeared into an office behind the counter. Redfern continued to examine the items on the bill. Who could Monique Gravelle have been talking to for so long?

"Here you are, sir." The woman handed him the dockets from the switchboard on which the operators carefully recorded the phone number and destination of each long-distance call in case of a subsequent dispute. Redfern riffled through them. All the calls had been made to Paris. All to the same number. He made a mental note of it and handed the dockets back.

"I'm afraid I have authorization to pay for only one long-distance call. I shall have to check back with our campaign headquarters for instructions. Thank you for your help." He turned his back on the surprised cashier and disappeared into the crowded lobby and out into the street.

When he arrived at the Château Frontenac, his room was ready for him. He gave the bellboy a dollar tip before he could start fussing with the drapes and the television set. As soon as he was alone, Redfern locked the door and slid the chain across. He picked up the phone and dialed the long-distance operator.

"I would like to place a call to Paris, please." He gave the number and waited for the connection to be completed. He could hear the single note ringing somewhere in Paris. There was a click on the line.

"Bonjour, Les Entreprises de Luzt, un instant, s'il vous plaît." Very deliberately, Taylor Redfern lowered the receiver back into its cradle.

Taylor Redfern, still in his overcoat, sat on the edge of the king-size bed in his hotel room. He placed a long-distance call to London through the operator. He drummed his fingers impatiently on the night table as he waited for Brian Windsor to answer.

"Brian? This is Taylor Redfern. Listen, I haven't got much time. I need your help."

"Sure, Taylor, good to hear from you. What can I do?"

"You remember that story I was telling you about? The Premier's assassination. Well, I'm close to cracking it."

"Great!"

"Yeah, but I need some information. There's a company in Paris called Les Entreprises de Luzt. I've got to get a complete background on them. What they do, their financial position, principals, share holdings, company officers, subsidiaries—anything."

"How do you spell it?"

"I'm not sure, could be L-U-S-T-E or L-U-Z-T. I assume it's the name of a person. If it is, could you find out all you can about him?"

"Okay, but I'm up to my eyeballs in a series on the unions. I could send Madge over to Paris if your paper could spring some money."

Redfern thought for a moment. He could not approach the *Chronicle* for expense money now.

"I'll send you my personal check. Will three hundred dollars be enough?"

"I'll tell Madge to bring her own sandwiches. No, it should cover it. It must be pretty hot if you're shelling out yourself."

"It could be the biggest story of the decade, Brian."

"Pity I can't go myself, then."

"What time have you got there?"

"Just coming up to four o'clock."

"Okay, can you get Madge on a plane tonight? And if you could sound out your financial contacts in the City, I'd appreciate it. I'm really up against it."

"Do my best."

"I'm staying at the Château Frontenac in Quebec. Room Nine-thirteen. I'll probably be out most of the time, though. Could you telex me here?"

"All right. Give me twenty-four hours. I guess I don't have to tell you to watch out for yourself."

"Thanks, Brian."

"Oh, and Taylor, have a glass of caribou for me, will you?"

The Silver Cloud purred down Whitehall past the Cenotaph and turned right toward the barrier at Downing Street. The policeman on duty spoke to the chauffeur and glanced at the corpulent man who sat in the back seat, absorbed in his own thoughts. Satisfied, the policeman moved the barrier and signaled to the chauffeur to drive through.

Holbrook Meadows was perplexed by the abrupt summons to No. 10. Only three days before he had chatted amicably with the Prime Minister at a reception following her annual address to the Confederation of British Industries. What could suddenly be so urgent? The coalition government had leaned over backward not to interfere with the operations of London-based multinationals. Int-Con had contributed handsomely to both Conservative and Labour Party coffers over the years; the company's taxes were scrupulously paid and if any irregularities had occurred in the transference of funds it would have been the Bank of England that would call—and they would come to see *him!*

The Rolls drew up outside the famous black door with its gold numerals. A lone policeman stood at ease on the top step. George, the chauffeur, stepped out of the car and opened the door for Meadows, who levered himself out of the soft leather seat. George held up an umbrella to protect his employer from the soft drizzle. Meadows waved it away as he walked the few paces to the steps of No.

10. The policeman saluted and pressed the bell. Almost immediately the door opened.

"Commander Meadows?" A butler wearing white gloves stood in the doorway.

"Yes."

"The Prime Minister is expecting you."

Of course she is, he felt like snapping back. She bloody-well demanded my presence here. Instead, he handed the man his coat and hat.

"Will you have tea or whisky, sir?"

"Tea. Lapsang Souchong with a slice of lime. Lemon, if you don't have it."

"Very good, sir."

The butler led the way to a comfortable sitting room. The Prime Minister sat at an escritoire, her back to the door.

"Commander Meadows, madam."

The British Prime Minister turned and smiled a welcome. She looks more and more like the cartoonists' caricatures of her, Meadows thought. More like a public-school matron than a statesman.

"Come in, Mr. Meadows. How nice to see you again." The dropping of his wartime rank put him on his guard. Was she deliberately trying to insult him? He walked over to where she was seated, her hand extended. In the year since her election as Prime Minister, her hair had turned from steely black to gray. She wore half-moon spectacles now, a recent affectation; the burdens of state had coarsened the unremarkable features of a woman Meadows had avoided socially for years. She looked like an overdressed librarian in her expensively tailored Chanel suit.

"Prime Minister, always a pleasure," he mouthed in the Byzantine ritual of greetings exchanged by the powerful.

"Come and sit by the fire and warm yourself," she said, rising and moving toward the sofa. "Did Fulford offer you a whisky?"

"No thank you, ma'am, tea is fine."

"It's the only thing that keeps me sane. I understand Winston and his brandy now."

"I'm somewhat at a loss as to why you wish to see me. Your secretary gave no indication." Meadows steered the conversation round to the business at hand.

"Taking you away from your bridge game, am I?"

"No, actually I had an appointment with my gun-maker at Purdy's, and I'm booked to fly to Paris on the dinner flight."

"Well, I don't think you'll have to alter your flight. I'll get to the point."

The Prime Minister stared at the gas fire for a moment.

"I received a telephone call today from the American Secretary of State. I shan't bore you with the details, but the upshot of it is that our transatlantic allies are unhappy with some of the things you chaps are up to in Quebec." She lowered her head to observe him over her glasses.

"I don't quite understand," equivocated Meadows.

"Let me finish. The Americans were very explicit. They want you and your people out of Quebec. Cease and desist. If you continue to interfere in the political process there, they have threatened to turn quite nasty."

Meadows blinked in astonishment. How could the Americans know what IntCon was doing in Quebec? And what concern was it of theirs, anyway? All he wanted to do was to sell uranium to France, a NATO ally. He started to protest, but the Prime Minister cut him short.

"Yes, yes, I know what you're going to say. None of their business. They have no jurisdiction over a British-based company. Under normal circumstances they don't, of course. But unfortunately circumstances are far from normal."

"Madam Prime Minister I assure you . . ."

"Mr. Meadows, I don't care for Washington's hectoring tone any more than you do. I find it most irritating to be dictated to by their Secretary of State. But we are, not to put too fine a point on it, in a desperate situation. I'm not giving away any state secrets when I tell you that the health of sterling and of the economy in general is perilous —even with North Sea oil. You understand the economic realities as well as I; the political realities, however, are a different matter. This country has become polarized between factions of the extreme left and the reactionary right. The center is no longer holding. Unless something dramatic is done to stop this slide into anarchy we run the very real danger of seeing constitutional government in Britain destroyed and the rule of the gun taking over."

Meadows shifted uncomfortably on the sofa. He was about to speak but checked himself as Fulford, the butler, arrived with his tea. The Prime Minister and the IntCon chairman waited for the butler to place the tray on the table and leave the room.

"I'm afraid we had no lime, sir."

"Doesn't matter," muttered Holbrook Meadows under the quizzical gaze of the woman across the sofa.

"You were about to say?" invited the Prime Minister when they were alone together again.

"I was about to say I am fully aware of the political climate. But where do the Americans fit in?"

"The President is to go before Congress next week with a comprehensive new foreign-policy program. It will be the most ambitious American initiative in Europe since the Marshall Plan—a program designed to shore up sagging economies in Western nations with massive technological aid and long-term credits.

"The scheme includes hard proposals for international energy-sharing and for currency stabilization. But the most innovative aspect of the plan calls for the dropping of all U.S. tariff barriers with participating countries."

"Good Lord!" exclaimed Meadows. "An international free-trading zone of Western nations?"

"Yes, but even more original than that. The United States will drop their tariffs unilaterally. Other countries in the plan will be allowed to protect their own key domestic industries where necessary."

"We can have our cake and eat it, too!" Meadows was excited. "Free access to U.S. markets without reciprocal advantages to them? That's fantastic. We could ship to them at supercompetitive prices."

"Precisely, and when it takes effect we can expect a dramatic increase in capital investment in labor-intensive industries."

"I think I'll have a whisky after all, if you don't mind," said Meadows.

The Prime Minister rose from the sofa and pulled a bell cord by the fire.

"As you will appreciate, Mr. Meadows, it's a very bold plan, and, from the President's point of view, a

very dangerous one. American unions and business groups
are naturally going to fight it tooth and nail. It's an
enormous gamble for the President. He'll have to battle
Congress every inch of the way, and this is the run-up to
a Presidential election."

"Then why is he doing it?"

"Well, what are the alternatives? We're on the verge
of economic and political chaos. Italy may have already
slipped over the brink. Spain and Portugal will be next.
The rise of the neo-Nazi party in West Germany threatens
their economic miracle. France has gone the other way.
So from an American viewpoint the choice is clear: withdraw into Fortress America and let the ravening hordes
sweep across Europe."

"The nineteen-thirties all over again."

"Exactly. Or they can make a bold and imaginative
move to try to salvage social democracy. Say what you
will about that man in the White House, he's really put
himself in the front line."

"Indeed," interjected Meadows.

"This isn't just a one-way traffic. There are conditions," the Prime Minister cautioned.

"I assumed as much."

"Before this country is eligible to participate in the
scheme we have to stem the shift to the left in the trade-
union movement. Washington has made some suggestions.
We can live with them although I confess I don't like
them much. In addition, we have to neutralize the National Front—their recent declarations about civil alliances
with like-minded German groups have made Washington
nervous. It will mean some rather brutal police action.
We shall be hearing a lot about totalitarian regimes and
loss of civil liberties in the next few months, I'm afraid.
However, that is the price we will have to pay."

"That could get rather difficult. The press . . ."

"Yes. The press. As I say, there is a price. Washington demands its pound of flesh. But think of what we
stand to gain in the long term. Naturally, the President
isn't going to put his head on the chopping block unless
he has some iron-clad assurances from us about the future. Every other country in the program faces similar
demands."

"I see."

"That, in general terms, is the scheme. And now I come to you. And the reason for your presence here today. The phone call from the Secretary of State added two new conditions to our participation in the program. Both concern you, Mr. Meadows. IntCon must withdraw all financial and material support from the candidature of Guy Lacroix. This must take effect immediately. And two, you are to stop all negotiations with France regarding future uranium supplies."

"But that's not possible!" spluttered Meadows.

"Quite possible, my dear Mr. Meadows; in fact, imperative."

"Madam Prime Minister, let me be frank with you. IntCon is in dire trouble. My company's primary revenue producer, a South African gold mine, is petering out. Without it, we face acute liquidity problems. If we can negotiate this uranium deal with the French, I'm confident we can work out a payment schedule with them that'll see us through the crisis. Without it, I must warn you we will probably be forced into receivership. And that would mean the loss of at least twelve hundred jobs in this country alone. How will that look in the House?"

The Prime Minister sipped her drink before replying.

"I don't like the prospect any more than you do. But I'm faced with two choices: the bankruptcy of a major company or the bankruptcy of a nation. If this American program does not go through, we'll be forced to default on our repayments to the International Monetary Fund. Under the circumstances, Mr. Meadows, I have no choice."

Holbrook Meadows fought for breath. The image of the Prime Minister blurred before him, and he felt a sharp pain above his heart. For a moment he wondered if this were a coronary. He lay back against the sofa and shut his eyes. A death sentence had just been passed on the company he had spent a lifetime building, and he was powerless to do anything about it.

The Prime Minister leaned forward and smiled.

"I think I hear Fulford coming. You look as if you could use that whisky, Mr. Meadows."

"I'm sorry, sir, Mademoiselle Gravelle is not here. Can anyone else help you?"

The secretary at the Belmont campaign headquarters had the abstracted air of someone of whom constant and unreasonable demands are made.

"Could you tell me where I can find her, it's very important," insisted Redfern.

The woman consulted a typed agenda on her desk. Monique Gravelle was proving to be maddeningly elusive.

"Doesn't she ever spend any time in the office?" Redfern asked. "I was here yesterday and she was out then, too."

"She has a very busy schedule, sir," replied the secretary without looking up. "The convention opens in less than a week. As soon as the carnival finishes. Ah, here it is. Monique Gravelle. Radio-Canada. Studio Two. She's supervising a television interview with Monsieur Belmont."

"Can I reach her there?"

"They're scheduled to be in the studio till noon. You've got forty-five minutes yet."

"Thanks. I'll try to catch her." Redfern turned and headed for the door. He hailed a passing taxi and ordered it to the Radio-Canada building.

The broadcasting center was a squat, modern structure in suburban Ste. Foy. Redfern knew his way around the building from his years as a correspondent in Quebec City. Studio Two was on the main level, a boxlike room traditionally booked for interviews with politicians.

The red light was on over the studio door as Redfern approached. He let himself into the darkened control room. The taping of the interview with Belmont was well underway: on the monitors the candidate's face in close-up was beginning to disappear behind a cloud of pipe smoke. Redfern recognized immediately the three journalists questioning the minister—a political reporter from *Le Soir* known for his pro-Belmont sympathies, a Radio-Canada talk-show host more at home with starlets than statesmen, and the *New York Times*'s Quebec correspondent, who spoke Parisian French and had a pained expression on his face whenever he had to listen to anyone who didn't. An excellent trio from Belmont's point of view, thought Redfern; the candidate was certain to shine under their collective caress.

Redfern nodded to the producer, whom he knew from years past. "Okay if I sit in?"

"Sure, but don't expect any fireworks. Those guys are pussycats. Someone did some careful screening. Cigarette?"

"Thanks." Redfern tried to remember his name. Yves something-or-other. Cloutier, was it? He couldn't recall.

"Which one is his campaign manager?" Redfern asked.

"You can't see her. Camera Two is blocking her out right now."

Redfern strained to see. The set was at eye level, an oasis of light in the darkness of the studio. The cameramen and technicians were no more than silhouettes. He couldn't see the woman.

The taping droned on, and Redfern smoked another cigarette. The smoke and the strain of looking into the darkness hurt his eyes. But Belmont, on the other side of the glass, looked relaxed and seemed able to deflect the questions with ease, embarrassingly so. His television technique was first class, thought Redfern as he watched him on the monitors. The man talked directly at the cameras; his gaze was level and open; he spoke fluently, and with conviction. A real father figure. The kind of man Quebeckers would normally love.

The producer pressed a key on the panel in front of him and spoke into a small microphone protruding from it.

"Okay. Give them the wrapup. Roll theme and credits. Coming to you, Camera Three."

The voices of the men faded as the theme music established itself, and the production credits passed in front of a long shot of Belmont and his interviewers. The taping was over.

Taylor Redfern felt a sudden surge of excitement as the studio lights came up and the producer thanked everyone for participating. The four figures on the set slouched in their seats, the cameras pulled back out of range, and then Redfern saw her. She was standing in profile to him holding a clipboard—a stunningly beautiful woman with shiny black hair that fell across her shoulders and down her back. She turned her face to the control room. Redfern squinted to focus his eyes on her. He could feel the blood rising in his neck: it was the woman he had seen in the National Assembly press gallery. There could be no doubt about it. He experienced the same tremor of fear as he had on that November day when she had directed the photographer toward him.

"Is that her . . . Monique Gravelle?" he asked the producer, his voice catching in his throat.

"That's her. Not bad, eh? How'd you like to have her slippers under your bed?" Redfern continued to stare at the woman. The light over the studio door switched from red to green.

"If you want to see her, you'd better catch her now," said the producer. "I think I heard them say they had to rush over to another meeting."

"Right, thanks," said Redfern, bracing himself for his entry into the studio.

Monique Gravelle was making some notes on her clipboard. Redfern walked up to her.

"Mademoiselle Gravelle."

The dark eyes glanced up at him, and he thought he caught a spark of recognition.

"Yes?" The voice, deep and rich, gave nothing away.

"My name is Taylor Redfern. I believe we have a mutual friend."

"Oh?"

"Yes. Kevin Reilly. Shall we go somewhere and talk about him?"

She looked over his shoulder as if seeking some escape route. Redfern knew he had struck a nerve.

"Yes. All right, but not now. Where?"

"I'm staying at the Château Frontenac, Room Nine-thirteen."

"No. It must be somewhere public. There's a bar on the Place Royale, the Bar des Amis. Do you know it? I'll meet you there at eight tonight."

"Come, Monique, we'll be late for the Rotarians." Jean-Claude Belmont caught them both by surprise. "Ah, Monsieur Redfern. I'm delighted you're taking an interest in my campaign. But I'm sorry, I shall have to spirit Monique away from you. You understand."

"Yes, of course, sir."

"Good, good. *Au revoir*. See you at the convention, no doubt." Belmont turned and headed for the studio door. Monique Gravelle moved to follow him, but Redfern caught her by the arm.

"Eight o'clock," he whispered. "You'd better be there or you'll be answering questions from the RCMP."

She shook herself loose with a frown.

"I'll be there."

Redfern watched the movement of her lithe body as she hurried after the departing minister.

Lawrence Wilde had never seen the President in such an ugly mood. The elected leader of over two hundred million Americans paced the Oval Office cursing everything Canadian and looking as if he would start biting the furniture at any minute. And this was the man who talked of "sweet reason and tolerance" at his inauguration? The man whose finger was on the trigger? The Secretary of State shuddered.

"If I may remind you, sir, your blood pressure."

"Blood pressure!" shouted the President. "And who the hell d'you think's responsible for my blood pressure? Those goddamned Canadians. No wonder they chose the beaver for their national symbol. They slap their tails and hide among their timber at the first sign of a fight."

Lawrence Wilde couldn't restrain a smile. The President's imagery was apt.

"How can you sit there grinning like a fool!" the President stormed on. He swept a letter from his desk with a ferocity that threatened to topple the Victorian inkstand. "You've seen it! 'Any overt intervention at this time would involve a clear risk of armed conflict,'" he read in a mincing voice. He threw the letter back onto the desk.

"What in God's name do they expect will happen if they don't intervene? That goon Lacroix isn't playing patty-cake. He means what he says. And those sons of bitches in Ottawa sit on their fat asses with their fingers in their ears waiting for the bang."

"Sir, there are genuine political and military concerns involved here. The Canadian ambassador—"

"Don't you play the devil's advocate with me, Larry. They're prevaricating, and I sure as hell am not going to fall into the same trap. They're scared shitless up there. That's the long and the short of it."

The Secretary of State said nothing. There was little to be gained by arguing with the man in such a mood. The Canadian stance made sense to Lawrence Wilde; the Canadian ambassador had spent the better part of the morning justifying it to him. At Wilde's suggestion, the Canadian Prime Minister had attempted to explain his position in a phone call to the President. But the President was so incensed that he hung up on him in mid-sentence—an unprecedented breach of international protocol. "I just couldn't take any more of the guy's sniveling," he growled when Wilde protested.

"You realize what they've done," continued the President. "They've told us to mind our own bloody business. Their domestic problem, my eye. If only it were."

Wilde waited for the President to calm down. His language was becoming more moderate and the telltale red blotches at his cheekbones were losing their vivid hue. He would run out of steam in a minute.

"All right, sir, what now? It appears they've called our bluff. It's our move." The President returned to his chair behind the desk and sat down. His face was impassive again.

"Let's examine the options. Number one, we can sit tight and do nothing and hope like hell the Canadians *can* handle the business. Advantage: we come out nice guys who don't mess in our neighbor's back yard. Pat on the head from the Afro-Asian block in the U.N. Much prestige in the Security Council. Well, you can forget that."

"I'm afraid we can't do 'nothing.' Time is against us," cautioned Wilde.

"Yeah. Option two. We get Lacroix. Turn the CIA, the FBI, those Cuban nuts, anyone else we've got, turn 'em all loose in Quebec and eliminate him, whatever the cost. Attractive. The only problem is they're all a bunch of bunglers. They couldn't finish the guy off if they had him blindfolded and roasting over the tomb of the Unknown Soldier. Besides, I understand his security is better than mine since that lunatic took a shot at him before Christmas, right?"

"That's the reading we get."

"So there you are. It probably wouldn't work and we're running out of time as you say. Now, option three. We send an emissary to Lacroix. Talk tough to him. Offer him some kind of a deal. Get him off his UDI kick in exchange for a substantial U.S. investment in Quebec, routed through France."

"It's worth considering, sir. Any other options?"

"Scarce tactics. Mass troops along the Quebec border. Try to panic them. Might work, seems to me those Canadians scare pretty easily."

"It could have exactly the opposite effect. The French Canadians can be bloody-minded when they're pushed to the wall."

"The hell they can! I'll tell you one thing, Larry. I'm going to order additional units into those border bases, surreptitiously or otherwise."

"I think it should be done covertly, Mr. President, at least for now."

"Hmmm. We'll see. By the way, did you settle that IntCon matter?"

"Yes, sir. They are no longer in the picture."

"Good. Bloody amateurs, always ruining the game."

"Sir, I'd like to know one thing. You have my support in whatever you do, that goes without saying, naturally. But I need an answer if I'm going to plan our strategy effectively."

"Yes, what do you want to know?"

"If it comes right down to the wire, sir, do you intend to go in?"

"Go in? You're goddamned right we go in. And with everything we've got. There'll be no pussyfooting, I can promise you that."

Stepping into Quebec City's Place Royale was like being transported back two centuries in time. The millions of dollars invested by federal and provincial governments to restore the seventeenth- and eighteenth-century houses to their original splendor had been well spent. The square was one of North America's unique tourist attractions: a living museum of early Canadian architecture—well-groomed buildings housing boutiques, fine restaurants, and cheerful bars.

Taylor Redfern stood outside the Bar des Amis. The boisterous sound of many voices singing the rousing chorus of *"Chevaliers de la Table Ronde"* rolled out of its inviting interior. He knew the bar well from his days as the *Chronicle*'s Quebec correspondent—a cozy place with old stone walls two feet thick, exposed wooden beams, and long, roughhewn tables. He had spent many pleasant evenings there with colleagues from the National Assembly press gallery. But it was hardly the rendezvous for a confidential meeting. He decided to wait for Monique Gravelle there and suggest they go somewhere else. He glanced at his watch: it was a few minutes before eight o'clock.

The Bar des Amis was already crowded. Waiters in their carnival shirts and sashes good-naturedly pushed through the throng with steins of beer and pitchers of caribou balanced on trays held high above their heads. A middle-aged man was standing on one of the tables, opening his throat for the steins of beer passed up to him by a cheering crowd. As Redfern watched, he reached the limit of his capacity and showered beer over everyone within range. Someone in a reedy tenor voice started a chorus of

> *Carnaval, Mardi Gras, Carnaval*
> *À Québec c'est tout un festival.*

Soon the entire bar had taken up the Winter Carnival theme song.

Redfern smiled. French Canadians certainly knew how to enjoy themselves. That's what made the Quebec carnival such an international attraction in spite of the habitual sub-zero temperatures that prevailed. He looked around in case Monique Gravelle had slipped in by another door. There was no sign of her. He took up a position by the bar where he could watch both entrances and ordered a beer.

Several of the waiters brought white canes up to the bar to be filled with brandy. Redfern watched the procedure with interest. The plastic canes were accessories to the official festival uniform, considered *de rigeur* by *le vrai Carnavaliste*. The hollow interior of these canes held twelve ounces of brandy or any other beverage. Essential for sustaining internal warmth while standing exposed in the bitter cold, watching the parade, the dog-team races, the ski jumping, or just ambling through the streets to see the ice sculptures. Redfern's attention was distracted each time the door opened, ushering in a blast of cold air. He looked at his watch. Almost half past eight. Monique Gravelle might be an excellent campaign manager but she had no sense of time, he thought.

While Taylor Redfern waited for Monique Gravelle, sipping his beer angrily, the object of his impatience was in his hotel room, ferreting through his belongings. The lights in the room were off; she used a small flashlight for her work. Quickly she ran her hands through the layers of clothing in the drawers and the pockets of jackets and trousers in the closet. She found nothing. Working with extreme care, she made sure there was no evidence of her search. In the bottom of the closet was a pile of dirty linen; she moved it about with the toe of her shoe. He certainly has a lot of washing, she thought idly, why doesn't he rinse it in the sink or send it out?

She lifted the pillows on the bed and pulled up the mattress. On the bedside table the radio clock read 8:35; she would have to hurry. In a drawer next to a Gideon Bible, she noticed a tin of aspirins and a notebook. She took a small camera from her purse and turned the pages of the notebook over one at a time, taking a shot of the scribblings on each. She examined the portable typewriter and Redfern's briefcase with its fresh note pads, copy paper, some newspaper clippings in a file dealing with the leadership race. She riffled through his contact book and replaced it. In one pocket of the briefcase she found a used airline ticket to London—what had he been doing there? Also in the pocket, scribbled on a piece of paper in pencil, was the name Charles Watson and a phone number. She put this back carefully and closed the case.

Finally, she checked the bathroom. His shaving kit stood on the basintop with a popular brand of cologne. Next to it, a small bottle of eye drops and a plastic box for contact lenses. There appeared to be nothing at all in Redfern's belongings that might be useful to her. The man carried his secrets around in his head, if he had any secrets. She gave the bedroom one final inspection, and just as she was about to cross to the door there was a knock. She drew back against the wall and slipped her hand into her purse, feeling for the tiny .22 revolver she carried.

The knock sounded again, more insistent this time.

"Message," a bellboy's voice called out. Monique could hear him preparing to use his passkey. In a moment, he would find her in the darkened room. Then she would be faced with disposing of him or answering some difficult questions.

"I've just gotten out of the shower," she called out. "I'm not dressed."

She could hear the key being withdrawn from the lock.

"Just slip it under the door, will you?"

"It's for Mr. Redfern," said the voice on the other side, unsure.

"That's all right. I'm Mrs. Redfern. My husband will tip you when he comes back. Thank you."

A white telex envelope appeared under the door. She waited until she heard the elevator door open down the hall. She replaced the safety catch on the revolver and dropped it back into her purse. Then she bent down and picked up the unsealed envelope.

She pulled the flashlight from her purse and opened the telex. She scanned the message, and, as she did, she felt her pulse quicken. She had been extremely fortunate; a few moments longer and she would have been gone. Redfern would have returned to find the message, and the game could have been up right there. She stuffed the telex into her purse. It would probably be several hours before Redfern became aware it had not been delivered. By then, she would have had time to deal with him. She opened the door fractionally and made sure the hallway was empty.

Finding a vacant room in Quebec during the carnival had not been easy. Monique, having checked out of the Hilton to escape the attentions of Taylor Redfern, had to settle for a fleabag in the lower town. Even rooms in the Hotel Touriste, which should have been condemned years ago, were taken, and it was only after a fifty-dollar bill had been pressed into the hand of the proprietor, a man with no teeth and less conversation, that she secured one. She registered under a false name, knowing Redfern would probably phone every hotel in the city once he discovered she had tricked him.

With the roomkey in her pocket, Monique Gravelle hailed a cab and ordered it to Palais Station. She picked up her suitcase from a coin-operated locker and carried it to a public telephone booth. Once inside, she placed a collect call to Paris.

"Les Entreprises de Luzt."

"Put me through to him immediately, it's Monique."

"Hold on, please. He's out, but he's left a number. I'll

have to locate him." The answering-service operator in Paris put Monique on hold.

She could feel the dampness under her arms. The fear of pursuit had set her adrenalin flowing. She could smell the animal scent that emanated from her in the confined space of the booth.

"I've rung through to his club. They've gone to find him. Apparently he's in the sauna. I should be able to connect you shortly." The woman's aggressive cheerfulness annoyed her.

"Thank you," she replied curtly.

"Hello, Monique. Is anything wrong?" She felt instantly reassured by the sound of de Luzt's voice.

"Not yet, but there could be soon. There's a reporter here who wants to do a story on us. Are you with me?"

"Yes. The one you told me about? Redfern?"

"Yes. We have a mutual friend, he told me. His first name's Kevin."

"I see." Monique could hear the displeasure in his voice.

"It's more serious than that. He's got someone in London looking into your company. I intercepted a telex at his hotel. Redfern hasn't seen it yet, but when he does, he's going to start pulling the whole operation together. Am I making myself clear?"

"Perfectly. Our American associates, the Company, have been deviling away too, my dear. Any sign of them where you are?"

"No, not yet. But they can't be far behind Redfern. Them or the Boy Scouts."

"Where are you now?"

"I'm at the station. I checked out of the Hilton. I'm now at a hole called the Hotel Touriste. Under the name of Suzanne Groleau. What do you want me to do?"

"First thing tomorrow, phone your office and tell them you've been taken ill. You won't be at work for a few days. Then stay out of sight. Have you completed all the necessary work there?"

"Everything's ready for the burial. The ledgers are done and the documents are complete."

"Excellent. All right, now stay in your room and whatever happens, don't let that reporter find you. I'm coming over myself to help you with the final phase."

"But, I can—" she started to protest.

"No arguments, Monique. We are almost there now. We have to move fast and get out. If Mr. Redfern wants to interview anyone, let him interview me. I know how to handle men like him."

André Lafontaine had felt uncomfortable ever since the Prime Minister suggested he be the emissary of the federal government to speak with Guy Lacroix in Quebec. He felt even more discomfited sitting opposite the Quebec Minister of Social Affairs in his campaign office, waiting for the younger man to finish his phone call. He had had no love for Lacroix before his spectacular rise in the Parti Québécois; now he had nothing but contempt for the man.

Lacroix slammed the receiver down. "Damned incompetents!" He glared at Lafontaine. "Well, what do you want?" he demanded truculently. "I haven't much time. The convention opens in a few days, you know."

Lafontaine contained his anger. The outcome of this meeting was too important for him to allow himself the luxury of trading ill-tempered banter with Lacroix. The Prime Minister had made it clear that if he didn't succeed in striking a bargain with the radical leader, the result could be bloodshed. Lafontaine cleared his throat.

"Monsieur Lacroix, I'm here to make you a proposition."

"On whose behalf?"

"The Prime Minister's." That was not exactly true. The proposal had been worked out by the Prime Minister in consultation with the U.S. Secretary of State. But there was no point in alerting Lacroix to the American involvement, at least not yet.

"Okay, my federalist friend, what is it?"

"The Prime Minister knows of your plans to proclaim UDI should you win the leadership convention next week."

"Should? You mean when I win."

"Whatever. I'm not going to argue with you."

"I've heard these rumors," said Lacroix loftily. "I've made no official statement to that effect."

"Officially, perhaps not. We have reason to believe that is your intention, though. Do you deny it?"

"I deny nothing, neither do I confirm it. What do you expect me to say?"

"All right. Let's assume for the sake of discussion that our information is correct. . . . The Prime Minister has authorized me to say . . ." Lafontaine paused as the words seemed to stick in his throat ". . . that we understand your frustration with the negotiations. The talks have not progressed as quickly as we all would have liked. I am authorized to assure you that if you abandon your idea about UDI, the Prime Minister will convene a constitutional conference within six months. Under that aegis, we could reach an amicable settlement on the entire Quebec situation."

Lafontaine sat back, waiting for a reply.

"Another stall," murmured Lacroix.

"I'm sorry, I didn't quite hear you."

"I said, you can tell your precious Prime Minister he can kiss my ass."

"Now just a minute, you—"

"No, none of your 'just a minutes.' You bastards in Ottawa have been playing games with us for years. You've done everything you can to get our government defeated, to peddle your influence in our referendums, to obstruct negotiations. Well, you're out of it now, *finis*. The people of Quebec know where they want to go and they're calling to me to lead them there. And, by God, I'm going to do it—and now."

With great difficulty André Lafontaine suppressed his desire to punch the man in the teeth.

"Monsieur Lacroix, our offer is made in good faith. I suggest you consider it carefully before throwing it back in our faces. UDI is a dangerous course. I don't have to tell you the consequences. You need only look to Rhodesia. What the Prime Minister is offering is an orderly transition, with protection for both sides and guarantees of stability. I wouldn't reject it out of hand if I were you."

"And why not?" retorted Lacroix. "What do you people think you're doing? You think a few beads and mirrors will satisfy us? Because that's exactly what you're offering. Beads and trinkets. The people of Quebec are not children. They don't need toys. They need liberty, and they need it now!"

"You can save your speeches for the platform, Lacroix." The dam had burst, and Lafontaine's temper erupted. "You don't impress me one bit with your rabble-rousing. Liberty, my ass. What kind of liberty do you honestly think our people will have? Yes, our people. Because I'm French Canadian too, in case you've forgotten. Are you blind, man? Don't you know what's going on out there? You've wrapped yourself in the fleur-de-lis and you can't see a thing. You make one move toward UDI and the Americans will be in here so fast you won't be able to tell the stars from the stripes."

Lacroix flicked a lock of hair from his eyes. The vehemence of Lafontaine's outburst had checked him. He seemed suddenly hesitant and unsure of his ground. Lafontaine pressed his advantage.

"Do you doubt that, Mr. Candidate? Do you doubt it? Well, let me tell you something. We've been talking to the Americans. They're building up forces in New York and Maine right now. They aren't going to let you get away with it. So you can take your pick: either you sit down at the bargaining table with us or let them stick a howitzer in your back and tell you what to do." He was angry at himself for saying so much; he had played all his cards, but perhaps it was better that way.

Guy Lacroix sat silent behind the desk for an unconscionably long time considering his response.

"Yes, Mr. Minister, I had anticipated the possibility of something like that," he said slowly, "but I didn't think the Americans would be so stupid."

His voice began to quicken, the momentum of his feelings forcing out the words. "Here's the message you can take back to your puppet in Ottawa and his masters in Washington. If one American or Canadian soldier sets foot on Quebec soil after I become Premier, for any reason, I will have no alternative but to call on France and the Soviet Union for military assistance. Furthermore, I have excellent reason to believe that such an appeal would be answered immediately." His voice became shrill and he rose to his feet. "If you want Quebec to be the Armageddon of the superpowers, then go ahead. Otherwise keep your filthy hands off Quebec and let us pursue our own destiny!"

Taylor Redfern lay full length on the bed in his room at the Château Frontenac, staring at the reflected light on the ceiling. He felt tired and dispirited; the neon flashes of excitement he had experienced when he thought he was near the truth had ebbed away in the Bar des Amis when Monique Gravelle failed to appear. Now she had vanished. He had checked the Quebec Hilton as soon as he realized she had no intention of keeping their rendezvous. He had pounded on her door until an irate young man with a towel around his middle answered it. Beyond him, Redfern caught a glimpse of a woman in the bed. He had shouldered his way into the room only to find to his acute embarrassment that she was not Monique Gravelle. The clerk at the front desk told him that Mademoiselle Gravelle had checked out of the hotel that afternoon, a fact which finally convinced Redfern that she had never intended to meet him at the Bar des Amis.

What should he do now? He could check with Belmont's campaign headquarters in the morning, but he knew she would not be there. Was she still in Quebec City? He could phone every hotel and rooming house, but if she had gone to ground she would hardly register under her own name. Besides, there were scores of hotels in the city. Or she could have just stepped onto a plane to anywhere. . . .

He rubbed his reddening eyes; the gloom of defeat enveloped him in the dark hotel room. Why had he let himself get into such a position? He could have long ago cooperated with the RCMP and told them all he knew. They had the resources to track down Monique Gravelle wherever she was. Maybe she had met the same fate as Sergeant Touraine. Who knew? Maybe he was next? He still carried Charles Watson's number with him. Why didn't he call? Then again he could just forget the whole rotten business and fly back to Vancouver and his family. Or just get drunk. Certainly a drink would help. He rolled over, switched on the bedside light, and dialed room service. He ordered two double Scotches to be brought up to the room. While he waited, he sat down at his portable Olivetti and began to peck idly at the keys. When his eyes focused on the white sheet of paper he found that he had ben subconsciously typing the name of Monique Gravelle over and over. At that moment of recognition the phone rang, making him start.

"Hello."

"Mr. Redfern?"

"Speaking."

"This is the overseas-message operator. I'm sorry to disturb you. We have just received three additional paragraphs to the telex that came in earlier this evening. Apparently they were delayed in transmission."

Redfern was puzzled.

"Telex, what telex?"

"It was delivered to your room over an hour ago, sir."

Redfern looked quickly around the room. There was no sign of it.

"There's nothing here. An hour ago, you say?"

"Yes, sir. I gave the message to the bellboy myself. It was quite long. I'm positive he delivered it. He's off duty now or I'd check with him. . . ."

"Do you keep a copy?"

"Oh, yes, sir. We keep carbons of all messages received."

"Good. Can you send up the copy right away along with what's come in. Tell the bellboy to deliver it to me in my hands personally, understand? He might have taken it to the wrong room. Tell him Nine-thirteen."

"Yes, sir. I'll have it sent right up."

Redfern looked at his watch. Brian Windsor had promised results within twenty-four hours; the telex must be from him. By the sound of it, he and Madge had come up with a fair amount of information. He tried to restrain his mounting excitement.

While he waited for the telex to be delivered, he pulled out the Quebec City yellow pages and flipped through the hotel listings. They took up several columns. If he tried to track down Monique Gravelle that way, it would be a tortuous process.

At a knock on the door, he tossed the directory onto the bed and crossed the room to open it. A service waiter in a white jacket entered with a tray holding two glasses of Scotch and a small pitcher of ice. A few doors down the hall Redfern could hear the riotous sounds of a party.

"Just put it down there," he said, pointing to the bed-side table. The waiter gave him the bill to sign and left without a word when Redfern handed him a modest tip. Surly bastard, thought Redfern; he started to close the door only to find a bellboy in the hallway about to knock.

"Mr. Redfern?" The journalist nodded. "Message for you, sir."

Redfern took the envelope and fished in his pocket. He had given his last change to the waiter.

"I'm sorry. I'm out of change."

"That's all right, sir. You can catch me next time. Have a nice evening."

The bellboy retreated down the hall. Redfern closed the door and, without thinking, slipped the chain into place. He sat on the edge of the bed and stared at the envelope in his lap. Before opening it, he took a gulp of Scotch.

The message was long; the telex had been folded into three quarto-sized sheets. It began with a rundown on Les Entreprises de Luzt. Brian Windsor had discovered that it was a privately owned company with all the shares concentrated in the hands of its sole principal, Antoine de Luzt, a resident of Paris. The actual corporate offices were registered in Liechtenstein, no doubt for tax purposes. However, Liechtenstein appeared to be no more than an address of convenience—probably a lawyer's office.

The company itself, a small investment firm, dealt almost exclusively in European stocks and some highly esoteric bonds. It was difficult to get a reliable reading on assets since it was a private firm and not required to publish annual reports. Its confidentiality was further protected by Liechtenstein's friendly disclosure laws. Very few of Windsor's financial contacts in London had ever heard of the company. Those who did know of it were generally vague. However, one broker had recently had dealings

with a buyer who picked up the option on a large bloc of
IntCon shares offered by his client. The purchaser turned
out to be Les Enterprises de Luzt.

IntCon and de Luzt, a fascinating combination,
thought Redfern. He took another gulp of Scotch to cele-
brate the connection.

The only other potentially interesting piece of information Brian Windsor had managed to unearth was a
suspicion that the company was something more than a
small investment house. There was nothing tangible, only
the hint that it was a shell—albeit a lucrative one—for a
larger operation; a front was the term Windsor used, but a
front for what? He had left the question open.

The additional paragraphs on a second sheet were
Madge Tillwood's findings on Antoine de Luzt himself.
She had had better luck with her informants. One of her
contacts in Paris was an international-affairs analyst at the
Sorbonne. He had recognized de Luzt's name immediately.
Redfern could hear the beat of his heart as he read Madge's
findings.

*Antoine de Luzt appears to be a well-connected interna-
tional operative believed to act for the French government
on assignments not officially endorsed. He is said to have
been instrumental in the successful abortion of the coup
d'état in the Ivory Coast four years ago, but there is no
proof of this.*

Redfern remembered that incident. The Ivory Coast
was a client state of France. An attempt to overthrow the
pro-French president had been brutally suppressed; hundreds of so-called conspirators had been publicly executed.

*De Luzt is also said to be the middleman in the sale of
Mirage jets by France to a number of Persian Gulf states.
Rumor has it that he is currently working for the govern-
ment to locate new sources of uranium for France.*

*As far as his personal background is concerned, his
family are military. He served with the French army during
the Algerian war, with the field rank of captain. He is
reputed to be an expert in brain-washing and debriefing
techniques, learned during that campaign. He was also
accused of torturing guerrillas but exonerated by a military*

court when France pulled out. Before that, he served with French forces in Indo-China in a similar capacity and was there until the fall of Dien Bien Phu. He returned to Paris after the French surrender. He appears to be independently wealthy, the right clubs and all that, although he has no formal job.

Family background, for what it's worth: Antoine de Luzt is descended from a noble family with extensive holdings in Burgundy. His father was a close advisor to Charles de Gaulle during World War II. The family still controls some excellent vineyards in the Côte d'Or region. De Luzt married in the mid-1950s. He has one daughter, born 1959. The mother died in childbirth. He has not remarried though his sexual predilections are well known. The whereabouts of his daughter is unclear. One final note. Antoine de Luzt is considered here to be an unscrupulous and ruthless man. He has no criminal record, but his reputation suggests a man who will let nothing stand in his way. If you think he's involved in this situation, be careful, Taylor. Will send you more info when I get it. Love, Madge.

A light dusting of snow drifted across the White House lawn, driven on by a biting northerly wind. It was unseasonably cold for Washington, and the members of the National Security Council summoned by the President were happy to be indoors, seated around the long table of the Committee Room.

"Everyone here?" The President scanned the faces of his staff, their colors heightened by the elements outside. At his back a huge map of Quebec, illuminated from behind, dominated one wall.

"General Webster is in Iran, sir," said Colin Dempster, his National Security Advisor. "Apart from him, all present and accounted for."

The President, who disliked military terminology and couched his own thoughts in the jargon of the football field, frowned at Dempster.

"All right, all right. Let's get the ball in play. The subject today, gentlemen, is Quebec." The President gestured at the map behind him. There was a stir of interest around the table. This wasn't going to be another routine review of military preparedness or a discussion of the minutiae of the disarmament talks. "I'm going to ask Lawrence Wilde to give us an update on the situation."

Lawrence Wilde rose from his chair and crossed to the podium behind the President. He asked for the lights to be lowered, and for the next twenty minutes the Secretary of State delivered a monologue on Quebec and its relevance to Washington. As Wilde developed his argument, the military members of the Council leaned forward, paying more attention to him than they had at the start; they sensed that they would be playing a major role in the coming weeks.

". . . so the British have complied with our requirements," Wilde was saying. "They have brought pressure on their extremist groups, and IntCon has been cut off at the knees. As far as the French are concerned, well, they continue to act like the French. They maintain a diplomatic charade—that they are not interfering in Quebec— but we know that they are. As a result, the President has decided that France will be excluded from the foreign-aid program to be announced next week."

"Those bastards have been sticking it to us for years," muttered General Henry Wilson, chairman of the Joint Chiefs of Staff. "Ever since de Gaulle. It's about time they got some of their own medicine back."

"Don't worry, Hank, they'll get theirs," said the President. "Go on, Larry."

"To recap, gentlemen. It appears highly likely that Guy Lacroix will win the leadership of the Parti Québécois at the February seventeenth convention. If I were laying odds, I'd give four-to-one on it. Now, if he is chosen leader at the convention, he will automatically become the new Premier of Quebec, since the Parti Québécois is in power.

"We have cast-iron evidence that in his inaugural speech he will proclaim a unilateral declaration of independence. He hasn't confirmed this publicly—he's being very careful not to rock the boat now that the boat is heading for port. But he hasn't denied it, either. We are convinced on the basis of information received from CIA operatives in Quebec that this is in fact his intention."

"What if he loses the convention?" asked Colin Dempster.

"Then we can all relax. His opponent, Jean-Claude Belmont, is a pragmatic man. We can deal with him. Lacroix, on the other hand, has visions of himself as some kind of Messiah. A burning idealist. The most dangerous kind. Now, we have tried to come to terms with Lacroix privately. After conversations with the Prime Minister of Canada, a contact was made by a senior French Canadian minister in his cabinet. A meeting between him and Lacroix was arranged. Of course, this was on my initiative, at the President's request. Lacroix was offered, in effect, a blank check if he agreed to drop the UDI idea in favor of more conventional procedures. His reply was colorful—he offered a portion of his anatomy for a Prime Ministerial embrace."

There was guarded laughter around the table. The President remained tight-lipped.

"Lacroix is clearly bent on a course of action," Wilde continued, "and he will not be swayed. Furthermore—and this brings me to the central point of this meeting—Lacroix told the federal minister that if Canada or the United States attempts to intervene militarily to stop him, he will call on France and the Soviet Union for assistance. The wording of his remarks suggests that he has already had secret discussions to this effect with both countries."

"The son of a bitch," ejaculated the Vice President. "Who the hell does this guy think he is?"

"More to the point, can he pull it off?" asked General Wilson.

"From the factors we programmed into the computer, it appears he can't, unless there is something we don't know about," replied Wilde. "But I shall let the Secretary of Defense speak to that."

Secretary of Defense Ronald Vaughan sifted through a stack of papers in front of him and pulled out two documents. He joined Lawrence Wilde on the podium and coughed theatrically into his fist before speaking.

"Thank you, Larry. First, regarding France. France, as we know, has vital interests in Quebec. But even so, we don't believe that any threat of French military intervention should be taken seriously. The French independent nuclear capacity, to put the worst case analysis, is pretty feeble compared with our own. In conventional terms they would be no match for the Canadians, let alone ourselves. Their logistical problems would be too great to sustain anything more than token skirmishes at battalion strength over a period of no more than one week. As a nation, the

French are extremely vulnerable to retaliation. They would have to be out of their skulls even to think of standing up against us. And they aren't crazy over there. Troublesome, yes, but not suicidal. Any support they might give to Quebec would be purely symbolic—a squadron of Mirage jets without French pilots or, perhaps, a nuclear submarine to show the flag in the Gulf of St. Lawrence. *Le Tonnant,* one of their SNLE class, is in the North Atlantic now. But if it came to the crunch we believe they would back off and head for home."

"With their tails between their legs," added the President gleefully.

"That makes good sense," said General Wilson. "But what about the Soviets?"

"They're a different ball game, General. May we have the house lights raised?" The Secretary of Defense was warming to his subject, and he wanted the attention of the meeting.

"The Russians, unlike the French, don't appear to have any vital interest in Quebec. But the opportunity to stir up some serious trouble in our back yard must be very tempting to them. Ever since we wooed Egypt and Somalia out of their orbit, they've been dying to have a go at us. Also, the new regime in Moscow has been extremely aggressive of late in the Mediterranean, the Middle East, and Africa. You know the Russians, they always have to prove something. They could miscalculate over Quebec, and we'd have a serious confrontation on our hands."

"Have there been approaches to the Kremlin?" asked General Wilson.

"We haven't wanted to alert the Russians to our concerns. It would be like handing them a loaded revolver with the safety catch off," interrupted Lawrence Wilde. "But it has come up in the normal ambassadorial horse-trading."

"What you're saying, Mr. Secretary of Defense, is that we could have another Cuban Missile Crisis on our hands." Brooks Dare, the deputy assistant to the President, voiced the thought in everyone's mind. The oldest official on the Council, he had been at the State Department when John Kennedy had faced down the Russians two decades earlier.

"Potentially worse," said Vaughan. "That would depend on how far the Soviets are prepared to go. The hardware they have at their disposal today makes the stuff they sent to Cuba look like firecrackers. But far be it from me to play the alarmist, gentlemen. Our assessment is that Moscow would not risk all-out war over Quebec. As I said, their vital interests are not involved here. We read it that they'll do a good deal of saber-rattling, but in the end they too will back off. But just to cover all the bases, I should add that we're not as sure about this prognosis as we are about the French position. I think that sums it up, Mr. President."

"Thank you, Ron," said the President. "Any comments, gentlemen?" Both Wilde and Vaughan took their seats again at the table as the President looked around with the air of a man who felt he had absorbed everything there was to be gotten from the meeting and expected everyone else to feel the same.

"On the basis of what we've heard today, Mr. President, the risks of military intervention in Quebec by the United States are acceptable," said General Wilson, adding quickly, as an afterthought, "should you deem it necessary."

Several of the men around the table nodded their heads in agreement.

"Is that the consensus of the Council then?" asked the President.

"Just a minute, sir." Lawrence Wilde was on his feet.

"What is it, Larry?" There was a note of impatience in the President's voice.

"I think we've overlooked two important elements in this. One is world opinion. The other is the reaction at home to any move we might make in Quebec. As far as world opinion is concerned, you just don't go marching into another country these days. Gunboats went out of style with Palmerston. Just think what'll happen at the U.N. if we send the Marines into Quebec. The Soviets would have us signed, sealed, and delivered as the aggressor, and think what that would do to our years of patient bridge-building with the Third World. Because they're behind Quebec in this, fair and square. Poor little Quebec, being exploited by the English. If we cross that border with anything more lethal than a tennis racket, we might solve the Quebec problem to suit ourselves but we'd be creating a host of new ones. Black Africa would take a running leap at the

Russians, and we could kiss them good-by for at least twenty years."

"You have a point," said the President.

"We would also run a terrible risk at home. Our people still remember Vietnam and Cambodia. Campuses across the country would erupt if we went into Quebec. It'd be the nineteen-sixties all over again. With the press dumping on us from a great height. I would also remind you, sir, and I realize I'm overstepping my authority here, but Congress could get very sticky about this. They don't go much for undeclared wars."

"Goddammit," exploded the President, "how in hell am I expected to run the country and conduct foreign policy if I have to worry how the whole world's going to react every time I sneeze? I'm not going to play with my hands tied behind my back."

Lawrence Wilde moved quickly to mollify the President.

"I believe there is a way to neutralize these problems, sir."

"Well, what? Speak up, man."

"We get Canada to invite us in."

"What the hell are you talking about? Those imbeciles in Ottawa would never do that."

"They might, sir. Under the right circumstances. I'll talk to you about the mechanics later, if I may. The point is that the federal government would call on us in the event of UDI to assist Canadian troops in overthrowing an illegal and traitorous regime in Quebec and in the restoration of constitutional government. We could hardly refuse such a request from our closest ally and trading partner, could we? And the idea's salable both domestically and internationally. Black Africa condemned Britain for years for not intervening in Rhodesia to overthrow Ian Smith's illegal regime. They could hardly turn around and condemn us for helping Ottawa in doing exactly what they demanded of Britain. We'd have them and the Soviets in a neat bind. And I'm convinced the same argument would work here at home. Especially if our intervention were massive, neat, and, above all, fast."

A slow smile spread across the Presidential features. "I like it. A good game plan, Larry. It makes sense.

But how do we get Ottawa to agree to help us legitimize it? They'd be scared that once we were in we'd stay."

"I don't think so. I think we could get their cooperation, sir. May I move to adjourn this meeting of the Council temporarily. I'd like a private discussion with you, and then we could reassemble for your final decision."

"All right." The President pushed his chair back. "Thank you, gentlemen. I'd like you all back here in one hour's time."

"Would you fasten your seat belt, sir. We're beginning our descent into Montreal's Mirabel Airport." The stewardess leaned over Antoine de Luzt and helped him locate the buckle end. De Luzt looked at his watch. It was just over three hours since the Concorde supersonic jet had taken off from Orly Airport in Paris. The plane's needle nose was in the landing position. From the ground, it looked like a great bird of prey. A triumph of aviation technology, de Luzt thought.

"And your table in the upright position, sir." De Luzt shuffled the pamphlets and literature on the Quebec Winter Carnival which he had been studying on the flight across the Atlantic.

"You sound like a sergeant major, my dear, barking out orders."

The stewardess reddened.

"It's IATA regulations, sir, not mine."

"Of course. Tell me, have you received confirmation of the executive jet I ordered for Mirabel?"

"Yes, sir, the captain says it will be on the tarmac for you when we land. We've made arrangements for immediate customs and immigration processing. You should be airborne within half an hour of landing."

"Splendid. I would like to say thank you by way of dinner, but I'm afraid I must go directly to Quebec City. Another flight perhaps."

The woman's brittle façade cracked for a moment as she allowed herself to smile.

"You almost asked me to dinner, and I almost accepted. I hope you had a pleasant flight, sir."

The Lear jet was waiting at the airport as promised. De Luzt met the customs and immigration officials in a mobile lounge en route to the terminal building. He had nothing to declare—he was a French businessman, visiting the Quebec Winter Carnival on holiday. Clearance was prompt, and the small executive jet was airborne twenty-seven minutes after the Concorde's touch-down.

The trip to Quebec City took only forty-five minutes, a fast hop over an undulating carpet of snow. On landing, de Luzt paid the pilot in cash and beat a hasty retreat to the terminal to escape the biting wind that sliced across the tarmac. Inside the building, dressed in a beaver hat and coat, was Monique Gravelle. Lovely as ever, de Luzt thought as she hurried to him. They embraced and Monique broke away to look up into his face.

"It's been a long time. It's so good to see you, Papa."

The Prime Minister of Canada awoke from a shallow, troubled sleep believing it was morning. He looked at his bedside clock: 1:35 A.M. There was someone moving about in his room.

"Who's there?"

"It's me, sir, Martin, sir, I'm terribly sorry to wake you." The portly figure of the Prime Minister's butler took shape against the windows. "The American ambassador, sir. He's downstairs."

"What? At this hour?"

"He says he must speak with you. It's vital. He instructed me to wake you, sir."

The Prime Minister had a premonition of disaster. Ambassadors did not go around rousing heads of government in the middle of the night unless the situation was critical.

"All right, Martin. Tell him I'll see him in five minutes. Make us some coffee, will you?"

The butler withdrew. The Prime Minister snapped on his bedside light and reached for his robe and slippers. He was still groggy from sleep. He went into the bathroom and splashed cold water on his face. All the while, he speculated on the catastrophe for which the American ambassador had wakened him. The President had been assassinated? Russia had dropped the bomb on China? The Queen had been kidnapped? World War Three . . . ?

Ralston Bishop was waiting for him in the living room. Although he was formally dressed for an audience with the Prime Minister, it appeared that he too had had a late summons since his tie was not quite straight and one of his cuff links was undone. He stood up as soon as the Prime Minister entered the room.

"Mr. Prime Minister, please accept my apologies for having you wakened. I'm afraid it couldn't wait till morning."

"If we wanted to work office hours, Ralston, we would have become bankers. Now, what's the matter? Let's sit over here," he said, motioning toward two chairs.

"I've just gotten off the phone. A two-hour conversation with the President and the Secretary of State. They asked me to see you immediately and impress upon you the urgency of the matter."

"It's too early for riddles, Ralston."

"As you know, Mr. Prime Minister, the President is deeply concerned about the course of events in Quebec. Both he and the Secretary of State are convinced that Guy Lacroix will win the leadership convention next week."

"You don't have to have a crystall ball to predict that," said the P.M. wryly.

"They also believe that Lacroix will proclaim independence when he is sworn in as Premier."

The Prime Minister recalled Lafontaine's report. There didn't seem much doubt of that either. He waited for the ambassador to continue.

"Therefore the President and the Secretary of State feel we must have a contingency plan."

"Contingency plan? What are you talking about?"

The ambassador sensed that the ashen-faced man in the dressing gown sitting across from him was beginning to dig his heels in. He spoke more deliberately yet continued to invest his words with a sense of urgency.

"The President and the Secretary . . ."

"Yes, yes. I know whom you're speaking for. Let's have a little shorthand. Just say 'they.' "

"Very good, sir. They are sure that the Canadian federal government would not tolerate an illegal regime in Quebec City."

"I thought we'd been through this already."

The ambassador plunged ahead, ignoring the Prime Minister's remark. "They are sure the Canadian government would wish to take appropriate action to restore constitutional government in such a situation. Appropriate military action."

"The hell we would!" The Prime Minister could feel the blood rising in his cheeks.

"The President and the Secretary of State have authorized me to advise you that the United States would be pleased to assist Canada in this matter. We are prepared to offer tangible support. All you have to do is detail what tactical military units you need to supplement your Canadian forces."

"Have you all gone mad down there? I have no intention of sending troops of any kind into Quebec."

The ambassador looked uncomfortable. He had lived in Canada for many years. He found his present assignment distasteful.

"Mr. Prime Minister, I informed the President that you would reply in essence as you have done. His words to me were that this offer is not coming in the nature of a request."

"And what the hell does that mean?"

"It means . . . it means that the President is insisting this course of action be followed."

"Am I hearing you right, Mr. Ambassador? Insisting? Who in God's name does he think he is, insisting?"

"He thinks he's the President of the United States, sir. He also thinks he holds all the cards."

The Prime Minister was on his feet, rage boiling in his stomach. At this moment, the hapless butler appeared with a tray and coffee cups.

"Get out of here!" shouted the Prime Minister. He turned on the ambassador. "And what do you mean by that, all the cards?"

"The President has instructed me to tell you that unless events are orchestrated to follow the scenario I have outlined, he will be forced to reconsider the traditional benefits which Canada has enjoyed as a most favored nation of the United States."

"Such as?"

"The Auto Pact, which is once again working in your favor. Quota-free entry of most Canadian goods into the American market. The free flow of American investment capital into Canada. Canadian exemptions from our laws governing convention expenses, foreign travel, taxes. That's just a start."

The Prime Minister sat down heavily. The blood that had risen in anger now drained away as if an artery had been cut. This man with the crooked tie and the unbuttoned shirt cuff was warning him that the United States would lay waste to the Canadian economy if he did not obey a President diktat. Any restriction on Canadian trade with the United States—which amounted to almost thirty billion dollars a year—would be harmful to the economy. Severe action as threatened by the President could close down half the Canadian manufacturing sector within a year. Controls on the inflow of investment money would be equally devastating. Government and the private sector relied heavily on Wall Street for funds; if that well dried up, the government would be forced to make heavy cutbacks in its public spending, which would be politically unacceptable to the electorate. The Prime Minister was appalled by the President's threat.

"Ralston, I just can't believe this."

"Do you want to hear it from the President himself?"

"No, no. I'm sure you're quoting him as he would wish. But I tell you, we are not without retaliatory powers of our own. The closing of our markets to American goods would seriously harm your own industries, certainly in the northern states. Then there's our natural gas and oil."

"We've gotten along without them before, and we've lived with delays on the new pipelines for so long that frankly we've begun to bring on stream alternate supplies."

"We control the St. Lawrence Seaway, don't forget," countered the Prime Minister.

"If Lacroix gets in, it strikes me Quebec will control it."

"Lacroix could never deny us rights there."

"And we have treaty rights with you. We would take it extremely seriously if you were to break them unilaterally."

The two men stared at each other like bulls pawing the ground. It was the ambasador who made the first conciliatory gesture.

"Mr. Prime Minister, I suggest we stop fencing. The President and the Secretary of State have considered the alternatives very carefully. I have been instructed to tell you that the United States is prepared to accept the consequences of an economic blockade of Canada. And that such action, if you don't accede to the President's request, will be taken immediately. You realize, of course, that the mere mention of a blockade would cause a run on your banks and a stock-market crash."

The Prime Minister had no choice, and he knew it. Either he went along with the President's outrageous demand and risked a possible civil war, or the Americans would ruin Canada's economy, an action which in itself would most likely lead to the breakup of Confederation. A sickening choice, whichever decision he made.

"I must consult my cabinet," he said in a barely audible voice.

"The President is aware of that," pressed the ambassador. "He has instructed me to ascertain what your recommendation to them will be."

The Prime Minister felt like a butterfly, anesthetized and waiting for the pin to fix it to the wall. He buried his face in his hands. Someone once said that living next to the United States was like living next to an elephant: well, the elephant had just rolled over. He looked up at Ralston Bishop. "You can tell the President I will do as he requests. We will go into Quebec and call upon American units for assistance. God help us."

Taylor Redfern sat in the Jacques Cartier Lounge of the Château Frontenac nursing a Scotch and considering his next move. Carnival hilarity bubbled around him, but he was oblivious to the laughing women and their drunken escorts. The telex from Brian Windsor had made him more afraid than he had ever been in his life. The vague sense of menace he had experienced over the past months now had a name and a history: Antoine de Luzt. He was convinced that de Luzt was the man behind the assassination of the Premier—of Touraine, too.

He was playing in the big leagues now, and he didn't even know the rules, if there were any. Antoine de Luzt was clearly an international agent acting on behalf of the French government, a brutal man with long experience in covert operations at the highest level. Redfern knew he was no match for such an adversary: what was a political reporter from a bankrupt Montreal newspaper doing meddling in affairs like this? What was one more murder to a man like de Luzt?

A drunken tourist stumbled against his table, spilling his drink. The man apologized vaguely and staggered off, repeating the performance at various tables in his path. Redfern used the beer mat to wipe the liquid off the table. He looked around for a waitress, but there was none to be seen. He shrugged, tossed a bill on the table and left. The lobby of the gigantic nineteenth-century hotel, which stood like a fortress over the city, was crowded. He wandered past brightly lit boutiques toward the writing room, looking for some solitude. He thought again of calling the RCMP, but once more he rejected the idea. The pieces were tumbling into place. If he could locate Monique Gravelle again, he was convinced he would have his story. To go to the police now would be to give it to the world.

The writing room was quiet. From the high windows Redfern looked down from the heights of Cape Diamond to the ice-covered St. Lawrence. He watched the progress of the ferries as they broke their way through the floes in their passage from Quebec to Lévis, its sister city on the south bank. The tranquillity of the scene had a quieting effect on him. A few people were strolling late on the Dufferin Terrace boardwalk, which overlooked the river. But the bitter February cold kept most holiday-makers inside. The river itself was choked with ice, except for the inky swirls of water where the ferries had gouged their way through. The lights of Lévis glimmered in the darkness, cheerful and welcoming. Redfern looked down river toward Île d'Orléans. A great silver disc of a new moon had risen; its ghostly light reflected off the snow.

He considered the possibility of buying a gun in the morning. He had carried a knife for protection for a while but had thrown it down the garbage chute when he realized how silly that was. A small gun might give him more confidence, except that he had never fired one in his life. He would probably end up shooting himself in the foot. In any event, hand guns were not so easy to purchase in Canada these days. New federal gun-control laws were being strictly enforced. A police permit was necessary before purchasing one. Forget it.

A crowd of noisy revelers barged into the writing room singing "Alouette" at the top of their lungs. Redfern pushed his way through them and out of the room. He wandered through the hotel until he found a quiet bar tucked away at the rear. He checked to be sure the tourists had not found it. There was a handful of solitary drinkers, so he decided to join them. He ordered a double Scotch and settled down to get quietly drunk.

It was past midnight when he wove his way back to the lobby. At the elevator he could hardly focus on the illuminated numbers. He groped unsuccessfully for the button as a man and a young girl entered behind him. The couple began to kiss and fondle each other as soon as the doors closed. Sheepishly, Redfern asked them to press number nine for him. The girl laughed and Redfern inspected his shoes for the rest of the ride. The elevator stopped at the ninth floor, and he stumbled out. He could hear the girl's laughter as he negotiated the corridor to his room.

It took him a few minutes to find his key. He had to turn all his pockets out, twice. He finally found it, wrapped in his handkerchief. He fumbled with the key and managed to insert it in the lock. The room rocked slightly as he closed the door behind him; he felt as if he were on one of those ferries bumping through the St. Lawrence ice. He staggered toward the bed; his eyes were killing him. He cursed his contact lenses. He wasn't going to make the same mistake he had made in London. Steadying himself, he made his way to the bathroom and switched on the light. He grasped the bottle of eye drops and unscrewed the top. He could feel himself swaying. With as much concentration as he could muster, he squeezed the rubber-tipped dropper and lifted it from the bottle. His hands shook, and just as he was about to bend his head back to administer the drops, the bottle spilled over his hand and slipped through his fingers. It smashed on the floor.

"Goddammit," he muttered. As he stared at the broken glass on the floor, he saw smoke rising from the puddle. At the same time he became aware of a sharp burning sensation on the back of his hand where the liquid had touched him. Immediately, he turned on the cold-water tap and thrust his hand under it. With a sudden shock of recognition Taylor Redfern, as drunk as he was, realized that someone had tried to blind him.

"How do I look?" Antoine de Luzt, with the bearing of a
Legionnaire, stood erect in front of the mirror, admiring
himself in his carnival costume.

"Like a lobster in a loincloth." Monique laughed.
She got up from the hotel bed and adjusted the sash
around his waist.

"For one thing, it ties at the side, not in the front. You
men have no dress sense."

"A little respect, if you don't mind," de Luzt said in
mock seriousness. He turned again to the mirror. "Yes, I
admit that's an improvement."

"Of course it is. Here, let's see how you look in the
balaclava." She tossed him a black wool headcovering
from the suitcase. De Luzt pulled it over his cropped gray
hair. Immediately he was transformed into a dark, menacing presence. Only his eyes and mouth were visible through
apertures in the woollen garment.

"You're sure this is what they wear? I feel like a
hijacker in this," he said in a muffled voice.

"No, it's perfect. Especially tonight," said Monique.
"They said on the radio there'd be snow and subzero
temperatures for tonight's carnival parade. You should see
some of the creations they'll be wearing against frostbite.
Don't worry. You'll be like everyone else."

"Good." De Luzt slapped his stomach in the mirror.
"A fine disguise." He pulled the balaclava from his head.
"So our little surprise for Mr. Redfern did not work." He
begun unwinding his sash.

"When I called his room this morning, it was he who
answered. He'd be in a hospital or looking for a guide dog
if it had."

"What did he say?"

"I hung up, of course, as soon as I recognized his voice. Either he hasn't used the drops yet or he found the acid in time. If he did, he's going to get smart."

"Well, I've dealt with more formidable adversaries than Mr. Redfern. He's by nature a gentleman. He doesn't have the instincts of a street fighter."

De Luzt began to rummage about in his suitcase, and from it he withdrew what looked like a long knitting needle —except that it was triangular in cross section, and, one inch above the point, the planes were grooved. The edges were surgically sharp. He fitted a short wooden handle to the end and secured it with a metal collar. Monique watched fascinated as he took the top off his white carnival cane and slid the triangular blade into it. With the slightest pressure the metal collar fitted snugly against the top of the sheath. He held the wooden handle under the tap in the basin for a while and then pressed the white cane top over the wood. As the wood expanded, it would wedge securely into the cane top. He held the cane up to the light to inspect his handiwork.

"If you didn't know, my dear, you could never tell. The perfect carnival weapon."

The curtains of Taylor Redfern's hotel room were drawn. The door was locked and the chain in place. In front of him on the table was a small tape recorder. He held the microphone in his left hand, as his right was heavily bandaged and throbbed painfully. When the cassette clicked to the end of side one, he put the microphone down. With his good hand, he turned the tape over and continued his dictation in a voice devoid of all emotion.

The black circles under his eyes testified to his sleepless night. He had been forced to call the hotel doctor—a diffident man who did not take kindly to being disturbed at one o'clock in the morning.

The physician had treated his hand with a soothing cream, wrapped it in gauze, and bound it in a thick crepe bandage. He advised Redfern to have it seen to in a couple of days. Redfern had felt he owed the doctor an explanation and mumbled about his car breaking down; the acid from his battery had leaked and it ran over his hand. The doctor nodded and then shook his head as if to say it didn't really matter. They could both smell the acid fumes wafting in from under the bathroom door.

When the doctor had gone, Redfern lay awake, staring at the ceiling and thinking of the agony if one of those drops had touched his eyes. He reacted to every sound in the corridor now, the low moan of the elevator and the periodic clunk of the steam radiator. Several times, he contemplated throwing his clothes into a suitcase and running; but he felt drained of energy. He couldn't lift himself off the bed. The doctor had tied the bandage too tight and the burn throbbed under the gauze. He decided not to loosen it, because the pain kept him awake and he was terrified of falling asleep. At one stage, he picked up the telephone to call Lois in Vancouver, but he was afraid his voice would betray him.

Toward dawn, he fell into a sleep of exhaustion and dreamed of faceless men with empty eye sockets pursuing him down endless corridors of ice. Gigantic animals with ravenous jaws reared up at him in frozen attitudes of attack. He awoke trembling and covered in sweat. Shortly after eight, as he dozed, the telephone screamed in his ear. He sat up in terror and lifted the receiver to stop its nerve-jangling ring. There was no voice at the other end. In a panic, he smashed it down and broke the cradle.

With a sudden compulsion to commit everything he knew to paper, he ran to his typewriter. Everything must be documented in case something happened to him. He began to type furiously with both hands, but the pain was too great. He tried to use his left hand only, but the speed of his thoughts outran his fingers and he pushed the machine away with a cry of frustration. He was shivering uncontrollably although the room was well heated. He threw on his overcoat and, keeping his wounded hand hidden, took the elevator to the hotel lobby. In one of the shops selling electronic equipment, he purchased a tape recorder and a half dozen cassettes on his company credit card and brought them back to his room. Methodically, he numbered the tapes and wrote his name and the date on each. He began to dictate the sequence of events which had led him to Quebec, from the day of the Premier's assassination to the previous night's episode with the acid bottle.

He incorporated everything, his suspicions, his nameless fears, even his love for his wife. On the final tape he dictated the telexes from London. Finally he said, "This is the complete and truthful testimony of Taylor Ellis Redfern, journalist, of Montreal. Should anything happen to me . . ." He paused and thought for a moment. He listened to the hum of the machine, which seemed to await the rest of the sentence. But he pressed the stop button and rewound the tape. He played the tape back, and when he came to "journalist of Montreal" he pressed the record button to erase what followed. He took the final cassette from the recorder and stacked it on top of the rest. The whole story was there, imprinted on those yards of flimsy brown tape. The sight of the plastic containers, so square and neat, made him feel curiously calm.

The question now was, what to do with them? He couldn't carry them with him. The acid bottle had proved to him how vulnerable his room was. He thought of sending them to the Prime Minister's office in Ottawa. But they might end up in the hands of some bureaucrat who wouldn't even bother to listen to them. Finally, he took a large brown envelope from his briefcase and painfully scrawled across it the name and office address of Cameron Craig. He took the cassettes out of their plastic boxes and dropped them into the envelope, sealed it, and stuffed it into his inside jacket pocket. He then picked up the phone and dialed the Air Canada reservations office. He would be on a flight out of Quebec City with a connecting link to Vancouver by three o'clock. As far as Taylor Redfern was concerned, the file on the assassination conspiracy was closed. He was getting out with his life.

The Oval Office looked rather like the nerve center of a war room: briefing maps stood on easels in a semicircle around the President's desk. In the middle was a large-scale plan showing all of Eastern Canada and the United States. Several locations were circled in yellow, red, and green. The smaller maps showed strategic areas in greater detail; on these were magnetic counters suggesting the deployment of men and armor.

Colin Dempster, the National Security Advisor, was outlining the principles of Operation Nighthawk to Lawrence Wilde; to Secretary of Defense Ronald Vaughan; to the Chairman of the Joint Chiefs of Staff, General Henry Wilson; and to the President himself.

"The key to the whole operation, Mr. President, is surprise. A quick, surgical thrust. We must secure all the strategic military installations—they're the ones marked in red on the map—within zero plus four."

"You mean we've got four hours," interrupted the President.

"Yes, sir. Central communications points and paramilitary positions—police stations and the like, sir—are marked in green. These are to be secured within six hours. The principal Quebec government offices, marked here in yellow, must be taken within two hours.

"It is essential that there be as little bloodshed as possible. The people of Quebec must be convinced from the outset that resistance is counterproductive. The entire operation must have the appearance of a move to restore constitutional authority in the province, not an attempted invasion."

"What about the media?" asked Lawrence Wilde.

"I was just coming to that. Use of domestic media will be extremely important in this connection. All commercial radio and television stations in the province will be ordered off the air. CBC stations, French and English, will remain on the air, but all programming will originate from Ottawa. Privately owned stations will be given specially recorded cartridges, sound only, instructing listeners and viewers to tune to the CBC for emergency information."

"What's the CBC going to say?"

"The Prime Minister will have recorded a message advising the people of Quebec to remain calm. He will say that combined Canadian and United States forces have entered Quebec for their protection and to assist in the restoration of legitimate government in the province. He will stress that we are joining the Canadian troops at his specific request. This message will be on a repeat pattern. Television will carry the same tape with a smiling still of the Prime Minister."

"The son of a bitch," murmured the President.

"Key political figures of the Parti Québécois and potential agitators will be taken into protective custody," continued Dempster. "The publication of all newspapers in the province will be suspended and a curfew imposed from dusk to dawn. This information will be part of the Prime Minister's message. He will also announce that he is invoking the War Measures Act."

"What about the Canadian armed forces? What's their role precisely?" inquired General Wilson.

"They have two assignments. The first is to assist our forces in securing military bases in the province. Units known to be loyal to Ottawa—that is, English-speaking units—will pinpoint and isolate those units whose loyalty may be questionable under the circumstances so that our men can contain and neutralize them. The Department of National Defence in Ottawa is already taking steps to ensure that there will be sufficient loyal manpower within each of the Quebec bases to make this possible."

"How are they doing that?" asked Wilde.

"They have transferred small, tactical English-speaking units into the province, ostensibly for training purposes. Most of the Royal Twenty-second Regiment, which is basically French, will have been airlifted to Ankara to take part in a NATO exercise in Turkey. That kind of thing."

"What's their other assignment?" The President smiled for what seemed like the first time in weeks.

"To maintain a high profile in the occupation of civilian installations. Most of our units will be under the nominal command of a Canadian officer. I say nominal because they will, of course, be responsible to their own officers. The point is that the Quebeckers will be less likely to offer resistance if they see Canadian troops in action rather than ours. We trust this will alleviate the possibility of open rebellion, which could lead to civil war."

"Okay, it's good. Now how do we pull it off militarily?" asked the President, visibly brightening with each new detail.

"I think General Wilson can give you a better picture of that, sir."

"We have been quietly moving crack contingents of Green Berets and Marines into Plattsburgh Air Force Base in New York State, and Loring Air Force Base in Maine over the past few weeks, sir," began General Wilson. "Many of these men have had Vietnam and Cambodian experience. The best. We've also been shifting several hundred transport helicopters into these bases and some Hercules transports as well. Forces in sufficient strength will be airlifted by transport planes and helicopters from each base at precisely the same time. They will arrive at civilian and military airports in Montreal within forty minutes and within seventy minutes in Quebec City. In the meantime, loyal Canadian units will have secured all air-fields and radar stations to ensure the safety of our men. And, of course, to make sure the alarm is not raised by the movement of aircraft across the border. Once on the ground, all units will move to secure their objectives. As soon as this phase of the operation has been completed, the RCMP will move in to arrest key figures before they go underground. Quite frankly, sir, I believe it will be as simple as a turkey shoot. The operation would begin, weather permitting, at midnight. By noon the same day, our forces should be in complete control. We just await your signal."

The President slapped the desk in front of him. "Well done, gentlemen. You've done a great planning job. I'm convinced Operation Nightwalk will work, both militarily and politically. I know how anxious you must be, General, to move from the theoretical to the practical, but we are still working on a contingency basis. If Lacroix should lose the convention or back down from his UDI plans, we put it on ice. There's to be no move until I give the direct order. Is that clear?"

"Absolutely, sir."

"You're frowning, Larry."

"No, sir. I just hope it doesn't come to that, that's all."

"Well, we must protect our interests, gentlemen. Thank you, you may go. Larry, I'd like to have a few words. I want to review with you the wording of our statement to the U.N."

The steeply raked copper roofs of the Parliament buildings in Ottawa, weathered green over the years, afforded the only color to the Gothic façade with its self-important towers and unnecessary arches—a symbol of permanence in a changing world, but permanence based on a Victorian model. John Penny, the Minister of Agriculture, stared out the window of the Prime Minister's office and thought how out of place these buildings were in the twentieth century. He could see all the way down to the bottom of Parliament Hill, where the eternal flame danced like a flag in the wind of a freezing February day. The gas-fueled flame had been lit in 1967 to commemorate the centenary of the Canadian Confederation; from his angle the action of the wind appeared to blow it out, but it fluttered upright gamely again. How vulnerable it seems, he thought, as he turned from the window to confront the Prime Minister once more.

The man behind the desk, his leader for five years, his friend for longer than he cared to count, had aged dramatically over the past two months. He looked ill and burned out. Penny hated himself for attacking again, but it had to be done.

"I'm sorry, sir, but I can't go along with it. How can you allow the Americans to take over like this? After all you've stood for. Look at that flame out there."

"Come on, John," said the Prime Minister wearily.

"No. Listen. That centennial flame. That stands for one hundred years of our history of self-determination. And you look at the wind trying to snuff the thing out. Well, it can't. But I tell you, the Americans can—if you let them dictate to you."

The Prime Minister heaved a great sigh that embraced his political dilemma and his personal fatigue. He knew his life as an active politician was finished. Even old friends and colleagues like John Penny were treating him like a pariah. Whatever the outcome of the Quebec convention next week, he knew he would no longer be leader of the party or head of the government within three months. Those were the political realities. Yet there were still some battles to be fought. John Penny had the authority and respect to challenge his leadership and lead a cabinet revolt against his decision to accept the American diktat. That could only result in more far-reaching consequences for Canada than Washington's plans.

"Do sit down, John. It's difficult talking to you when you're pacing up and down."

The minister took a chair by the desk.

"For many years, all my life I guess," said the Prime Minister slowly, "I've believed in the independence of this country. Oh, I've recognized our vital links with the American economy and the need to keep more or less in step with Washington's foreign policy. That's politics, the art of the possible. But I also saw us as masters of our own destiny in most essential areas. I supported the initiatives that ended in our establishing links with China and Cuba long before the Americans. I supported controls on American investment in our industry and resources. You may recall I was one of the most vocal opponents of a continental energy system. Because I've always believed we should hold our reserves against *our* future domestic needs rather than sell them off to the Americans. And I've been proven right. I supported the legislation that drove *Time* magazine out of Canada and helped build a healthy magazine industry here. I guess when I come to write my autobiography I can say I was something of an economic nationalist—but never to the point of foolhardiness. I've always been pragmatic. And damn it, we made tremendous strides in fostering our own sense of economic and cultural identity during those years. I suppose on that tenuous thread I wove a flag which obliterated everything else. I thought we were becoming masters in our own house— that's ironic, isn't it? It's exactly the same slogan the Québécois used. That's what I thought, that we were free to handle our own affairs at home and abroad without interference."

The Prime Minister paused and took a deep breath. John Penny waited for him to continue.

"Well, I have to admit that I was wrong. Disastrously and fatally wrong. I failed to see that none of the issues we stood up to the Americans on was really vital to their national interest. All of them were areas in which they could afford to pay lip service to the idea of Canadian independence, however reluctantly. My whole political philosophy, my whole career was built on a false assumption, and now I have to pay the price. You've seen what's happened. The Americans find themselves faced with events in Canada which they regard as highly detrimental to their security. They have violently disagreed with the way my government proposed to handle those events. They're not prepared to back down, so they've done what they've always been capable of doing in the crunch. They've picked us up by the scruff of the neck and given us a good shaking. I'm sorry, John, that's the reality of the situation. If this government chooses to resist, the result will be far worse for Canada than acquiescence."

"But why did you agree to this, Mr. Prime Minister?

You don't have to be their hatchet man. The country will not think the less of you if you resign. At least you would be stepping down on a matter of high principle."

"Someone will have to do it, John. My career is finished anyway. If I resign now, I'd simply ensure that my successor is ruined as well. Because whoever he is, he'll find that there's no other option. I'm not being a martyr, but I'd rather have the can tied to my tail than allow it to happen to you or Avery Walton or whomever."

John Penny studied the drawn face of the Prime Minister. In abrogating his leadership, he seemed diminished physically, yet Penny felt an overwhelming sadness for the man who was destroying himself in the belief that he was helping his country. "All right," he said, avoiding the Prime Minister's eyes. "You have my support."

Great clouds of snow driven on the wind swirled around Quebec City. From his window in the Château Frontenac, Taylor Redfern peered down at the street below, but the blizzard virtually erased everything. At 2:00 P.M., just as he was about to leave the room for the airport, he received a call from Air Canada saying that Ancienne Lorette airport had been closed down and no flights in or out of Quebec were expected before the following morning.

The sickening movement of snow past his window heightened his sense of panic. The claustrophobic feeling of being imprisoned in his hotel room in a hostile city began to fray his nerves. He had to escape. He put a call through to the bus depot: all services had been suspended; highways leading out of the city were already impassable. The last train, which had left for Montreal at noon, had been forced to turn back. He was trapped in the city. And his life was in danger.

He felt he would go mad if he had to wait entombed in his hotel room until the snowstorm abated; and yet if he left the one secure place he knew, there was no telling what horrors awaited him in the blinding snow outside. There was only one thing he could do: go to the police.

He put on his overcoat and battled his way through the drifting snow to the police station down the hill from the Château Frontenac. The streets were all but deserted. The snow was drifting in deep waves. He sank up to his knees at each step. At the police station, the duty sergeant listened to his story impassively, glancing occasionally at his bandaged hand while sucking on the end of his pencil. He made no notes but passed Redfern on to a detective who questioned him at length about the whole affair. Redfern impatiently answered his questions until he realized that the man was not taking him seriously. With a shock of insight, he understood that he had been living with the conspiracy for so long that it was reality for him; to other people it must have sounded like the babblings of a madman. He suddenly recalled a piece of long-forgotten trivia —how many nuts and publicity-seekers had given themselves up to the police when John Kennedy had been assassinated.

"Listen, I'm not one of your crazies off the street," he said defensively. "I'm a journalist with the *Montreal Chronicle*." He reached inside his pocket for his press pass, but it wasn't there. He remembered he had left it in his briefcase at the hotel. "If you need proof you can call my editor, Cameron Craig. You can call collect."

"Sure," said the detective, doodling on his pad.

"You've got to believe me. My life is in danger. I need police protection."

"Mr., ah, Redfern. Every man we have will be on duty at the carnival parade tonight. All leave has been canceled. I couldn't possibly detail a man to you. I suggest you be your own protection, if you feel someone is after you."

"Not someone. A man called Antoine de Luzt. An international agent."

"Yes, yes. You should enjoy the carnival and forget about this."

Redfern laughed in spite of himself. The detective was treating him like a demented child.

"Surely they're not going to hold the parade in this weather?"

"They hold the parade in any weather. This is Winter Carnival. Enjoy yourself. It's not a time to worry."

Redfern trudged back to the hotel and locked and chained the door. He placed a call to Charles Watson, the RCMP lieutenant, but there was no answer. In desperation, he called Cameron Craig.

"Cam, this is Taylor. Before you start—"

"Taylor, if you're not in Montreal, you're fired, so don't tell me where you are."

"Cam, for Christ's sake, shut up and listen. I can't tell you on the phone what's going on. I'm in Quebec City at the Château Frontenac."

"Are you all right?" Craig's ebullient manner turned instantly to one of concern.

"I'm in trouble, Cam. This phone might be bugged. I don't know. I've got to get out of this town, but it's snowed in."

"Yeah, I heard on the news. Now listen to me carefully. There's a guy in Quebec named Armand Corriveau. He's the editor-in-chief of *La Voix du Québec*. He'll be in the book. Tell him I told you to call. He's an old friend. Ask him to put you up at his home until you can get out of the city. If he wants to talk to me, tell him to phone. Meantime, I'll see what I can do for you at this end. In this blizzard I don't know what, but I'll try. But get to Armand."

"Thanks, Cam."

The snow had slackened now, though the evening clouds, a gun-metal gray, promised another bout. Redfern riffled through the phone book, searching for Armand Corriveau's number. As he did, he could hear the sound of carnival revelers singing on the sidewalk below his window. He found the number and dialed. Corriveau told him to come immediately. He ordered a cab and a bellboy to collect his luggage since his injured hand prevented him from carrying anything. As he waited for the bellboy, he looked down on the growing crowd of revelers gathering in front of the hotel, laughing and singing in anticipation of the parade which would be starting shortly.

They were warmly dressed in parkas and ski suits, and most wore balaclavas on their heads. Carnival canes were much in evidence and they were already being drained of their sustaining alcohol. Some youngsters were wrestling in the snow. Snowballs were flying around the square. Everyone seemed to be having a grand time.

There was a knock at the door. Redfern unchained and unlocked the door for the bellboy. But instead, he found himself staring at Monique Gravelle, wrapped in her fur coat, and a tall man in a red Hudson's Bay coat, wearing a black balaclava. On reflex, he took a step backward and slammed the door in their faces. But the man's hand caught it before the lock engaged and forced it open. He stepped into the room, and Monique followed. She drew a small pistol from her purse. Redfern flattened himself against the wall, breathing heavily.

"Mr. Redfern, I believe. Allow me to introduce myself. My name is Antoine de Luzt. I understand you have already met my daughter, Monique. Why don't we all sit down? I think it's time we had a talk."

Antoine de Luzt pulled the balaclava from his head and motioned to Redfern with sinister politeness to sit at the writing desk. The reporter's eyes darted around the room looking for an avenue of escape. He began to shake uncontrollably as de Luzt moved two armchairs between him and the door.

"My dear," said de Luzt to his daughter, holding a chair for her with elaborate courtesy. Monique had the silver-plated revolver trained on the journalist even as she unbuttoned her fur coat and sat down.

"You've aroused my curiosity, Mr. Redfern," said de Luzt affably, as he took the chair next to his daughter. He slid the carnival cane from his sash and placed it on the floor beside him. "It's very rare that anyone gets so close to me or one of my operatives. I flatter myself that we run a discreet operation. I'd be interested to know how you managed it."

"Go to hell," Redfern spat back at him. "You're discreet enough to try to blind me!"

"A warning to stay away."

"What kind of a sadist are you?"

"Come, Mr. Redfern, that's not very polite. I'm paying you a compliment in my own clumsy fashion." De Luzt smiled. "I'm most impressed by your diligence. You're a professional, like myself. I admire that."

"Thanks for nothing," responded Redfern, trying to mask his fear.

"I'd really like to know how you found out about us." De Luzt pressed the point. He needed to discover the weakness in the Quebec operation to make sure that the same mistakes weren't made again.

Redfern sat staring from father to daughter with a frown of defiance on his face.

"All right. Let me put it this way, Mr. Redfern. I'll make a deal wtih you. There must be some unanswered questions in your mind. I'll trade information with you. Your answers for mine."

"And then you'll kill me." Redfern said flatly.

"Perhaps. On the other hand, it may not be necessary. Our work is almost finished here. If what you have to say is satisfactory, perhaps a further deal can be negotiated." De Luzt had no intention of letting Redfern out of the room alive, but he needed the information. Men with a straw of hope can use it to build a fortress in their minds.

Redfern, for his part, had to keep the conversation going.

"Okay, it's a deal. But I get to ask my questions first. If I'm going to die, at least I want to get the full story."

"Journalists," said de Luzt to Monique, and they smiled at each other.

"Very well, Mr. Redfern, ask away." It doesn't really matter, thought de Luzt. He's a dead man anyway.

"The assassination of the Premier. Did you engineer it?"

"Yes, I must accept the credit. The plan was mine and Monique carried it through with consummate skill."

"How did you manage it? Did you buy Kevin Reilly?"

"Money? No. Far too crude. That type doesn't respond to money. Remember his background, Ulster Catholic. Study your Irish history, my friend. The Irishman is prepared to risk all for an ideal. A beautiful race. You don't buy people like that. You manipulate them."

"How did you find him?" Redfern forgot his fear under the rhythm of his cross-examination of de Luzt. His fascination for the story had rekindled.

"You have a good mind, Mr. Redfern. You ask the right questions."

"Should you be telling him all this, Papa?" It was the first time Monique had spoken since she had entered the room.

"Mr. Redfern has earned the right to know, my dear. We searched for the better part of a year for the right man. He had to be impressionable and a man of emotions. You know what I mean, a heart person rather than a head person. Not overly intelligent; otherwise he would have realized he was being used. He had to be capable of moral outrage, the kind only the Jesuits can instill in you. On a more practical level, he had to know firearms and reach for them instinctively. It goes without saying that he had to be heterosexual or Monique's charms would not have worked."

Redfern glanced quickly at Monique; her face was impassive. It struck him as indecorous that a father should discuss his daughter's sexuality in front of a total stranger.

De Luzt continued, "He had to be single, without close family ties. As you see, the requirements were very exact. We had a psychological blueprint, you might say, of the man we were looking for. Kevin Reilly was the perfect specimen. It took us a long time to find him."

"Then what? Once you had found him?"

"Then it was up to me," said Monique, with a wave of her revolver. "My father is an expert in behavior-control techniques. What I know, I've learned from him."

"You brainwashed Reilly?"

"Over a period of months, yes. First, I had to make him grateful to me. That was easy enough. He was a drifter. He lacked self-confidence. Especially with women. I only had to let him make love to me once. After that I was on a pedestal so far as he was concerned."

"You don't go out and shoot a man because of sex," countered Redfern.

"You know very little of life then, Mr. Redfern. Lust can be as strong a motivation as greed. The seven deadly sins," said de Luzt. "Seven old friends."

"Once he had formed an emotional attachment to me, the next step was to get him to depend on me for advice and direction. I started with small externals—like choosing his ties and telling him what clothes he should wear. Gradually, he came to trust me, and he allowed me to make other decisions for him."

"She was a very good pupil, don't you think, Mr. Redfern?"

"When I had established that kind of hold over him —he couldn't get up in the morning without asking me what he should be doing—it was just a question of sparking a sense of frustration and outrage in him."

"Tapping the black Irish soul, you might say, Mr. Redfern," added de Luzt. "The wellsprings of violence."

"That wasn't easy," said Monique. "Kevin was a very passive man. He let things happen to him. He wasn't a doer. I had to make him one. I had to plant the seed and make him think that it was in him all the time. I had to make him believe that the English in Quebec were the victims of a ruthless oppression. And then had to make him do something about it. Believe me, there were times when I thought the whole thing was wasted. He talked a lot, especially when he got drunk. But that's all he ever did. He was like that in bed too. If his father hadn't been fired as a night watchman because he couldn't speak French, I doubt if Kevin would have lifted a finger against anyone. I was lucky there. I played on that until he was ready to go out and shoot every French Canadian in sight. Then I had to make sure he shot the right one."

"You could say my daughter held the rifle and Mr. Reilly pulled the trigger."

"Incredible." Redfern could hardly believe what he was hearing. "Why, though? Why go to all that trouble to kill the Premier of Quebec? Why not just go out and get a hired gun?"

"You really do want your money's worth."

"You said yourself I earned the right."

"Why kill the Premier?" De Luzt asked the question as if he were about to conduct a seminar in political assassination. "Only the French government can answer that fully. I can speculate, though. I'm sure I don't have to tell you that the French have had an ongoing interest in the Quebec independence movement since it surfaced in the early nineteen-sixties. Ever since General de Gaulle's visit to Montreal in nineteen sixty-seven, it's been the policy to encourage the province in its bid for independence. How nice it would be for France to have an independent French-speaking republic in North America. We French, as you know, enjoy the idea of extending our power and prestige beyond our own boundaries.

"I know that for the last two or three years, Paris has felt a lack of conviction on the part of the Québécois. The government in the province appeared to be watering its wine. Our friend the late lamented Premier was moving toward a Canadian option rather than the bolder course of independence to which he was originally committed. Those who control the political destiny of France must have felt that an important opportunity was slipping away. Something had to be done, something dramatic, to push Quebec over the brink before the chance was lost. That is where I came in. At the invitation of certain individuals in the government, I have, in the past, performed some not inconsiderable services for France. I was asked to look into the matter. It was my assessment that if Quebec were to become independent, the Premier must be supplanted by Guy Lacroix. The question was, how to supplant the Premier? Politically, he was too entrenched to be removed. Assassination was the only course.

"As far as your second question is concerned, a hired gun wouldn't have worked. The killing had to appear to be politically motivated to give weight to Monsieur Lacroix's position. English Canadians, in an attempt to thwart the legitimate aspirations of the French Canadian people, had gunned down their leader. A simply political equation. But for it to be credible we had to have the right assassin —and what's more we had to ensure that the assassin would be immediately identified."

"And that's where Touraine came in, right?"

"Yes. The sight of twenty-five thousand dollars was too much for the man. He had never seen so much money in one place. He would have shot his own mother for it. I believe he smuggled it across the border to a New York bank. Maybe he felt it would be safer there."

"Did you have him killed, too?"

"I learned in Algeria, Mr. Redfern, that men whose loyalties are bought for money are the first to crack under strain. He might have said something to incriminate my daughter. Especially after you published that story on the payoff. Most inconsiderate of you. That's why we deposited him in your garage—as a warning. What a pity you didn't take the hint."

"But who killed Touraine?"

"There is a lot of muscle in Montreal, that's the word, isn't it? I believe you met one such in an alley. One of Monique's disreputable friends."

"You mean, La Discocave?"

"Run by a gang which controls much of east-end Montreal. I have made some generous contributions to them from time to time. Charity is always rewarded, Mr. Redfern."

"What about IntCon, how were they involved?"

"IntCon? They are businessmen; they look for opportunities. They were sitting on huge uranium deposits in Quebec and they saw the chance to exploit them."

"But weren't they involved in the assassination?" Redfern was still convinced of IntCon's complicity despite Holbrook Meadows's annihilation of his theory.

"No." De Luzt laughed. "They are probably not above it, though."

"What about the infrared night-sight on Reilly's gun?"

"We furnished Mr. Reilly with the best equipment available. I got that sight myself from a contact in Belgium. IntCon knew nothing of it, even though it was one of their classified items at the time."

"But I don't understand. IntCon did play a part in the affair."

"Oh yes, they threw over a million dollars at Lacroix when they saw what was at stake."

"What made IntCon so sure they could make a deal with Lacroix to develop their uranium?"

"You certainly ask a lot of questions, Mr. Redfern."

"Yeah, I've got time."

De Luzt looked at his watch. Monique was growing impatient.

"All right, but not much longer. The French government and IntCon had started secret talks. After our operation began in Quebec, France's prototype nuclear-breeder plant nearly blew up. The whole plant had to be closed down. The government had been counting heavily on that plant, and two more to follow, to fuel the chain of nuclear-power stations under construction across the country. And, of course, to enhance their military arsenal. When the plant failed, France was in a desperate situation. It needed unlimited supplies of enriched uranium at a time when the world wasn't selling. The Quebec situation began to take on a totally new dimension. There was all the uranium they could want sitting in the ground leased to IntCon. And the power necessary for the enrichment process was there at James Bay. If France could influence events to ensure Lacroix's victory, their needs could be met. My little project suddenly became the nation's number-one priority."

"So Monique was sent to work for Belmont to sabotage his campaign." Redfern turned to Monique. "And you put the finger on Raymond Mercier."

Monique shrugged her shoulders as if to erase the memory of the man.

"He could still win, you know. Belmont," said Redfern.

"I wouldn't put money on it, Mr. Redfern. By the time the convention opens, everyone in Quebec will believe Belmont is an embezzler who stole from his own campaign funds, falsified the books, and deposited large amounts in a Liechtenstein bank. It's all been arranged."

"No one will believe that," said Redfern.

"Frankly, it doesn't matter what they believe. The whiff of scandal at the convention will be sufficient to sink him. Now, I'm afraid you have exhausted your questions."

"Wait. Was it you in the press gallery that day, at the lying-in-state?" Redfern asked Monique.

"Yes. I heard you had talked with Kevin's parents. You were asking about me. I had you photographed. That's how they recognized you at La Discocave. The bartender had a photo of you under the counter that night."

"One thing I don't understand is how you were able to operate so freely. The contacts, the entrées, how did you manage it?"

"I've lived in this province for several years," said Monique. "I was a member of a separatist group at the University of Montreal with many of the people who are now in the government. When I came back here after my father took on this assignment, I had plenty of friends."

"How did you get Belmont to sign a reference for you?"

"I studied under him. I was his star pupil. He remembered me well."

"Mr. Redfern, I think we have been patient with you long enough," interrupted de Luzt. The air of ironic self-mockery was gone now. "It's time we heard from you. I want to know how you tracked Monique down and who else knows about her?"

"What if I don't tell you?"

"I believe we have a deal."

"I've just upped the ante. I want a guarantee of my life. Otherwise, I'll tell you nothing."

"Who else knows about Monique?" Redfern could see the sudden dilation of de Luzt's pupils as a charge of anger passed through him.

"I told you. I want a—" He felt the blow across his face almost before he saw de Luzt move. His mouth tasted of blood. De Luzt was standing over him, his hand raised to his shoulder. Monique sat languidly smiling in her armchair.

"I do not play games, Mr. Redfern. Either you volunteer the information I want, or you will force me to remember some techniques which proved extremely effective in Algeria."

Redfern, still stunned by the blow, gingerly felt his lips with the fingers of his good hand.

"What do you say?"

"Perhaps he needs a little more persuasion, Papa." Redfern cringed as de Luzt raised his hand, but before the blow fell there was a sharp knock at the door. All three of them froze. Then Redfern shouted, "Come in! Use your key!" Monique slipped the revolver into her coat pocket at the sound of the key in the lock. As the door swung open, Taylor Redfern leaped to his feet and bolted past de Luzt and Monique. With all his force, he grabbed the startled bellboy by his shoulders and threw him at de Luzt, who had vaulted over the chair after him. Redfern ran down the corridor to the fire stairs, which he negotiated four at a time. He could hear the sound of his footsteps ringing on the concrete. Was it an echo in the stairwell or was de Luzt behind him? He did not stop until he had reached the main floor nine stories below. He burst through a door into the lobby of the Château Frontenac, which was alive with carnival merrymakers escaping the bitter cold of the night outside.

Redfern jostled his way through the crowd. Over his shoulder he caught a glimpse of de Luzt emerging from the fire-stairs exit, the black balaclava once again covering his face. He began to thrash his way through the mob of people, who seemed to sway in front of him like a field of corn. He ached all over, and the cassettes in his jacket pocket dug painfully into his ribs with each contact. At the far side of the hall by the reception desk, Redfern spotted a hotel guard, but he was probably unarmed and with the crush of people he was almost impossible to reach.

He worked his way to the revolving doors and pushed his way into them. As the doors spun he was sucked into the freezing, black night.

The wind cut through the streets like a bacon-slicer. He had no overcoat, no hat or gloves. Only his sports jacket, which he wrapped around himself. He could feel the cassettes and he knew he had to get rid of them. He hurried along the icy sidewalk and under a stone arch to Place d'Armes, a small square in front of the Château.

The Carnival parade had begun. Crowds six deep, pressing together for body heat, ooh-ed and ahh-ed at the gaudily lit floats as they passed in procession. Ice duchesses and fairy-tale characters muffled up against the cold waved mittened hands at the spectators. A light snow fell, but not enough to spoil the view. Clowns and animal figures skipped along beside the floats, rushing into the crowd and dragging people into the street to dance with them. The giddy mood of celebration was all-pervasive, and if the bands marched only to the beat of drums, it was because metal mouthpieces would have frozen to the musicians' lips; but nobody seemed to miss the music.

Redfern stood shivering at the periphery of the crowd. The wind seemed to freeze the very marrow of his bones. He looked around for a way to escape, but all the streets in the area had been cordoned off and there were no taxis or cars in sight. The sidewalks on both sides of the road were choked with people; he would never be able to push his way through. He looked back and spotted the red-coated figure with the black balaclava darting through the crowd toward him. In a frenzy, he ran at the wall of people in front, fighting his way through until he reached the barrier. He clambered over it and tried to lose himself in the carnival parade. Immediately, he was grabbed by a giant rabbit with a fixed grin that danced him in circles until he was dizzy. He tore himself loose and rushed across the street, avoiding the ponderous floats and the mischievous Disney characters who skipped through the streets beside them.

As he stood for an instant looking for a break in the crowd of spectators, the major float of the parade, bearing the waving figure of Bonhomme Carnaval and the carnival queen, bore down on him. He dodged out of its way and, as it passed him, grabbed onto its side. The crowd roared as two parade marshals ran over and hauled him off the float. Before they could give the journalist a friendly warning, he sprinted off down the street. He had caught sight of de Luzt again, and he tried to break out of the street through the crowd. Half tripping, half sliding, he scrambled on his knees through the legs of spectators and burst out into a small park at the center of the square.

Suddenly, there were no more people in front of him. He turned back to see the heads of the parade watchers silhouetted against the lights of the floats. De Luzt was nowhere in sight. There was a red and white box in front of him bearing the legend *"Postes Canada."* Redfern took the envelope containing the cassettes from his pocket, and, though it had no stamps, he pressed it into the box with a feeling of relief.

He sat down on a bench and tried to collect his thoughts. What he needed now was a policeman. He strained his eyes in the darkness and thought he saw a patrolman on crowd-control duty at the bottom end of the park. Redfern ran toward him, sinking, knee-deep into snowdrifts with each stride, his feet numb from the cold. But he was going to be all right! De Luzt could do nothing once he had police protection.

The officer stood unmoving as Redfern, out of breath and hardly able to speak, ran up to him. The man was apparently engrossed in the parade.

"Thank God," said Redfern, pulling at his sleeve. "You must help me. There's a man . . ."

"Eh? Que voulez-vous? Parlez français."

Redfern stared into the man's face. His eyes were glazed, and he appeared to rock on his heels. He was dead drunk!

"Oui, oui, je parle français," Redfern nodded furiously, still holding the policeman by his arm. "Please, you must help . . ."

"Circulez, circulez . . . move along, move." The policeman motioned Redfern away with his nightstick as if he were a mosquito.

"But you must understand. Listen to me!" On the far side of the square, where he had entered it, Redfern saw the red-coated figure. "Oh my God!" He pulled at the policeman's arm.

"Aidez-moi . . . help me!"

Redfern made a lunge for the holster that hung from the man's belt. With frozen fingers, he grappled with the leather harness to get at the police revolver inside. The drunken policeman lurched backward, swearing at him, and began to strike out wildly with his nightstick. He caught Redfern a glancing blow across the back of his neck and the reporter fell to the ground. The lights began to spin, and hot tears of rage and frustration coursed down his cheeks. He staggered to his feet and forced himself to run. De Luzt had spotted him and was racing across the park in his direction.

Redfern headed for a small street which led off the square. The street was lined on both sides with ice sculptures. A circus elephant reared up on its hind legs, its trunk higher than the buildings behind it. A panther, painted black, its mouth a gash of red, eyed the reporter as he ran by. Dragons, whales, and sphinxes, dog teams and polar bears bore witness to his passage. Blackamoor heads mounted on twelve-foot poles leered down at him, mocking his pain and his terror.

He turned a corner and almost collided with the Carnival Express, a motorized train for people too lazy or too drunk to see the ice sculptures on foot. Several of its occupants were wrapped in blankets; some held out canes to him as he passed them like a long-distance runner.

The street now opened onto a huge plaza. Above him, a series of Bonhomme decorations turned slowly in the wind. In front stood the crystal battlements and towers of the ice palace, illuminated at its base and center with colored lights like a Disney castle. The frozen flags of the carnival cracked from flagpoles on each tower. Redfern looked back. The blackhooded figure of de Luzt dogged his footsteps, gaining on him as he ran. He staggered toward the palace, his sides aching and his lungs on fire from the effort of running.

The entrance to the ice palace was lined with an avenue of majestic ice sculptures, each a work of art in its own right. They seemed to form a passageway straight to the center of the palace. Redfern felt drawn to it, as if this winter fortress offered him sanctuary.

Inside, the palace was a maze of clear, shimmering blocks of ice. As soon as he entered, Redfern came to the sickening realization that he had trapped himself. There was no way out. He turned to retreat, but it was too late. De Luzt was running down the avenue of sculptures—his own personal blackhooded fury. In seconds, de Luzt would spot him.

Redfern turned and raced deeper into the palace, past sparkling walls of ice. He had expected to find crowds of people filing through the maze, but it was deserted. The play of light on the outside walls sent shards of color across his path. Through the translucent blocks of ice, he caught sight of de Luzt's red coat.

The refraction effect of the ice made it impossible to tell exactly where his pursuer was, however. Cautiously, Redfern moved away from the image of de Luzt, magnified by the ice and reflected by its many facets. But as he moved, so too did the red-coated figure, like a malevolent shadow. With a shock, Redfern realized that if he could see de Luzt's image in the ice, de Luzt could see his, too.

In a panic, he attempted to lose de Luzt by doubling back on his tracks, hoping to find the path that would lead him out of this frozen prison. He made a quick turn to the left, then to the right. The red-coated image appeared to diminish in size.

He edged his way down a corridor, watching the reflections of the ice walls. Suddenly, he could no longer see de Luzt. The corridor forked; he hesitated for a moment, then went to the left.

He immediately realized it was a mistake. The icy passage came to an abrupt end in a small chamber, like the center of a pyramid. The walls of ice soared fifteen feet around him, enclosing a square of velvety black sky. Along the base of the walls, set three feet apart, spotlights played upward on the ice, bathing the heart of the palace in primary colors.

There was only one way out, the way he had come in. But as he turned to run, the entrance was blocked by the hooded figure of Antoine de Luzt. For a moment the two men stood motionless, staring into each other's eyes: they became part of the ice structure around them. They made no sound. In the distance, Redfern could hear the drums of the carnival parade as it turned into the plaza. De Luzt advanced toward him, reaching for the cane at his side. Redfern tried to scream, but no sound came. He dug his fingernails into the wall of ice behind him as he watched de Luzt draw a long, thin blade from the cane. Redfern edged sideways, feeling the cold, slippery surface of the ice at his back, his fingers searching for the end of the wall.

"I'm sorry, Mr. Redfern." De Luzt moved toward him, the steel blade pointed at Redfern's chest.

"No, please," whispered Redfern, but his words were inaudible. Then, with the last of his strength, he launched himself at de Luzt, his hands extended to gouge his assailant's eyes. De Luzt stepped aside and the force of Redfern's momentum hurled him into the wall of ice on the opposite side of the chamber. He turned to see de Luzt bearing down on him, the thin blade aimed at his eyes. Desperately he dodged again, almost stumbling over one of the spotlights. It could be a weapon, something with which to defend himself. He knelt down and began to pull frantically at the deeply embedded fixture.

"I'm afraid it is of no use, Mr. Redfern." Antoine de Luzt was standing over him, the sword blade all but touching his neck. With a howl of desperation, Redfern turned and launched himself upward, grabbing de Luzt around the waist. De Luzt, momentarily thrown off balance, braced his right leg behind him and plunged the blade deep into Redfern's back. Redfern sank to his knees, a look of surprise on his face. He stayed there for several seconds in an attitude of prayer, his blood beginning to cover the ice in a spreading stain. Then, with a deep sigh, he fell forward.

De Luzt jerked the blade free and bent to turn Redfern over. Nothing must be left to chance; a second thrust through the heart would ensure permanent silence. He raised the blade to strike.

A piercing scream from the corridor stopped him. Four teen-aged girls were standing there, terrified. It would only be a few moments before they attracted others. Cursing, de Luzt leaped to his feet and ran toward them. The girls scattered in panic, falling over one another to get out of his way. De Luzt pushed past them and raced from the ice palace, quickly losing himself in the parade crowd outside.

Taylor Redfern lay in the middle of a warm, red pool, moaning softly.

A distant bell tower chimed the half hour. Jean-Claude Belmont had heard it mark the time throughout the night. He swung his legs out of bed and looked at his watch: 6:30. The morning sky was turning from gun-metal gray to shades of pink. There was movement outside his hotel room. He saw a morning newspaper being slid quietly under his door like some grotesque white tongue. He sat on the edge of the bed staring at it, acknowledging its presence but unable to pick it up.

Today could have been the pinnacle of his political life. Today the Parti Québécois convention could have elected him Premier of Quebec. Instead, he was isolated, publicly disgraced, and facing a possible criminal action which, if proven, could end in his imprisonment. He still could not fully grasp what had happened. . . .

Yesterday afternoon, the police had raided his campaign headquarters while he and most of his staff had been attending the convention's tribute to the late Premier. A receptionist and two volunteer sign painters were on the premises, but none of them had the presence of mind to demand search warrants; nor did they offer any resistance when the police broke into locked filing cabinets and took away cartons of papers and account books.

When Belmont heard of the raid, he immediately assumed it to be a crude attempt by Lacroix to discredit him on the eve of the convention vote. Lacroix, he reasoned, was not above using his Provincial Police connections for his own political ends. He saw the raid as an expression of Lacroix's insecurity—the Minister of Social Affairs might not have the leadership in his pocket after all. Certainly, the feeling on the convention floor was that it would be fairly close. Belmont's organization had done well in the rural ridings; he had drawn strong delegate support in such areas as Lac St. Jean, the Eastern Townships, the St. Maurice Valley, and Abitibi. If he could hold Lacroix to something approaching a standoff in the major urban centers—especially Montreal and Quebec City—he felt he had a chance of winning on the convention floor. The polls, which at one time had given Lacroix a commanding lead, had begun to reflect a modest swing to Belmont. He still trailed badly, but anything was possible at a convention.

Only after he received a call from a friendly reporter at *Québec-Matin* did Belmont realize the enormity of the charges against him. He stood accused of misusing campaign funds; accountants had been appointed to audit his books, and any irregularities could result in his arrest.

He had called an immediate press conference to deny any wrongdoing, but before the assembled journalists—who were delighted to have such a story to enliven the day—Belmont found himself at a disadvantage. Since the police refused to allow him or his staff access to the impounded ledgers, he had only his protestations of innocence to offer. When closely questioned on the matter of campaign funds, he could only answer that he had left the administration of the money to Raymond Mercier and, later, to Monique Gravelle. Mercier had resigned in disgrace, one of the radio reporters pointed out, and Monique Gravelle had disappeared mysteriously. Belmont had to admit that he did not know Monique's whereabouts; she had telephoned a week earlier and said her mother had been taken seriously ill and she had to return home. There had been smiles around the room when Belmont had added, "To the cynical mind, I know it would seem highly suspicious that the two principals involved in the bookkeeping are no longer on the scene. I promise you that I am not trying to impute blame on those who are not here to defend themselves, but I can assure you that I am innocent of any suggestion of financial impropriety." He knew as he said it that the press would crucify him.

The late-night television news had confirmed his worst fears. He watched in fascinated horror as film clips of the actual raid were shown. Obviously, the press had been tipped off in advance. A Provincial Police spokesman was quoted as saying that preliminary examination of the ledgers showed that entries had been carefully altered to conceal the siphoning off of substantial amounts of campaign money. Deposit receipts from a Liechtenstein bank had been found in a locked filing cabinet in Belmont's office. The total amount tallied roughly with the discrepancy in the ledgers. A complete audit, however, and a thorough investigation would be conducted before any criminal charges were laid. The news broadcast ended with some reaction from convention delegates. It ranged from concern to outright disgust.

The next few hours had been a frantic scramble as Belmont and his aides worked to produce a special statement to delegates for distribution at the convention. In it, he denounced the entire affair as a hoax, hinting that it had been spawned in Lacroix's camp as a means of sabotaging him. Belmont doubted that it would influence the delegates now, but there was little else he could do. He had to make some move to wipe off the mud.

The newspaper, protruding under the door, could not be ignored. He stood up and walked across the room like a condemned man. He recalled something his law professor had once said to him: they never remember the good you might have done, only the magnitude of your fall. He pulled the paper free and, bracing himself, flipped it open. The headline was even worse than he imagined it would be. Across eight columns it read: "Belmont Accused of Embezzlement."

The noise of the convention floor echoed around the hockey arena. The delegates engaged in ritual handshakes as they moved from group to group in a crazy quadrille more reminiscent of an Oriental bazaar than a meeting to elect a party-leader. The seats, which a few nights earlier had been filled with hockey fans, were now alive with delegates wearing straw hats and waving pennants in support of their particular candidate. The walls were decorated with bunting, and huge portraits of the dead Premier hung like totems from the rafters.

In a training room off the main hall, hastily transformed for the occasion into a convention site office, Jean-Claude Belmont pleaded with Gilles Boucher, the convention chairman.

"What do you want me to do, Gilles, get down on my hands and knees and beg?"

"Jean-Claude, what you're asking is beyond my power."

"Please, Gilles. The vote has got to be postponed."

A growing chant of "La-croix, La-croix, La-croix" could be heard rising in the arena outside.

"I can't do it. You know the rules. I don't have that kind of discretionary power."

"No, but you have the power to accept a motion from the convention floor. I could propose a motion postponing the vote until the status of the candidates is clarified. The convention is its own master. It can do anything it likes."

"Look. Even if I did accept such a motion, it would be defeated. Listen to them out there. They want to get on with it. You know what happens, the momentum of it takes over."

"Yes, but at least give me a chance. Once you accept the motion, I can speak to it. I could explain the circumstances. I could make them understand how unfair it would be, how dangerous even, to go ahead right now."

"Always the master of procedure, aren't you, Jean-Claude?"

"Then you'll do it?"

Boucher played with his gavel and thought for a moment. He had been selected for the sensitive role of convention chairman because of his impartiality. He was a colorless party man who owed allegiance to no one and, as such, was acceptable to both sides. What he lacked in intellect, he made up for in loyalty to the party.

Outside the training room a band struck up. Boucher had to shout to make himself heard.

"It would give you an unfair advantage. Any speech by you on such a motion would attract far more attention than anything Guy Lacroix might say. Candidates are allowed only one opportunity to address the convention. You had yours on opening night."

"Unfair advantage!" Belmont was no longer the dispassionate lawyer. His anger flared, and he pounded the table in front of him. "How the hell can you talk about unfair advantage after what Lacroix did to me yesterday?"

"Now, you don't know that Guy was in any way involved in that."

"For God's sake, man, take your head out of the sand. Who do you think tipped off the press? Little Red Riding Hood? Of course he's involved in it. All I ask is the chance to restore some semblance of balance."

Boucher shifted uncomfortably in his chair and occupied himself with his gavel.

"Well? What do you say, Gilles? Stop playing with that damned thing and answer me. The afternoon session is due to start in ten minutes."

Boucher tossed the gavel onto the table and hid his hands from view like a scolded child.

"All right, Jean-Claude." He frowned to give himself the appearance of gravity. "It's against my better judgment, but I'll do it."

Belmont flopped back into his chair. He smiled sadly at Boucher. At least, now he had a chance. The chant of "La-croix, La-croix" had died away, and he could hear his own name being taken up and hurled back like pebbles at the opposing camp.

"Thank you, Gilles. I won't forget this. Now, as to the wording . . ."

The convention floor was like hell's own circus. Rival bands hired by the two camps blared at each other at the threshold of pain. Lacroix's red and white placards bobbed up and down throughout the hall; Belmont's blue and gold were much less in evidence. All the razzmatazz that the public-relations firms could dream up had been focused on the convention floor, which now took on the appearance of a gladiatorial arena: girls dressed in the candidates' colors handed out red carnations for Lacroix and yellow roses for Belmont. Campaign buttons were distributed to anyone who would wear one. Students of such gatherings noted that Lacroix buttons far outnumbered those worn by Belmont supporters. Posters of the two men hung in equal number about the walls, in strict accordance with convention rules.

Belmont had attended many of these conventions; he knew what to expect, but as he entered the hall the pulse-quickening atmosphere of the occasion caused the adrenalin to run. In the past, he had been able to sense the mood and inclination of the floor just by standing there a few moments, but today he had lost confidence in his own judgment, and he looked around desperately for some physical signs of assurance. He found little satisfaction in the spontaneous delight exhibited by the Lacroix supporters, who shouted to each other and sang. His own faction was more subdued, waiting, analyzing, talking quietly. As he made his way through the crowd toward his special convention box, Jean-Claude Belmont felt his past slipping away from him like sand through an hourglass. A few members shook his hand and wished him luck as he passed, but many of the rural delegates pretended not to notice him and busied themselves in conversation with their colleagues.

His passage through the hall was marked by isolated clapping, but even the band bursting into his campaign song did not lift his supporters or wring cheers from them. Yet he walked proudly through the hall, smiling and nodding as he went. He reached his box and kissed his wife, who was already seated waiting for him. The photographers clustered around, sensing his torment, waiting for the confident façade to crack. Two radio reporters thrust microphones at him and asked how he thought the vote would go. "I may have something to say a little later," he said, half apologetically.

Across the floor, the Lacroix band struck up to herald the entrance of their champion. The cheering started as a low rumble, as if a subway were passing underneath the hall. Belmont could hear the sound of individual voices calling Lacroix's name, but as the sound expanded these were lost in the all-enveloping roar of his supporters clapping and stamping their feet. First, twin lines of red-pants-suited girls marched in, clearing a path before them. Then came the band, in red uniforms, blasting away to further excite the mood of the delegates. Behind them, accompanied by his two closest advisors, came Lacroix, both arms above his head, waving at the delegates, his face flushed with excitement. As soon as he became visible to the crowd the cry started: "La-croix, La-croix, La-croix," a hypnotic chant that built to a crescendo. As it died away, his supporters drummed their feet on the floorboards. Belmont, aware of the photographers around him and the television cameras trained on him, inclined his head toward his wife and chatted to her, feigning indifference to the reception of his rival.

At length, Lacroix reached his box and took his seat. Gilles Boucher, on the platform, let the demonstration continue for a few minutes and then rose and rapped his gavel to bring the convention to order. The noise hardly abated with the first call to order, and it was a full ten minutes and much action with the gavel before the delegates seated themselves and prepared to listen.

Boucher felt the heat of the television lights on him. He cleared his throat. *"Mesdames et messieurs, bienvenue . . .* welcome."

He droned on through his introductory remarks—announcements regarding charter flights home, cars blocking entrances, fund-raising. Belmont fidgeted in his chair. He stole a glance at Lacroix, who was busy giving a television interview. He returned his attention to the podium.

". . . and that concludes the announcements," Boucher was saying. "Now, ladies and gentlemen, I do not have to tell you that the main order of business this afternoon is the election of a new party leader." He waited for a reaction to his attempt at humor. As there was none, he looked grave once more. "However, before we proceed, it is my duty as chairman to inform you that, under parliamentary rules, a motion to adjourn can be put forward at any time. And I must tell you that I have received such a motion. To adjourn this convention *sine die."* A buzz of uncertainty rose from the convention floor. Belmont looked over at Lacroix. The Minister of Social Affairs appeared to have stopped in mid-sentence. With a gesture of irritation he was waving the TV reporter away.

"This motion," continued Boucher, "has been proposed by one of the candidates, Jean-Claude Belmont. Under the rules, I have accepted it and agreed to allow the delegates to vote on it." There were cries of "Shame" from the floor. Lacroix had risen to his feet and tried to interrupt with a point of order. Belmont silently entreated Gilles Boucher not to be swayed from his declared intention.

"I shall now call upon Monsieur Belmont to propose the resolution for adjournament."

Belmont rose quickly from his seat and made his way to the podium amid a chorus of jeers and catcalls.

His heart was racing as he stood at the microphone,

facing some two thousand delegates. He could feel the waves of hostility rising up at him from the convention floor. He had gambled his entire political future on this moment. He looked down at the faces turned up to him, and he could not recognize one of them; all the party workers, the riding representatives, the ministerial advisors—men and women who had in the past responded to his leadership, whose ideas and political philosophy had been shaped by his oratory—were now his judge and jury. The angry buzz around the floor died away as he prepared to speak. The podium was suddenly illuminated as the television cameras closed in for Belmont's address with their unerring instinct for blood.

"Thank you, Mr. Chairman. My friends, fellow workers for independence, I shall be brief. You're all aware of the events which took place at my campaign headquarters here in Quebec City yesterday. You are all also aware of the interpretations that have been placed on those events by the press. You have heard my denials of any wrongdoing, and I repeat them here before you today and in the sight of God. Those of you who have worked together with me over the years must know in your hearts that I am incapable of the actions which have been attributed to me. You must know that I am innocent of the charges made against me. . . ." He felt the tears begin to form in his eyes and his voice faltered. He took a sip of water.

"However, it is only natural that there should be doubts and that these unfortunate and ill-timed events have cast a shadow over my record and over my candidacy to be your leader. I have been advised to step down, to withdraw from the race. But that would only be an admission of my guilt. I am staying to fight, my friends. My innocence is shield enough against the obloquy of the press. I will not stand down!"

There was a scattering of applause that quickly died away.

"Therefore, I come before you to ask that the vote—a crucial vote in the history of our people, ladies and gentlemen—be delayed until such time as the accusations against me have been cleared up. We have been waiting for four hundred years to fulfill our destiny. Will you not give me a few days?"

"Time for more fake photographs?" yelled a heckler in the crowd. There was laughter around the hall. Lacroix covered his face with his hand and whispered to an aide. Belmont struggled to control his voice.

"I ask you to delay the vote until members of this party are able to assess the relative merits of the candidates before you without the cloud of suspicion and intrigue that hangs over us."

"You! You!" shouted back individual voices from around the hall.

"Call the vote." "Let's get on with it." Belmont could see nothing beyond the glare of the lights. The voices assailed him from the darkness. He gripped the edge of the podium and his voice became plaintive.

"I've given this party my complete loyalty and devotion ever since I helped our dead leader to create it. I ask nothing more than the opportunity to be judged on my record. I ask only for equity and fair-mindedness."

"Was it fair to smear Guy Lacroix?" The voice pierced the blackness like an arrow. The crowd on the floor became restless.

"Vote, call the vote."

"Point of order."

"Call the vote."

"Vote! Vote! Vote!" The chant was taken up in all parts of the hall. Belmont held his hands up for silence, but his audience was past caring for his self-justification. The chant became a roar, augmented by the clapping of hands in rhythm to the words. Belmont felt a hand on his shoulder.

"Easy, Jean-Claude." It was Gilles Boucher. "I'd better take over." Belmont retreated from the rostrum, his head lowered in defeat. Boucher banged his gavel vigorously for order. The convention expressed its will in the continuing chant. The television cameras followed Belmont as he slunk away into the shadows.

Guy Lacroix allowed himself the hint of a smile as Belmont disappeared from view. As a candidate, Belmont was finished; he had been publicly disgraced on the convention floor, and the image of a man trembling on the brink of an emotional breakdown had been carried into the homes of Quebeckers throughout the province. The chairman still had not controlled the chanting delegates, and, as the television lights swung round to focus on Lacroix, he flicked the lock of hair from his eyes and stood up with his arms raised in an attitude of victory.

"I put the motion that this convention be adjourned until further notice!" Gilles Boucher shouted above the din. "All those in favor say aye . . . all those against. . . . The motion is defeated."

The explosion of sound which greeted the announcement seemed to contain the knowledge of a greater victory. The tidal sound washed around Guy Lacroix and appeared to lift him bodily onto the shoulders of his supporters. With shining eyes and a face transfigured with a rapturous sense of his own mission, Guy Lacroix, the next Premier of the Province of Quebec, acknowledged the ecstatic homage of the party faithful.

The President sat in front of the television screen fingering the ice in his bourbon on the rocks. The chinking sound of ice against glass distracted Lawrence Wilde, who was trying to concentrate on the results of the convention vote as they flashed on the screen.

"Do you mind, sir?"

"Mind, you're damn right I mind," snapped the President, without taking his eyes from the TV set.

"No, sir, the ice. I can't hear the announcer."

"Well, turn the sound up, for Christ's sake."

The cameras focused on a jubilant Guy Lacroix as he made his way up to the podium, his hands clasped above his head like a boxer in triumph.

"The son of a bitch. I said it then and I say it now, Larry. That guy's a son of a bitch."

Lawrence Wilde watched the figure of Lacroix luxuriating in the ecstasy of victory. He disappeared in the middle of a pushing, heaving mob of well-wishers, all trying to touch him as if he were some mystical totem.

"Maybe his friends will do us a favor and trample him to death."

"What?"

"Nothing, sir. Just hoping the roof would curl back and lightning would strike, that's all."

"The only lightning that'll strike will be ours."

"Yes, sir."

Lacroix's victory had come as no surprise to the Secretary of State. Reports crossing his desk for the past three weeks had predicted it as inevitable. The police raid on Belmont's campaign headquarters had sealed the contest. The vote of 1,547 for Lacroix against 468 for Belmont was even worse than the most pessimistic prognosis. As Wilde watched Lacroix emerge, tousled but happy, from the welter of excited supporters, he noted ironically how like the President he behaved in his hour of triumph. There was an aura of gloating arrogance about the man, as if he would exact revenge on his opponents now that his power was absolute.

Lacroix had reached the podium and was waving wildly to the crowd, which responded with a deafening roar. Great nets strung from the ceiling loosed hundreds of red and white balloons which drifted down into the hall, where they were immediately burst by cigarettes. The security guards around the room moved in nervously. A girl in a red pants suit broke through the cordon and was greeted with another roar as she grabbed Lacroix and kissed him.

"Damn kid, wet behind the ears. He wouldn't last five minutes in Congress," muttered the President.

Lacroix held his hands out, motioning the crowd to silence. The delegates began to sit down in their seats, waiting to hear the first words of their new leader. A quivering silence descended over the Quebec Coliseum. Lacroix turned to his left and slowly scanned the room with his eyes. When he had completed a sweep of the room, he raised his arms like a revivalist preacher and, throwing his head back, he shouted, *"Vive le Québec Libre!"* No hockey crowd had ever emitted such a collective bellow of joy.

In the improvised war room of the White House final plans for Operation Nighthawk—the American occupation of Quebec—were being discussed. An Air Force general was briefing the National Security Council, chaired by the President, when a scretary entered the room and discreetly handed a note to Lawrence Wilde. When he had read it, Wilde interrupted the briefing.

"Excuse me a moment. Mr. President, I have just received a transcript of Premier Lacroix's address to the

National Assembly from our Consul-General in Quebec City. There's no doubt about it now."

"Read it out, Larry."

"Let's see . . . here's the relevant passage. He's just reiterated the statement he made at the convention last week that Quebec must have complete independence with no strings attached. He goes on:

> *'As you know, it has been the policy of this government to conduct negotiations in good faith with representatives of the Canadian government to achieve this. It is with regret that I report to this House that these negotiations have not progressed as we would have wished. Therefore, I am advising members today that the Government of Quebec is breaking off any further talks with the Government of Canada on this matter. We have taken over the machinery of independence ourselves. It had always been our most cherished hope that Quebec could gain its historic freedom in a spirit of peace and good will. Because of the intransigence of Ottawa, it appears that this will not be so. But we will have our freedom, my friends, no matter what the circumstances. Since negotiation has failed, it is time for positive action.*
>
> *'The motion I am placing before this House today will achieve that end. Because we must move quickly for our own self-preservation, the government has chosen to limit its debate to forty-eight hours. We have been discussing the issue in Quebec for over one hundred years. We have heard all the arguments for and against. Forty-eight hours should now be ample time.*
>
> *'There are those outside Quebec who will oppose our nationhood. They have threatened us with force of arms. But Quebec has powerful allies. If any state or military group attempts to interfere with the birth of our nation, they will learn this to their cost.'*"

"Exactly what does he mean by that?" Secretary of Defense Ronald Vaughan wondered.

"We're not sure." Colin Dempster, the National Security Advisor, answered the question. "We believe Lacroix may have been talking to the Russians. Certainly France will show the flag in some form. But our original assessment of the situation remains unchanged. We do not believe either France or the Soviets will intervene. A lot of noise, but nothing up front."

"Are we a hundred per cent sure of that?" demanded the President.

Dempster swiveled around to face him.

"No, sir, we're not. But the risk is worth taking, according to the Pentagon."

"Thank you, Colin. Anything else, Larry?"

"Nothing of significance, sir. Just more rhetoric. The motion itself is worded quite simply: 'Resolved, that the National Assembly supports the Government's decision to declare Quebec a sovereign and independent nation under the terms and definitions contained in the charter of the United Nations; and to seek immediate membership in that world organization.'"

"When is the vote?" asked the President.

"Tomorrow night, sir. Eight o'clock."

The President looked down the table.

"Gentlemen, we have discussed this matter many times. We all know what is involved. I believe that it is imperative we move before the vote is taken, in terms of the reaction from the international community. Are there any dissenters from this view?"

No one spoke.

"All right then. Midnight tonight, it's Operation Nighthawk."

Cameron Craig had not left his desk for twenty-four hours. The remnants of meals taken on the run littered the top of his desk. He was short-staffed, and the fast-breaking UDI story, hard on the heels of the Belmont scandal and the leadership convention, had meant that the newsroom of the *Chronicle* had been stretched to the limits of its capacity. Even Morgan had been co-opted into daily reporting, a fact which Craig would later use as a measure of his own desperation. The editor himself was working as a rewrite man, a caption writer, and a copy editor.

"Are these the only shots you have of Lacroix?" he

growled at the photo editor. "They're six months old, for crying out loud."

"Okay, Cam, you get me a photographer in Quebec. Spring the money and you'll have one in two hours."

"Where's Henderson? I want that copy on the Premier's speech. Do I have to do everything myself?"

A secretary came in with cardboard cups of coffee and some doughnuts. "Where do you want them!" she asked.

"Where do I want them? Just leave them!" Craig yelled. "Can't anyone make a decision around here except me?"

The secretary scuttled out and nearly collided with a copy boy, who placed the morning's mail in the editor's IN tray.

"Sir?"

"What the hell do you want?"

"Sir, there's an envelope with postage due. A dollar eighty."

"Postage due," mimicked Craig in disbelief, looking at his photo editor. "I'm up to my ass in the biggest story of the year and he bothers me with postage due. Out!"

"But what do I do with it? It's addressed to you, but it has no stamps on it. The post office says . . ."

Cameron Craig snatched the envelope from the boy and threw it across the room. It hit the wall and landed on top of a pile of newspapers.

"Now get your ass out of here or you'll be one copy boy who didn't realize his lifelong dream of becoming editor." The boy shrugged and turned on his heel.

"All right, where were we?"

"You were saying you wanted an up-to-date photo of Lacroix."

"Yeah. What about a line drawing?"

By nine o'clock that night the temperature in Montreal had dropped to twenty-one below. The frigid wind off the St. Lawrence sliced along the boulevards. Cameron Craig left the cheery comfort of Auberge St. Michel with its red-checked tablecloths and roaring fire to walk back to the office. He clenched every muscle against the cold and wished himself away from Montreal, from Quebec and the whole rotten business.

He was depressed because Taylor Redfern had been in

a coma for over a week now; not even Redfern's wife had been allowed to see him in the intensive-care unit of the Hôtel Dieu Hospital in Quebec. That's where they took the Premier and Kevin Reilly, he said to himself. Craig was depressed too because of the editorial he had to write for the morning's edition. The theme was the implications of UDI. The new government threatened to impose press censorship, and Premier Lacroix had let it be known that he wouldn't shed a tear if the *Montreal Chronicle* folded. Craig had received a call before he left for dinner from the publisher, who suggested that an editorial favorable to the new regime might not come amiss "in these difficult financial times." Not that he wanted to interfere, of course, but it was better to have a newspaper than not. At least write something neutral . . .

In his office, Craig sat down at the typewriter and rolled some copy paper into the carriage. He stared at the blank sheet, but his thoughts would not fall into place. Angrily he tore the paper from the machine and threw it into the wastebasket. He lit a cigarette and stood staring out of his window down onto the ice-choked river. Wearily he rubbed his eyes. What were the other English editorial writers saying? Perhaps they could provide an idea.

He crossed to the pile of newspapers stacked against the wall. Lying on top was a brown envelope—the one he had thrown in anger earlier in the day. He picked it up and looked at it. Stamped on it were the words *"à percevoir* —postage due." He recognized Taylor Redfern's handwriting, and with a sudden surge of excitement he tore it open and shook out six small cassette tapes. He reached in the desk for his tape recorder and ejected the cassette, replacing it with Redfern's first tape. He pressed the start button and turned the volume up full. After a few seconds he heard Redfern's anguished voice.

"It is now nine forty-five A.M. on February fifteenth. I am dictating this in Room Nine-thirteen of the Château Frontenac in Quebec City. I am committing to tape all that I know about the conspiracy to assasinate the late Premier of Quebec. . . ."

Two hours later Cameron Craig slumped back in his chair, stunned. It took him ten minutes to rally himself. His first instinct was to call for a copy typist, but instead he picked up the phone and dialed the night operator on the *Chronicle* switchboard.

"I want you to put a call through to the Prime Minister." He glanced at his watch. It was 11:48 P.M. "Yes, I know it's almost midnight, but this is an emergency. He's probably at his residence, but find him. Wherever he is!"

As he waited for the connection to be made, he calculated how many column inches there were in Taylor Redfern's testimony.

"C'mon you guys, move your butts, get moving."

Lieutenant Vin Michaels of the Green Berets, his face blackened like those of his men, snapped out orders as the troops ducked under the whirling rotors and scrambled aboard the gunships. Behind him, stretched down the tarmac of Plattsburgh Air Force Base, another fifty helicopters were being loaded with men. At the end of the runway, black against the floodlights, M-551 Sheridan tanks rumbled up the tailgates into the cavernous bellies of the C-130 Hercules transport planes. These would be coming in as soon as his men had secured Dorval Airport, just west of Montreal.

Lieutenant Michaels looked at his watch. It was 11:57 P.M.

"Everybody aboard, Sergeant?"

"Yes, sir, we're ready." Sergeant Nealms was standing in the door of the lead helicopter, a walkie-talkie in his hand.

"Okay." Michaels swung himself up into the cockpit and began to buckle himself into the seat next to the pilot. The radio crackled with flight instructions from the tower. Above the birdlike screech of the rotors he shouted back to Sergeant Nealms. "Get that door shut, Sergeant. We lift off in less than two minutes."

"Right, sir."

"Are we on schedule?" he asked, turning to the pilot.

"Yes, sir. Orders are just coming through now. We'll be in the first wave. Our estimated flying time to Dorval is thirty-five minutes. There's a slight headwind. We lift off at the signal of a white flare."

Lieutenant Michaels glanced back at his platoon, seated on the hard wooden benches, waiting in silence to go into action. He felt that familiar thrill of anticipation as the

helicopter revved and seemed to strain against some in-
visible leash that kept it anchored to the ground. He had
not seen combat since those last, terrible days of Vietnam.

Through the windshield, far away at the end of the
runway, he saw a ball of light which rose like a comet and
hung momentarily several hundred feet above the tarmac
before bursting into a phosphorescent star. As it fell to
earth, it illuminated the entire airfield in a bright metallic
wash. The helicopter shuddered momentarily and then
lifted off. They were on their way. They were going in.

ABOUT THE AUTHORS

GORDON PAPE is a journalist and publisher of the *Canadian,* Canada's most widely circulated magazine.

TONY ASPLER is a novelist and an executive producer with the CBC.

Bantam Book Catalog

Here's your up-to-the-minute listing of over 1,400 titles by your favorite authors.

This illustrated, large format catalog gives a description of each title. For your convenience, it is divided into categories in fiction and non-fiction—gothics, science fiction, westerns, mysteries, cookbooks, mysticism and occult, biographies, history, family living, health, psychology, art.

So don't delay—take advantage of this special opportunity to increase your reading pleasure.

Just send us your name and address and 50¢ (to help defray postage and handling costs).